Revelations

Tattoos and Tears
Book 2

By Amiee Louise

REVELATIONS TATTOOS AND TEARS BOOK 2

First edition. October 2, 2025.

Copyright © 2025 Amiee Louise.

ISBN: 978-1968759261

Written by Amiee Louise.

1

Peyton

I am aware of the noises and hear muffled voices in the background, but my brain can't focus on what's going on. I hear the sounds of sirens and the familiar noise of the London traffic. I desperately want to scream out, but my vocal chords do not cooperate and all I see is perpetual darkness.

The next thing I know, I wake up in an all-too-bright room with blinding fluorescent lights above me. My vision is blurred, and I struggle to focus on my surroundings. All I am aware of, is that every part of my body hurts and aches. I go to move, and my body protests. I try again to focus, and that's when I see him—Sam, my gorgeous rock star. His familiar handsome face is spoiled with concern and sadness.

"Ruby, she's awake."

His voice is gruff and broken. Ruby's face comes into focus and I turn my head.

"Thank God. Peyton, hey it's me, Ruby."

I open my eyes, feeling more aware of my surroundings.

"Hey, sleeping beauty," Sam says, stroking my hand.

"Sam." My voice is hoarse and doesn't sound like my own.

"It's OK. I'm here. You're in the hospital, angel." I frown, and he gives me some water through a straw to hydrate my dry throat. "You were in an accident."

Sam's jaw clenches and I know instantly there's something he is keeping from me.

"Sam, what happened?"

I sound anxious, though I'm not sure why. He looks from me and then to Ruby. She wipes a tear from her eye and sniffs, as if she is building up the courage to tell me.

"You were in a car accident, sweetie," Ruby finally says. "Forensics have gone over your car with a fine-toothed comb. They reckon it was deliberate—someone cut your brakes."

Sam's face turns angry. His jaw is clenched, and he starts to pace around the room, running his hands through his hair.

"W-what? Why? How?"

I struggle to take in what Ruby has just said. *Deliberate... someone cut my brakes on my car on purpose. Why would someone want to do that?* I can't process this information and I go to sit up. I scrunch my face in pain, and like lightning, Sam rushes over to the bed.

"*Jesus*, angel, please try not to move," he says, his voice soft with concern. A tear spills from my eye.

"Sam, it hurts."

He strokes my hand. "I know, baby, I thought I'd lost you."

I see the angst in his eyes; he looks as if he hasn't slept in a few days and my heart clenches.

"Skip's outside guarding the room in case the person who did this tries to come here and Cole's back at the apartment going through the CCTV footage from my building. I'm not going to let anyone hurt you, angel, I promise. Whoever did this they're not going to fucking get away with it," Sam spits out angrily.

A guard outside my room—what the fuck? This is all too much for my brain to process right now, and that's when the tears come. Tears spill from my eyes and they won't stop. I am sobbing uncontrollably, and Sam holds me, comforting me as best as he can.

A few hours pass, and I have been drifting in and out of sleep, hearing the low humming beep of hospital machines around me. I can hear Ruby and Sam talking in hushed tones.

"She's been out for five fucking days, Sam, who would want to do this to her?" Ruby sobs softly. I can hear Sam's footsteps pacing around the room.

"I really don't know, but I'm going to find out, and they're not going to fucking get away with this, Ruby, I can promise you that."

Sam's phone starts ringing. "I need to take this, it's Cole. I won't be long."

I hear him leave the room and the chair scrapes along the floor, as Ruby takes his place next to my bed. I open my eyes to look at her.

"Hey, how are you feeling, sweetie?" she asks softly, and I clear my throat.

"Sore."

Ruby smiles. "I know, babe. You gave us all such a scare. Thank God you're all right."

A tear rolls down my cheek as I choke out, "I'm so sorry."

Ruby shakes her head. She holds my hand and strokes it reassuringly. "Shush, none of this is your fault, Peyton, I promise you. You've got nothing to be sorry for."

I sob softly, "How long have I been in here?"

"Five days. It was touch and go at first, the crash was really bad. Your car took the majority of the damage; it's a complete wreck."

My eyes widen. I know I am lucky to be alive, but my *beloved* car?

"Sam's been such a rock in all this. He called your parents and made the arrangements so that you could have a private room. He even dealt with the police and the press. That boy is a saint among men, babe, I'm telling you. Hold onto him."

I look at her and cock my eyebrow.

"You couldn't stand him the other day." I say, smirking; it's good to know that I haven't lost my sense of humour. Ruby laughs and Sam comes back into the room. A look passes between Ruby and him.

"What's going on? Before you even think of fucking lying to me, just tell me what the hell is happening."

Sam clenches his fist.

"That was Cole on the phone, he has gone over the CCTV footage from the parking garage and he found something he thinks I should see. *Motherfuckers!*" Sam shouts, running his fingers through his hair frantically. Ruby stands up and brushes his arm reassuringly.

"I'll go and get us some coffee. You two should talk."

Ruby winks, and I smile weakly. She leaves the room, and Sam takes the seat next to my bed. He links our fingers together and strokes my knuckles.

"*Christ*, I've been in hell these past few days, angel. I've been relentlessly questioned by the police because it happened on my property and my parking garage is now a fucking crime scene. I swear I'm going to get the person who fucking did this, baby, I promise you."

Another tear rolls down my cheek, and I feel like all I have done since I have come around is cry. I'm actually pathetic.

"I can't remember anything, Sam."

He looks at me. "Shhh, it's all right. You had a traumatic brain injury, angel, and some temporary short-term memory loss is normal, apparently."

"What happened?" My voice is hoarse with unshed tears.

"You were pulling out of my parking garage, your brakes failed, and you crashed into an oncoming bus. It could have been so much worse; it's lucky that the traffic lights were on red, or it would have been utter carnage. I had no idea what was going on until I got the call to say you'd been rushed into hospital." He squeezes my hand and kisses the back of it gently. "Even now, you're still beautiful."

He smiles that familiar smile and strokes my face. I roll my eyes.

"Flattery will get you everywhere, Newbolt!"

We both laugh, and I hear a commotion outside the door. Sam gets up and opens the door.

"I'm her friend and her boss, dickhead, fucking let me through. I *need* to see her now." I hear Seb's frantic raised voice and Sam goes over to Skip to diffuse the situation. Seb kicking off outside my hospital room, I *do not* want to see that. I have seen it with my own eyes before and it isn't a pretty sight. Seb, being ex-SAS, is badass and could probably knock someone on their arse by just looking at them.

"It's all right, mate, let him through."

Skip nods curtly and gestures to let Seb through the door. He is clutching a large bouquet of purple gerberas and a Starbucks take-out cup. He comes in and then backs up when he sees me lying in the hospital bed. *Great, I must look really bad.* He comes closer.

"Hey, honey, how are you feeling? I bought you your favourite Starbucks coffee, espresso macchiato. I know you must be desperate for a decent cup of coffee, and I bought you flowers," he rushes out in a soft voice.

"Thank you so much, babe, I appreciate it."

Sam looks over at me. "I'll leave you two to it. I need to make a couple of calls, I'll be back in a little while, angel. I promise."

He kisses me on the cheek, nods to Seb, and leaves the room, shutting the door behind him. Seb is standing awkwardly next to my bed.

"Sit down, babe, for fuck's sake. You're making the place look untidy!"

He laughs. "Still not lost your sense of humour then, honey?"

I shake my head and the door opens. A nurse comes in and smiles brightly at me.

"I hope your visitors aren't wearing you out, Peyton?"

She is short woman, plump, and looks to be in her late fifties. She has skin the colour of dark mocha, friendly hazel eyes, and a warm infectious smile. Her greying hair is tied up in a neat bun and she takes the flowers from Seb.

"I'll put these in some water for you, petal."

I nod and realise she knows my name, but I don't know hers.

"Thank you..."

She smiles. "Estelle."

I smile back, and she leaves the room. Seb sits down on the chair next to my bed.

"I came as soon as I heard you were awake; I was so worried about you, honey. I was here when you were bought in, I called Sam straight away."

The look of pain and anguish in his eyes is apparent, as I regard him intently. There is an awkward silence between us, and I can tell by his body language that he is holding back. We haven't had chance to talk about the kiss from last Friday night either.

As if reading my mind, he says, "I'm so sorry about what happened on Friday, babe, I don't know what I was thinking."

I lean my head back in the pillow and tell him, "It's OK, honestly, it was just a moment of madness, and I was really drunk."

That old chestnut, you're fooling no one, Harper. I shake that thought away and he smiles.

"Great, so I took advantage of a drunken woman. Well played, Seb!"

"It's fine, let's say no more about it, and forget it ever happened."

He nods, and with those words, our kiss is forgotten. We are back to being just regular Peyton and Seb.

"How are things at the shop?"

He takes my hand. "Things are good, busy, but good. You don't need to worry about a thing, honey. Parker's back temporarily from paternity leave and I have a guest artist in from across town. You remember Harley? Harley

Hernandez from Black Tiger Ink. I've postponed my trip to America until you're back on your feet."

My eyes widen, and I suddenly feel bad for letting Seb down. A tear rolls down my cheek.

"I'm so sorry, Seb." I sob. Seb strokes my knuckles and places a gentle kiss on the back of my hand.

"Hey, honey, please don't cry, none of this is your fault, you didn't ask to be in here. It's all under control. You're a friend first and an employee second, babe. You take as long as you need. You're my shop manager, and your job is totally one million percent safe."

I have never felt so useless. I fucking hate hospitals. Seb stays for an hour or so and I find out that he is an uncle. Parker and Riley had their twin boys, born prematurely on the weekend, Joshua and Zeke. He gushes and shows me pictures on his phone. I am really happy for him and the new addition to his ever-expanding family. He leaves promising that he will be back to visit soon. I am in the hospital room on my own at last and my eyes feel heavy. Soon, I am a slave to sleep.

The next morning, I am barely awake, and I hear raised voices.

"I fucking *own* you, Sam, I made you what you are today, and I can crush you. I'll make damn sure your career is ruined and in tatters. No one in the music industry will touch you with a ten-foot pole." J.D.'s familiar cold voice fills my ears.

"I don't give a fucking shit, J.D, because I've got something you'll never have."

J.D sighs and sounds bored. "And what might that be, Sammy?"

"Love. I've got a woman who loves me more than life itself and someone who I love unconditionally. Being so close to losing her has made me realise that life is short. I intend to spend the rest of my life with her proving that she is the only woman I'll ever want."

Sam's words warm me inside. *He wants to spend the rest of his life with me.* Wow! Peyton Leigh Newbolt definitely has a ring to it! J.D.'s voice cuts through my thoughts.

"That's not who you are, Sammy. You're one quarter of the biggest rock band in the world. You should be balls deep in a different groupie every night of the week, more than one, just like the old days."

I inwardly wince at J.D.'s crass words.

"Every night was a party; now all you want to do is be with her. It's fucking sickening. Do you think the fans want to see you with a girlfriend? No, they want to carry on fantasising about their favourite rocker sprawled naked in their beds, willing to tend to their every fantasy, not settled down with some tart who got lucky."

Sam growls. I know that J.D knows how to get under his skin, and I can feel the anger radiating off him in waves.

"Don't you fucking dare talk about her like that *ever*. She's more than that, and I love her so much it hurts. Why don't you understand that, J.D? Is it really that hard for you comprehend?"

J.D is about to speak, but their altercation is interrupted by the door opening.

"Good morning, Sam." Estelle's voice fills the room.

"Morning, Estelle." I hear the smile in Sam's raspy voice and she sighs. My eyes flutter open; Sam comes over to my bedside and strokes my hand. "Good morning, my beautiful girl."

He kisses my forehead and Estelle comes to stand next to him.

"If you could give me a minute to examine her please, Sam?"

Sam nods and salutes. "I'll be just outside, angel."

He leaves the room with J.D. hot on his tail. I can tell that their argument is far from over.

"Our hospital has never had so many famous people through the doors! You're a very popular girl, Peyton." I smile. "Marlowe Newbolt from the Lightning Bolts was here; even now he's still dishy!"

Her laugh is warm and infectious; I find myself laughing with her. *Marlowe, Sam's dad was here?* I vow to ask Sam when he comes back.

"That rock band that your man is in Rancid something-or-other, all the boys have been here. My daughter is itching to catch a glimpse; she's their biggest fan."

I smile warmly and instantly like her. I vow to get the bands autographs for her daughter for being so kind to me. She takes my blood pressure and checks me over.

"Your Sam is so charming and generous; all the nurses are falling over themselves! I've never seen such a mess of hormones in all my life."

We both laugh. We chat easily as if we have known each other forever and she informs me of my injuries. My left shoulder is dislocated, mild ligament damage to my knee, two cracked ribs, cuts and bruises. My stomach churns at the extent of the damage that has been done to my body; I shudder at the thought that it could have been so much worse. I am so lucky I wasn't killed, but I thank God that the dislocation is not my tattooing arm. Estelle leaves the room and Ruby breezes in. She is wearing her black power suit and dragging my Ed Hardy overnight bag behind her.

"Good morning, sweetie." She leans down and hugs me. Her familiar scent fills my nostrils and I smile.

"Morning, Rubes, what's with the power suit?"

Ruby smiles brightly. "I have just had a job interview with another advertising firm, Isaac Carter's arch rival Carlisle Cassidy!"

She pulls the chair out and sits down.

"Are you sure that's a good idea?"

She rolls her eyes, and tells me, "Hell yes of course it is! Revenge is a dish best served cold and all that! I have access to some of Isaac's most crucial and important clients. I'm sure with my fabulous powers of persuasion I can convince them to come to this new firm. Isaac-fucking-Carter will wish he'd never clapped eyes on me once I've finished with him."

I reach for her hand and brush it reassuringly. I just hope she knows what she is doing. Ruby is known for being a tad reckless at times. She smiles and swiftly changes the subject.

"How's the invalid doing today?"

It's my turn to roll my eyes. "I'm not a fucking invalid!"

I put on my best sulking face and she laughs.

"All right, babe, keep your knickers on!"

Laughing, I watch as she pulls the bag onto her lap.

"I bought some of your stuff from the flat—thought you could do with some of your stuff with you. I bought your phone, your Beats headphones, some clean pyjamas, some toiletries. I've packed your iPad and Sam has bought you a new Kindle e-reader in case you get bored! I'm telling you, that boy has thought of everything!" Ruby giggles.

"Thanks, Ruby."

We chat for a while longer and she leaves a few hours later, promising she will be back. She closes the door and I am suddenly all alone. I pull out my phone and put my headphones on. I choose Ed Sheeran's "Give Me Love", I need something relaxing and soothing. I lie back on my pillows, close my eyes, and drift off.

***

"Can you hear me, love? We're going to get you out."

A kind, gentle voice breaks through my unconsciousness. I am aware of the dull cacophony of mid-morning Monday in London. My eyes flutter open, and I'm vaguely aware of my surroundings. My vision is blurred, I am disoriented and— Ouch, that fucking hurts. I can smell a strong, warm, metallic smell lingering in the air that makes me feel nauseous. *Am I bleeding? Am I dreaming? What happened? Where am I?* I have all these questions floating around and around in my head.

"Hey, what's your name, sweetie?"

I look up into warm, blue eyes and a friendly smile. He has a shaved head and is wearing a green paramedic uniform.

"Peyton," I manage to whisper.

"Hey, Peyton, I'm Jake. I'm a paramedic, and the firemen are going to get you out. I just need you to stay really calm for me."

I nod, and he smiles reassuringly. That's when the panic sets in.

"Where's Sam?"

He looks at me, a puzzled look across his face.

"I want Sam; you have to get him for me, please?" I plead. "He is my boyfriend. Please, you need to get him, he'll be worried."

Jake whispers to his colleague, a young woman with short red hair.

"OK, we'll get him for you, Peyton, I promise."

He smiles. My shoulders sag, and I wince in pain. The pain is excruciating, and I am in agony. I have never felt pain like this before.

"Where does it hurt, Peyton?"

I let out a breath.

"Everywhere," I sob.

"It's going to be all right, Peyton. Look, you need to stay really calm for me. I need you to move your head from side to side. I need to check you haven't broken your neck, can you do that for me?"

I look at him and his face is calm and impassive, I nod and move my head from side to side.

"Good girl, can you wiggle your fingers and toes?"

I do as he says, and he smiles warmly.

"Brilliant, you're doing really well, Peyton; we'll have you out soon."

I look around. I see a bus pulled to the side of the road and my car is askew in the middle of the road. There is an ambulance and two police cars. There is a police cordon around the area and a large crowd gathered to see what is going on. There are around six or seven police officers talking to witnesses. I turn my head, and I hear shouting from the street.

"Oh, my God! That's Peyton's car. Peyton! Please, you have to let me through."

Seb's deep frantic voice fills my ears, and I hear a gentle voice trying to calm him. Jake looks up and then back at me.

"There's a gentleman asking for you? He says his name is Sebastian Henry?"

I nod, knowing they will not let him anywhere near me if he is not family, so I improvise.

"He's my brother."

Jake narrows his eyes, but nods to a tall police officer and Seb comes over to the side of the car, leaning his head in the driver's side window.

"Peyton, honey, what happened?"

I shake my head and wracking sobs escape me.

"It's going to be all right, babe, the firemen are going to get you out, I promise."

Worry mars his rugged features and he reaches in for my hand. I accept it, and Jake whispers to Seb, who just nods.

"Peyton, darlin', the firemen are going to get you out now. I need you to look at me. Don't take your eyes off me, it's going to be all right, you have to trust them, imagine you're in a real life action film!"

He smiles, but it doesn't reach his eyes. I smile back and lock my eyes on his. I flinch as I hear a whirring sound and the sound of cutting metal.

"Eyes on me, honey."

My terrified eyes lock with his. Seb smiles and strokes my knuckles softly in a reassuring gesture.

"Good girl, it's all right, you're doing brilliant. Keep looking right at me, I'm here and I'm not going anywhere, babe."

"Seb, please, you need to get Sam for me. I want Sam."

"Shhh, it's going to be all right. I'm here; I'll get him for you, honey, I promise. I need you to keep looking in my eyes; don't take your eyes off me."

Then it went black.

***

I am jolted awake and my eyes fly open. I'm back in the bright hospital room and Sam is sitting next to my bed, gripping my hand.

"Hey, did you have a bad dream, angel?"

His handsome face is a mess of angst and days of pent-up worry. My skin is clammy, and my eyes glaze over. I will myself not to cry again.

"Hey, shhh, it's all right. I've got you, you're safe. Nothing's going to happen. Not while I'm here, angel," he whispers and climbs up on the bed. There clearly isn't enough room in the tiny hospital bed for his large, muscular frame, but he snuggles into me and pulls me close to him. I am tucked under his arm; I have missed his strong safe arms around me and his familiar soothing scent.

"Do you want to tell me about it?"

I look up at him and swallow the lump in my throat.

"I remembered something about the crash."

He looks at me and strokes my face.

"That's really good, you don't have to tell me if it's too painful."

"No, I want to; Seb was there, why didn't he tell me he was there?"

I feel Sam tense next to me.

"It should have been me, baby; I should have been there for you."

His jaw tenses, and I get the feeling that his green-eyed monster is making an appearance at Seb's involvement in my life.

"He was with you until they cut you out, he was picking up some stuff from a tattoo supplier near to my building and he saw your car in the middle of the road. He stayed with you and went in the ambulance with you. He called me straight after. I was rehearsing with the boys, but I came as soon as I heard, baby, I promise you."

The fact that Seb was there is really bothering him. *Bloody men!* We talk about my flashback in detail and Sam thinks I am making progress. I actually can't wait to get out of here. I hate hospitals—they're full of sick people. The day passes without any more drama and another quick visit from Ruby. She got the job at the new advertising firm, and I am pleased that she has finally got back on her feet. She deserves to be happy. She leaves promising me that we will definitely celebrate when I get out of here. I fall into a dreamless sleep that night and don't wake until the next morning.

I am finally allowed out of bed and I am glad to be somewhere other than lying in that Goddamn hospital bed. I have a crutch and my shoulder is strapped up in a dark-blue sling. I am escorted to the shower room by Estelle and we chat easily as we walk, enjoying the distraction. I am glad to finally wash the remnants of the crash away, relishing the hot water against my skin. After my shower, I am feeling a bit more like my usual self. Hobbling down the brightly lit corridor in my favourite pyjamas with the aid of just my crutch, Estelle is a few steps behind me just in case I fall.

I see Sam pacing the floor with his hands in his hair. He has a deep-set frown line forming on his forehead.

"Where is she? No, I won't bloody well calm down! You have to tell me where she is!"

His voice is thick with worry. I can see the tension radiating from him as the muscles in his arms and back bunch and tense. He turns around, and his green eyes lock with my blue ones, lacking their usual sparkle. He is in front of me in two large strides, scooping me up in his arms and squeezing me as gently as he can manage. I can feel him trembling against me and he lets out a breath.

"Thank Christ you're all right, angel, I think I died a million and one deaths not knowing where you were. Where's Skip?"

I suppress my smirk at this completely new, possessive, protective side of Sam.

"Hey, I'm OK, I was taking a shower. Skip—I sent him home, he looked bored," I say nonchalantly. Sam's jaw tenses and he frowns.

"He is there to protect you, angel, it's his fucking job, and it's what we pay him for."

"*Jesus fucking Christ,* Sam, if the person responsible was going to finish the job, don't you think they would have done it by now? It was probably some jealous fan or one of your legions of scorned women."

He winces at the last phrase. *Low blow, Harper.*

"So far I haven't seen any bunnies boiling in pots, no horse's heads have magically appeared in my bed, and there's definitely been no crazed lunatic hovering over my bed ready to hold a pillow over my face. So, you need to relax and stop bloody worrying so much, baby. Please, you'll make yourself ill."

Sam narrows his eyes. "Why aren't you taking this seriously? This isn't funny, Peyton, your safety is my number one priority right now, and I need to make sure you're safe. What if I'm not here? What if I can't get to you in time? *Jesus,* it doesn't bear fucking thinking about." He drags his hands through his hair and squeezes his eyes shut as if to calm himself. "Please let me call Skip and get him to come back."

I sigh and lean heavily on my crutch. I reluctantly agree, "OK, if it makes you feel better, but I don't like being guarded, Sam, it's not necessary. I'm a big girl, I can look after myself."

His mouth forms a straight line and I know he is keeping his mouth shut. He towers over me and lifts my chin until I look up at him. He looks older, tired, and has a few days' worth of stubble on his face. I reach up to stroke his face.

"Baby, when was the last time you slept properly?"

He lets out a deep breath and he looks truly exhausted. "The night you came to mine and you cooked me breakfast."

We both smile at the memory.

"Sam, honey, go home and get some rest, please."

He shakes his head. "I'm not going anywhere, angel."

He carries me back to my hospital room. I settle back into the hospital bed, glad that I could stretch my legs and freshen up. I feel so much better and almost human again. Sam takes his place next to the bed and his mobile starts ringing. He rolls his eyes and sighs.

"I'm sorry, I need to take this, babe. I'll be right back."

He kisses me gently on the lips and leaves the room. A few minutes later, the door opens again, and I am surprised to see my mum, dad, Dexter and Eden. My mum rushes in, a look of pure worry on her beautiful face.

"Peyton, darling, thank the Lord you're all right." She hugs me tightly.

"Mum, I'm fine. Ouch, you're hurting me."

She pulls away and cups my face in both of her hands.

"Look at the state of you, Peyton, my beautiful girl, you're clearly not fine. When you're well enough, you're coming back to Brighton with us, so we can take care of you properly."

My dad brushes her arm. "Let's not be too hasty, love, she's a big girl. Peyton can make up her own mind."

My dad hugs me and kisses me on the forehead. "We've been so worried, sweetheart."

I smile, and it takes everything I have not to cry again. "I'm sorry."

Mum sits down on the chair next to my bed and takes my hand in hers.

"This isn't your fault, darling, it was just a silly accident, it could have happened to anyone."

I keep my mouth shut, because this definitely *wasn't* an accident.

"We're just glad you're OK, we were out of our minds with worry. Sam called us when it happened; we've been popping in and out. We're staying at Sam's apartment, it's very swish."

Mum chuckles. *Why has Sam not mentioned any of this to me before?* I have a right to know that my parents are staying with him. I'm actually infuriated with him right now. Dexter moves closer to my bed and hugs me.

"I'm so glad you're all right, sis, you scared the shit out of all of us!"

"Thanks, Dex."

Eden is in the far corner of the room biting her nails and rolling her eyes profusely. She is, as ever, dressed immaculately in a dark grey playsuit, black tights, red heels, and a red skinny belt. She has her signature red lipstick on, and her hair is tumbling down her shoulders in chocolate waves. I narrow my eyes at her.

"That will teach her not to drive around in an ancient rust bucket. I bet she loves the attention of being in here. Sam pandering to her every need like the pathetic sap he is," she says with disdain. Dexter turns around and looks straight at Eden.

"If you're going to upset our sister then I suggest you just go, Eden, I've got no idea why you're even here."

My dad leans in to Dexter and whispers some words of reassurance. He looks exasperated, runs his hands through his hair, and puffs out his cheeks.

"This is fucking bullshit!" he shouts and leaves the room, closely followed by my dad. I have never seen Dexter angry before. Eden smiles slyly, and I look at her.

"I don't want you anywhere near me, Eden. Just go; you crossed the line when you tried to kiss my boyfriend."

She rolls her eyes again. "You're not still banging on about that are you, Peyton? Get over it, I have. He wasn't even that good."

I clench my fist until my knuckles turn white, and I know I am about to lose it with her.

"Just *go*," I shout coldly.

"Not as good as Callum, though."

My eyes widen in shock. *What the fuck does Callum have to do with this?*

"That shut you up, didn't it, sis? Callum and I slept together; it's been going on for a long time, even way before he left you."

My mouth forms an O shape and I can't get my head around what I have just heard. It must have been her voice I heard when Callum called me last week.

"Eden, love, I think you should leave now," my mum steps in.

"Why does she always have to get her own way all the time, Mum? She's always been the golden girl. I'll always be the black sheep of the family."

I roll my eyes. *Here we go, typical Eden, the eternal victim.*

"Me and Callum are in love."

Her voice sounds petulant. My heart drops and my stomach lurches. I think I'm going to throw up, and I reach over for the cardboard bowl next to my bed. Sam comes in; his face contorts when he sees my glazed eyes and dry heaves over the bowl.

"What's going on, angel?"

I shake my head. "Get her out of here, Sam, please, I don't want her here."

He looks confused, but nods. He escorts Eden out of the room, and I hear her high-pitched shrieking at Sam. I swing my legs out of the bed, wincing as my ribs protest in pain, and my mum is by my side in seconds. I hold onto my mum's hand, and I sob. Wracking, gut-wrenching sobs. I don't know if it's because of the revelation of Callum and Eden, the fact that my mum and dad are here, or being in here is overwhelming me. My mum holds me tightly.

"It's all right, my beautiful girl."

Sam comes back into the room. "Is everything all right, Sophia?"

My mum nods. She rubs my back soothingly and my sobs calm instantly. She kisses the top of my head.

"I hate seeing you like this, darling; please let your dad and I take you home."

I look up at her and sniff, trying to compose myself.

"I can't, Mum; I'm the manager of the shop now. I've got responsibilities."

She smiles brightly. "That's fantastic news, sweetheart. Why didn't you call and tell us sooner?"

"I've been so busy at work; it's been nonstop for the past few weeks."

She kisses me again and pulls away. "I'm going to see if I can get a decent cup of tea around here. We'll leave you and Sam to it."

She gets up and leaves the room. Sam crouches down in front of me, his frown line jumping in place.

"Do you want to tell me what's happened, angel?"

I look at him then I remember I'm mad at him. I get up from the bed and limp over to grab my crutch. Ignoring my body's protests and ignoring him as I head for the door.

"Baby, talk to me."

I hold my finger up.

"Just don't," I spit angrily.

"Are you mad at me?"

He sounds hurt and I look at him.

"Furious," I say coldly. "Number one, why didn't you tell me that my parents were staying with you? Don't you think I had a right to know? The nurse also told me that your dad's been here. Why would he come here? As for Skip guarding my room, what do you know, Sam? You're keeping something from me."

He stops me from leaving the room and backs me up into the door. He is so close I can feel his breath on my cheek and his scent intoxicating me. He puts his hands on either side of my head, effectively trapping me. His green eyes lock onto mine, and I can't look away. How can I go from seething mad to oddly horny within a few minutes? *Damn you, Newbolt!*

"I didn't know your parents staying at my place would be an issue, it was either that or let them find a hotel. I have four other bedrooms that aren't currently in use, so why not? What's the problem?" I go to speak but he stops me. "As for my dad, he knows how much I love you, so he wanted to check you were OK, you're with me so you're technically family. As it happens, he wanted you moved to a private hospital, but it was touch and go we didn't know if you were going to make it through the night. I was in pieces, Peyton, you have no idea how close I was to losing you. It almost killed me."

I can see his heart beat jumping through his white skull t-shirt and his eyes glaze over at the thought. Even upset, he still looks impossibly handsome.

"Jax and Cole found me in my apartment snorting coke and drowning my sorrows at the bottom of a vodka bottle. So they locked me in my bathroom for a while. You have to understand I was an absolute fucking mess. I was literally losing my mind. That's how much I love you. You don't get it, people throw the word love around like it's just a word, but they don't get it. If this has taught me anything, it's that the future is never set in stone. But I know one million percent that I want a future with you."

I melt into a puddle at his words. I want to be mad at him for keeping things from me, resorting to drink, and drugs. However, I oddly have an understanding of what he must have gone through this past week. I look up at him, and by the look on his face, he is expecting me to scream and shout. But, it doesn't come. Instead, I wrap my good arm around his neck and pull him closer. I stroke the silky soft hair at the nape of his neck. Our faces are inches apart, his breathing is hitched, and his heart is pounding. I press my lips to his frantically; I am filled with pure want and desperate need for this man. I stroke his tongue with mine and grip his nape tighter; I can't get close enough to him. He carefully lifts me off my feet with ease, as if I'm weightless. I wrap my legs around his waist and he pushes me against the door.

"God, you've got no idea how long I've waited for this."

My breath catches, and I am panting for him, desperate for his closeness.

"Tell me you want me to take you; I need to hear you say the words."

Our eyes lock.

"Sam, please take me," I pant, my voice sounds almost desperate with pure want. With me still in his arms, he holds me with one arm, pulls the blinds, and locks the door with the other. He smiles his familiar smile and he knows he has me right where he wants me.

"Take me like this, against the wall."

He cocks his eyebrow and nuzzles my neck.

"I don't want to hurt you, baby."

"I don't care. I need you, Sam, and I need you to take it all away."

He crashes his lips against mine and pushes my vest top down my shoulders. He is kissing a burning trail from my neck to my collarbone. He carries me over to the bed and puts me down, gently laying me down. Taking his time, caressing and undressing me until I'm lying on my hospital bed completely naked. He kisses a trail down my breastbone, down to my stomach; he bypasses the place where I want him to touch me the most. The door handle rattling interrupts us.

"Peyton, love."

Shit! My mum.

"Are you all right in there, sweetheart?"

Sam stifles his sniggers and straightens up. He clears his throat and lowers his voice.

"She's fallen asleep, Sophia."

He winks at me and I put my hand to my mouth trying to stifle my laughs.

"OK, when she wakes up, tell her we're going for some lunch, please, Sam."

"I will, Sophia."

I hear her heels click down the corridor. We both burst out into hysterical belly laughter. I don't think I have laughed that hard in a long time—my ribs are screaming in protest, but I feel so much better.

Sam nudges my thighs apart with his knee and strips off his t-shirt in one swift move. I will never get tired of seeing him naked in front of me; it is definitely a remarkable sight. He looks visibly thinner; his hips are narrower; his muscles are more defined and toned. I lick my lips as he strips off his dark-grey combat shorts and his black boxer briefs. His impressive erection springs free and he kicks off his shoes. Even his toned legs have more definition. What has he been doing while I have been in here?

"See something you like, baby?" His voice is dripping with seduction and I bite my lip. "Baby, don't do that please, I'm barely hanging on to my self-control right now."

I look up at him and deliberately bite my lip again. He growls and picks me up in a lithe move. My good arm wrapped around his neck, his hand supporting my bum, and the other around my waist. He walks us over to the wall and presses my back against it. I shiver at the coldness, and my whole body erupts in goose bumps. He lifts me up and impales me on his waiting stiffness. I mewl softly in his ear and nip his earlobe. He is gently moving me up and down in a slow, leisurely pace.

"Am I hurting you, baby?"

I shake my head. "Please just make love to me, Sam, I need you," I whisper softly, and he smiles his heart-stopping smile

"You don't have to ask twice, my lovely!" he says huskily. "Look at me, angel."

I look in his green eyes and am mesmerized by the feelings he evokes in me. Pure earth-shattering bliss when we're making love and pure love and absolute adoration when we're just Peyton and Sam. He lifts me up and impales me again—we have never have made love this slow before. It feels so good, I moan in his ear.

"Oh, Sam."

He quickens his painfully-slow pace and he is growling in pleasure.

"Don't stop, baby," I beg. "Please don't stop."

As his pace quickens, I feel my orgasm bubbling to the surface.

"Peyton, fuck, fuck, *fuck*, baby, I can't hold it."

I tug his nipple ring and he spurts his hot seed inside me, causing my orgasm to explode at the same time.

"Sam, I'm coming!"

He squeezes me tightly.

"I've got you. God, I love you, Peyton," he whispers as we both come down from our orgasms. He lifts me and takes me back to sit on the edge of the bed. He kisses me deeply on the lips, and for the first time in a few days, I actually feel better and almost back to my normal self.

We both dress in a relatively comfortable silence. I lay back in my bed, and Sam opens the blinds and unlocks the door. There is a tap on the door as soon as he unlocks it.

"Peyton, can I come in?"

Estelle's voice comes through the door. Sam smiles and winks mischievously at me, as he opens the door. I see Estelle look up at him and she swoons on the spot. I roll my eyes; does he really have that effect on all women he meets?

"H-Hello Sam."

He chuckles softly and nods. "Estelle," he rasps, and I hear screams outside. Estelle turns around and I see her literally melt on the spot.

"Looks like you've got company, Peyton."

I laugh as the other three band members come into view in the doorway.

"I'll come back later."

She winks and nods at the boys as she leaves.

"Peyton!"

Jax rushes over to my bed and hops up on the bed to join me. I scoot over, and he makes himself comfortable.

"How are you feeling, babe?"

"I'm good, thanks, Jax."

He smiles brightly, and I find myself smiling back. Brody saunters in, turns the chair around and sits so his legs are either side. Lucas has a sweet look of thoughtfulness and concern washing over his face.

"Hey, Peyton," Lucas' American lilt echoes around the room. "This guy has been a complete wreck since you've been in here, honey." He laughs and points to Sam.

Sam hits him playfully, and I laugh. It is good to know he has had the boy's support while I have been in hospital. Brody is being unusually quiet around me today, maybe since he was there when I walked in on Sam, so I decide to break the ice.

"Hey, Brody."

He looks up and stares at me. He smiles.

"All right, darlin', it's good to finally have you back with us."

He winks, and I have never noticed he has a split tongue before. It reminds me of a snake—that must be where he gets his nickname.

"Will you guys do me a huge favour?"

Jax smiles and winks. "Anything for you, sweetheart, you know that."

He pulls me into him for a hug and smiles. I love his sweet, affectionate demeanour and his all round, kind-hearted personality. He and the other boys have accepted me as one of their own. I know Jax would do anything for me because Sam is like a brother to him. He clearly looks up to Sam, and I am grateful of the influence they seem to have on each other.

"Take Sam home, please? He looks exhausted, and I know he hasn't slept for a while. Just take him home, and make sure he gets some proper rest."

Sam folds his arms and his brow furrows in a completely adorable roguish way.

"I don't need rest, baby, I'm absolutely fine."

I narrow my eyes at him. "I'm fine, seriously. Skip's outside, and the nurses are here. I don't need twenty-four-hour surveillance, honey."

He lets out a breath before saying, "OK, if it makes you happy, angel, but I don't like it. I'll be back as soon as I've showered, eaten, and grabbed a few hours' sleep."

He comes over to the bed and kisses me gently on the lips. Jax rolls his eyes and makes a vomiting gesture. Sam pushes Jax off the bed and he rolls off onto the floor. We all burst out into hysterical laughter. Jax gets up with a look of mock hurt on his face and grabs Sam from behind. In a second, Sam spins around and has him in a playful headlock—I love playful Sam.

We spend an hour or so chatting, laughing, joking, and catching up. Their company is a welcome distraction, and before long, they are all leaving, kissing me on the cheek in turn as they leave. Sam reluctantly leaves with them, promising me he will be back soon.

I am suddenly exhausted and drift off into a deep sleep.

***

"Stay with me, Peyton. Please, please, don't die on me, honey."

I hear the dull sound of sirens and I can feel Seb's large calloused hand stroking mine. It takes all my strength, but I manage to lightly squeeze his hand. He lifts my hand to his lips and plants a soft kiss on the back of it.

"Peyton, can you hear me?"

I am aware of a shadowy presence behind me, squeezing precious oxygen into my lungs.

"It's Seb. I'm here, darlin', you need to stay with me."

I hear his voice crack, I want to open my eyes and reassure him, but my body won't allow it. I feel him move and hear the sound of a phone keypad as if he is dialling a number.

"Sam, yeah, it's Seb. Look, there's been an accident. Yeah, a car accident. Peyton's been hurt; I'm in the ambulance with her now. Yeah, it was pretty bad. She is in a bad way. You need to get to the Whittington Hospital in Islington now, mate. I'm not sure. She was asking for you. OK. I know it's a stupid thing to say, but please try not to panic, our girl is a fighter. See you soon, mate. Bye."

I hear Seb disconnect the call and he resumes stroking my hand.

"Sam's meeting us at the hospital, honey, you need to hang in there, and everything is going to be all right. I promise."

***

I am jolted awake and my eyes fly open. I am aware that I'm alone; the room is deathly silent, and it is dark. I must have been asleep for a while. These flashbacks are scaring the shit out of me. I stare up at the ceiling and lose myself in thoughts of what ifs, and after a while, I fall into a restless asleep again.

The next thing I know, the morning sun is beaming through the window. My eyes adjust to the bright light and the door opens. Before he steps into the room, I sense his presence, and then he walks in, all six foot four inches of hard muscled, delicious male. He is freshly shaven; his hair is styled into his soft spiky style and he looks refreshed and so much more rested. He is back to looking like my gorgeous tattooed God. His green eyes lock with mine, and their familiar sparkle is back with a vengeance, temporarily disarming me and making my breath catch in my throat.

"Good morning, beautiful."

He strides in and plants a chaste kiss on my lips. His scent instantly calms me, and he perches on the edge of the bed, clutching my hand in his.

"Mornin', handsome." We both chuckle. "You look so much better now you've slept, baby."

He smiles, and I scoot over, making room for him in the small hospital bed.

"I feel better. Thank you for making the guys take me home. I haven't slept that good in a long time."

I snuggle closer to him and the doctor walks in. The doctor is a middle-aged Asian man called Doctor Rizvi. He smiles.

"Good morning, Miss Harper, how are we feeling this morning?"

I smile back and nod. "Yeah, I'm still feeling a little sore, but I'm fine."

He nods curtly, checks my chart, and examines me. When he is finished, he stands at the side of my bed.

"I don't see why you can't go home today."

My face lights up, and Sam gives me a reassuring squeeze.

"I'll prepare your discharge notes."

He nods and leaves. I am so glad and relieved that I can finally go home, so I can begin to put this situation behind me and move on.

2

Peyton

Sam and Skip have packed up all my stuff in preparation for me to go home. Skip nods and I smile warmly. He takes my stuff down the corridor.

"Are you ready, angel?"

We collect my medication from the pharmacy on the way out, and Sam wraps his arm around me and helps me down to the car, where hordes of paparazzi photographers are at the kerb. I am almost blinded by the flashbulbs and feel myself start to panic. Sam must sense it and puts his large hand protectively at the small of my back—I am instantly reassured. He opens the car door.

"Sam, over here."

There are shouts from different directions, and I am suddenly overwhelmed.

"Peyton, is it true that the crash wasn't an accident?"

My stomach somersaults at those words. I climb into the car and he crowds in behind me slamming the door behind me.

"*Fuckers,*" he curses. "I'm so sorry about that, angel, one of the drawbacks of being a rock star, constantly hounded by scumbag photographers."

"Please stop apologising, babe, none of this is your fault."

I have stayed away from the internet for a while, but I can imagine what crap they have been saying. I try to push that thought down into the pit of my brain and I look up to find him regarding me intently.

"How are you feeling?"

I smile and put on my best fake smile. "Yeah, I'm good."

He narrows his eyes, but he doesn't say anything else. He just wraps his arm around me and pulls me close to him while I rest my head on his shoulder.

"I thought you could stay at my place for a while, baby. Your parents, Dexter, and Eden have all gone back to Brighton when they found out you were coming home today. So I was thinking I can take care of you while you recover."

He cocks his head waiting for my response. I couldn't think of anything better than letting the man I love take care of me.

"I need to grab some stuff from the flat, if that's OK?"

He nods and smiles. "Yeah, of course, we'll swing by yours first then onto mine. I want you all to myself tonight, just you and me." I smile warmly. He chuckles softly. "We can get takeaway and I'll even stretch to a girly film, your choice!"

"That sounds like heaven, baby."

He plants a kiss on the top of my head. I am unusually quiet on the journey back to our flat. The thought that someone would want to hurt me deliberately makes my blood run cold. My thoughts are interrupted, as we pull up at the kerb and I climb out, promising Sam I will be as quick as I can. He kisses me gently on the lips and I make my way up to the flat. I open the door and the place is unusually tidy. Ruby is usually such a messy cow! I hear metal clinking as I step into the flat, my heart beat starts quickening and I panic that someone is in the flat.

"Ruby! Is that you? Have you finally come to your senses, you kinky bitch!"

I hear Jax's familiar voice shout. "I'm sorry, OK, you've made your fucking point, please just undo the cuffs, babe."

I look positively perplexed and walk to Ruby's bedroom. The door is ajar; I push it open further and find Jax in the middle of Ruby's bed, completely naked, handcuffed and blindfolded.

"Ruby? Come on, it's not funny anymore, stop teasing me, honey, please."

His voice is soft and pleading, I clear my throat. "Jax?"

He jumps.

"Peyton! *Fuck! Shit!* I'm sorry!" he curses, and I burst out into hysterical laughter.

"What the hell happened here, Jax?"

I try to avert my eyes from his naked form sprawled out on Ruby's bed, his impressive length resting on his pelvis. His dirty blonde hair is mussed; his body is toned, tattooed and bronzed. He has a body to die for, even though he is smaller than Sam, but very muscular. His legs are long and lean; I can't see an inch of fat on him, or an inch of skin that isn't covered in tattoos.

"Erm, Ruby handcuffed me. I stayed over, and she said she was teaching me a lesson. I didn't for one minute think she'd go to work and fucking leave me here."

I stifle my laughter and he clinks the handcuffs against the bed frame.

"Please, Peyton, babe. You need to un-cuff me."

I put my hand to my mouth to stop myself from laughing. I take a breath to compose myself.

"Honey, where are the keys? And how long have you been here?"

He squirms on the bed before answering through clenched teeth, "Erm, I don't know. She left my phone where I couldn't fucking reach it."

I avert my eyes away from his length to throw a cover over him.

"Hang tight, sweetie, I'll call her, just give me a sec."

I go out into the living room and the door swings open.

"Angel, is everything OK?"

Sam's tall frame walks into the flat and stands with his hands casually in his pockets. I look at him and smile.

"Yeah, everything's fine, babe."

He lets out a relieved breath.

"I was so worried; you said you'd only be ten minutes. I've literally had you murdered in fifty different ways."

I shake my head and roll my eyes, exasperated. *My possessive mercurial rocker is back.* He walks over to the kitchen.

"We've ... got a situation. I'm handling it, please don't go in Ruby's room."

He looks at me and cocks his pierced eyebrow.

"You can't say something like that and not expect me to go in there, babe!"

He leans in the doorway and bursts out into hysterical laughter.

"Jax! What the fuck, man!"

The handcuffs clink against Ruby's bed frame and he thrashes against the cuffs.

"Sam! Get the fuck out!"

Sam gets his phone out. "The boys have *got* to see this!"

He starts photographing Jax on his phone.

"Sam! You fucking dare send that to the boys they'll never let me forget it!"

Sam throws his head back and laughs hysterically, I roll my eyes. I take my phone out of my bag and dial Ruby's number, and she answers on the third ring.

"Hey, Rubes."

"Hey, babe, how are you feeling today?" she says in her familiar singsong voice and I clear my throat.

"Yeah, I'm good thanks, babe, how are you? I've just got back from the hospital."

She giggles mischievously. "I take it you found Jax then?"

I smirk. "Yep, sprawled out stark bollock naked, blindfolded, and handcuffed to your bed. What the fuck did he do?"

She laughs and says, "Let's just say he promised me that we were exclusive. We agreed we wouldn't see other people and I needed to teach him a lesson."

Poor Ruby, falling for yet another unfaithful man.

"I think you proved your point, babe, I need to un-cuff him. Where are the keys?"

I hear Sam laughing hysterically in the background and him typing on his phone.

"Sam! You fucking prick!" Jax shouts.

"You need to tell me where the keys are, babe, or I'm going to have a world war on my hands."

She is laughing hysterically down the phone. "All right keep your knickers on, babe! They're in my drawer next to my bed; I was going to come back at lunch to let him loose," she says innocently. I shake my head and walk back to her room. I sit on the edge of the bed and open the drawer, rooting around until I finally find the keys.

"Found them. I'm staying at Sam's for a few days. I'll call you."

"OK, babe, love ya."

"Right back at ya, Rubes, bye."

She hangs up and I unlock the handcuffs. I release Jax's arms and he struggles free of the blindfold, his eyes adjusting to the bright daylight streaming through the window.

"Christ, I need to take a piss."

He jumps off the bed still naked and bolts to the bathroom, cupping his manhood with both hands. Sam shakes his head and laughs. We go into my room and Sam helps me pack some of my stuff together. I grab my hair straighteners and zip up my bag. Sam takes it out into the living room where Jax is now fully dressed. We both smirk as we see the look on his face. His face is flaming red from blushing and he can't meet my eyes. *Poor Jax!*

"Do you need a lift home, mate?"

Jax nods. We leave the flat, and Skip drives us all to Sam's place. He pulls up at the kerb and Sam ushers me out of the car. I've never paid much attention before, but his building is actually impressive. Even though it is one of the smallest buildings in the area, it is all chrome and black glass from the outside with a plaque on the wall reading *Vengeance Towers*. How apt! Jax takes the stairs, still unusually quiet, leaving Sam and me to get into the waiting lift. He snakes his arms around my waist and pulls me close to him.

"I'm so glad you're all right, baby, I don't know what I would have done if..." He stops himself from carrying on his sentence and closes his eyes. I bury my head in his chest, relishing the closeness and desperately trying to reassure him. This side of him is a completely new side that I haven't seen before, and I'm not sure that I like it. I am vaguely aware that we don't go up to Sam's floor. We get off on another floor.

"I just need to check on something, angel." Sam's voice is soft, and he takes my hand, leading me down a light grey corridor with grey slate flooring all the way down. He taps the door, and I hear Cole's deep rumbling voice.

"Come in."

Sam swings the door open. Sam doesn't say anything but gestures me in before himself. I step into the room closely followed by Sam and I am faced with some sort of surveillance room which I haven't seen before. There is a bank of small flat screen TVs mounted on the wall, and Cole is sitting in front of them with his feet up on the desk, his hands casually behind his head. His wearing black dress trousers, a white shirt with two buttons undone, studying the footage closely.

"How are you getting on, mate?"

Cole takes a deep breath. "Nothing to report so far, mate, I'm still checking the footage from the night in question. I made a copy and handed one to the police, but I'm hoping to find something they might have missed. It's looking less and less likely if I'm honest."

He looks at me and nods. I smile, but I know it doesn't reach my eyes.

"I've forwarded the footage to Diego Sanchez; the guy's a genius, best at what he does, he might be able to come up with something."

He watches the screens carefully and rewinds the footage back.

"The person who did this... I want them fucking caught, Cole." Sam's voice is harsh and cold. He turns from Cole to me. "Do you think I'm letting you out of my sight knowing that there's still some fucking psycho out there who wants to hurt you?."

There's that possessive streak again. I don't know whether to be alarmed or grateful at his protectiveness, so I brush his arm.

"You can't keep me locked up in your castle in the sky, babe. I need to work."

His muscles tense and his nostrils flare.

"Then quit. I'm more than happy to take care of you, angel, I'm a very rich man."

I shake my head. "No. I'm not quitting; I happen to like my job. It's who I am, it's what I love, it's my passion. I'm not giving it up for you or some jealous psycho who's gunning for my blood."

Sam looks up to the ceiling and takes a deep breath.

"Stubborn woman, fine. If you need to work, I'll drive you myself every morning. I'll meet you for lunch and pick you up after work if that's what it takes. I've spoken to Seb and someone will be watching the shop twenty-four seven. If I can't drive you myself, then I'll send Cole. You're all right with that, aren't you, mate?"

Sam's tone of voice tells me it isn't a request—more of an order. Cole just smiles and nods, giving me a knowing look as if to say, *just humour him*.

"Yeah, sure, Sam, all part of the job description, mate."

Cole suddenly sits up straight in his seat and pushes himself closer to the screen. He backs up the footage; Sam leans on the back of Cole's chair and looks closer.

"Can you push in on that please, mate?"

I am daunted and unnerved by the amount of security Sam has in his building. It is all very hi-tech and very big brother is watching. I look at what has caught their eyes.

"Are you seeing what I'm seeing, mate?"

Cole backs it up again and zooms in further. I can't take my eyes away from the screen. A tall figure moves with precision and grace in front of the camera. It all happens so quick, but slowed down, it looks like a tall, slender, young girl wearing black jogging bottoms and a pink Rancid Vengeance hoodie. She has long, straight, bleached-blonde hair, black-rimmed glasses, and a black baseball cap. The same girl is picked up again in the parking garage, but disappears into a blind spot, which was near to where my car was parked. She's gone for approximately ten minutes, according to the timer on the screen, and then reappears outside the front of the building. I stand there opened-mouthed, and Sam leans down on the desk.

"*Mother fucker,*" he growls. "How the fucking fuck did we miss this?" He bangs his fist down on the desk.

"Sam, calm down, mate. Not in front of your lady, it won't help things."

Cole's voice is calm and soothing; it is the most I have heard him speak since I met him. I am still in shock at what I have seen on the screen. I was right; maybe it was a scorned woman or just a jealous fan that's responsible for this. Sam gets his phone out of his pocket and starts frantically tapping at the screen. He holds it up to his ear.

"Yeah. It's Sam. We've got something. You need to get down here right now. I'll make it worth your while. No, the longer you leave it, the longer my girl is in danger. You of all people should understand that. I don't give a fuck. Good, I'll see you in ten. Yeah, make sure you do. OK, bye."

Even agitated, he still looks gorgeous; he hangs up the phone and plants a kiss on top of my head.

"Everything's going to be all right, baby, I promise."

He smiles, and it feels like ages since I saw that beautiful smile on his handsome face.

"I need to make some more calls, angel. I'll be right back." He winks and kisses my cheek. "Look after my girl, Cole."

Cole smirks and salutes. "Yes, boss!"

Sam smiles and leaves the room, leaving me in the company of Cole.

"Is he like this with all the women he's been with?" My curiosity gets the better of me. Cole takes a sip of his coffee and laughs.

"Nope, just you, sugar. No other women have come close to the way he is with you. He's a good guy; he quite clearly worships the ground you walk on. I've never seen him this way with anyone before. He actually wakes up with a purpose and it's refreshing to see." Cole's voice is warm, and I relish the information he is giving me.

"What was he like before? You know, the drugs?"

Cole hangs his head. "He told you about that, huh?"

I nod and regard him intently.

"He was a complete mess. I thought he was going to kill himself before he hit twenty-five. He and Brody are not good together, they're a bad influence on each other. Sam knows it and everyone else knows it. J.D and the band won't fire him because they all have some twisted loyalty to him. All except for Jax. Jax sees what effect he has on Sam, and he resents Brody for it. I know the whole rehab thing was hard on you, Peyton, but you have to understand he was trying to protect you and he was a completely different person back then. He cared for no one, he shagged around with countless groupies, no feelings, no emotions, nothing. It was like he was dead behind the eyes. Since you came along, he has changed, he has a purpose, and he's hopelessly in love with you."

He smiles a genuine wide straight smile and continues, "I know it's none of my business, but you need to be a little more understanding. I like you, you're a genuine girl, and you make him happy. When he found out you were in that accident, it was as if his whole world was crumbling around him. When stuff like that happens, it triggers off something inside his head, something just clicks, and he hits the self-destruct button. He was devastated, I had never seen him that broken before. Not over a woman, anyway. He would give his life to protect you, but he doesn't like stuff happening that he can't control. The whole driving you to work? Please just humour him, it will make my job so much easier and more bearable."

I smile and take in all the new information that Cole has given me. I perch on the edge of the desk.

"The night of the accident, he said you and Jax locked him in the bathroom?"

Cole lets out a rich rumbling laugh.

"We did a little bit more than that, sugar. We found him slumped in the bath with six empty bottles of vodka and lines of coke all over the toilet seat. He was a total mess. He was passed out, so I turned the shower on him to get him to come around; I know how to handle him when he is in this kind of state. I called his dad and he came to the hospital to sit with you while Sam was having his episode. We cleaned up the bathroom and he finally came around. We locked the door and left him there to stew for a while. There's nothing like cold turkey to get him to come to his senses. He is nowhere near as bad as he was in the early days, but I handle him, he seems to listen to me."

I nod. I have never seen Cole this chatty before and I'm enjoying getting to know him and the part he plays in Sam's life. He is not just his security guard and chauffeur; he seems to play a bigger role in his life than he lets on. Not only is he a close friend to Sam, he is also a mentor and a much-needed calming influence.

"Do these episodes happen regularly?"

He looks at me and smirks. "You sure ask a lot of questions, sugar!"

I narrow my eyes at him and try a different approach. "What happened on the night of the album launch after I left?"

He cocks his head and leans back in his chair.

"Look, sugar, it's really not my place to be telling you any of this."

I raise my eyebrows and ask, "Did something happen after I left? I caught him and Brody snorting cocaine in the office."

Cole leans back heavily in his chair, and he is about to speak when the door opens, abruptly and prematurely ending our conversation. Sam walks back into the room, and a few minutes later, there is another tap on the door. Sam opens it and greets the two men inviting them into the room.

"Cole, could you play the footage again, please?"

Sam comes closer to me and edges his way between my legs. He wraps his arms around me.

"I promise we won't be much longer, but the police need to speak to you, baby."

He feels me tense against him and he runs his hands up my spine.

"It's going to be all right, we're going to get this bastard if it's the last thing I do, angel, I promise you."

The two men are studying the footage with careful eyes. Sam unwraps me from his embrace and pulls me to my feet. One of the men comes over to Sam and smiles warmly.

"Babe, this is Tate Jackson, he is our P.R guy. Tate, this is my beautiful girlfriend, Peyton."

Tate reaches for my hand; I take it and smile back.

"Pleased to meet you, Tate."

He nods. "You too, Peyton, it's a pleasure. I've heard a lot about you."

"All good, I hope."

He smiles. "Of course, darlin', this man is definitely smitten."

"All right, mate. I've got my rock star reputation to keep up!"

Sam and Tate laugh. Tate turns to Sam. "How do you want me to deal with the press then, mate? They're asking all sorts of questions about the accident, it's getting harder to shake them off with the old 'we don't know any more at this stage, it's still pending a police investigation'. I'm not sure how much longer I can fob them off before they start making shit up."

Tate folds his arms. Sam puts his hand to his head and sighs.

"Just try and hold them off for a few more days please, mate, the police need to speak to Peyton first."

Tate nods. "I'll make a few calls and call in a few favours. I'll sort it, mate, just leave it to me."

Tate winks and Sam shakes his hand. The other man who stepped into the room comes over to us.

"Miss Harper, I'm Detective Wilson Scott. I need to ask you a few questions about the accident, if that's OK with you?"

I nod, and he smiles, but it doesn't reach his eyes. Tate leaves telling Sam he will be in touch about the press release. Sam leads us out of the room, and we step into the lift and go back up to his apartment in complete silence.

"Do you want tea or coffee, mate?"

The detective nods and says, "Tea would be great. Milk, no sugar. Cheers."

Sam nods and he goes into the kitchen. I sit down on the corner sofa and the Detective sits at the other end. He takes out a notebook, and I suddenly feel uncomfortable.

"Miss Harper—"

I stop him. "Peyton, please."

He nods curtly. "Could you describe to me what you were doing when the accident occurred? Where were you going?"

"I stayed at Sam's the night before. I was pulling out of the parking garage to drive to work, I'm a tattoo artist at Saint Sinner Ink in Islington."

He takes down what I have said, and he nods. "OK, what happened immediately prior to the accident?"

"I had to stop because there was a bus coming, I pumped the brakes, but nothing was happening. I don't remember anything after that, I'm really sorry, it's all kind of hazy."

He writes it down. Sam comes back into the room with the tea and coffees. He puts the cups down on the table and sits down next to me. He puts his hand on my thigh in a gesture of reassurance and sips his coffee with his free hand.

"Is there anyone you can think of who might have a grudge against you?"

I am taken aback by that question. *Talk about going right for the jugular. Someone who could have a grudge against me?* I visibly shudder at the thought. I shake my head and squeeze Sam's hand.

"No, no one that I can think of."

Then I start thinking of all the times that J.D has threatened me. But he couldn't really be capable of something like this, could he? I push that thought to the back of my mind and decide not to say anything to Sam or Detective Scott. Before I know it, the detective gets up and puts his notebook in his jacket pocket.

"Thank you for your time, Miss Harper, this will be an on-going investigation, and we'll be in touch."

Sam and I both stand up and shake his hand in turn.

"Can I walk you out?" Sam asks. The detective nods and Sam kisses the top of my head. "I won't be long, angel."

Sam escorts him out of the apartment. I wonder what Sam could possibly have to say to the detective without my presence.

We spend the rest of the evening watching Netflix in Sam's living room snuggled up on the sofa. I am glad of the normality and it starts to feel like we are a normal couple with a bright future ahead of us. I fall asleep in Sam's lap, and the next thing I know, I am being carried into Sam's room. I open my eyes as he deposits me in his large comfortable bed.

"Come on sleepy head; let's get you ready for bed," Sam says. I go to get up, but he pushes me back down. "No, let me, baby."

I am too tired to fight him. He strips off my jeans, my white vest, and my shirt until I am lying on his bed in my underwear.

"You're so beautiful," he says huskily and strokes my cheek with the back of his hand. I smile and lean into his hand. He bends down and kisses me gently on the lips, tucking me into bed. I feel like I am five years old all over again!

"I need to make some more calls, baby, and I've got some stuff that needs my attention, but I'll be in soon, I promise."

Before he has left the room, I am a slave to sleep. I don't know how long I have been asleep, but Sam writhing in his sleep next to me suddenly wakes me.

"Peyton, angel, I'm sorry, I'm sorry, I'm sorry. Please forgive me, don't leave me, I need you, I'm so sorry." His voice is broken and desperate; his face is glistening with a thin sheen of sweat. He looks troubled and his face is contorted. His fists are bunching the bed sheets and his brow is furrowed. *No. No. No. Peyton.* Please don't leave me."

Seeing him so distressed physically makes my heart ache in my chest. He normally looks so peaceful and content when he is asleep. I move closer to him and gently stroke his face.

"Sam, baby, I'm here, wake up," I tell him, my voice soft. He continues to bunch the sheets and writhe in his sleep. I shake his arm gently and speak louder, hoping I will get through to him. "Sam."

Suddenly, he sits bolt upright, his arms are flailing, and he strikes me in the face. The slap echoes through the bedroom, I am physically shocked and shaken at his outburst. I let out a shriek and his eyes fly open. He looks at me and my eyes are glazed.

"*Fuck,*" he curses. He is covered in sweat; his eyes are wide and pained; I don't think he can believe what just happened.

"Baby, it's OK," I try to reassure him, and he shakes his head.

"I'm so fucking sorry," he whispers. I stroke his arm and he recoils from me, snatching his arm away from my touch as if I have burnt him. I watch as he gets out of bed and the moonlight casts a glow on his defined, undulating muscles and I can see the fine detail in his intricate back tattoo.

"Sam!"

He strides out of the room running his hands through his hair in a pair of black boxer briefs, ignoring me calling out his name. I am physically shaken by his behaviour and curious at what his nightmare was about. I pull the covers off, grab Sam's t-shirt from the floor, pull it on, and go out into the apartment to look for him. I look all over the apartment for him and eventually find him sitting on the balcony floor with his knees brought up to his chest. His head is leaned back against the window as he sips a glass of amber liquid with a trembling hand, his face sullen and tear-stained.

"Baby."

I make my way over to him and crouch down next to him, the cool night air causing me to shiver.

"Don't," he says, his voice a low rasp. I am inches away from him, so I brush his arm reassuringly. "I said don't," he chokes out and recoils from my touch.

"It's all right. What were you dreaming about?"

He lets out a strangled sob. "I fucking hit you. How can you even still be here? You need to go."

"You didn't mean it. I'm not leaving you, look at the state of you."

His face is pale; his eyes are haunted and scared.

"Please, you need to go right now," he pleads. He hugs his knees closer to his chest and I can see his whole body is shaking uncontrollably.

"Sam, please talk to me, I'm not going anywhere."

He shakes his head and scrambles to his feet, completely ignoring my presence. He strides over into the kitchen and picks up his phone.

"Cole, yeah, I know what time it is, I'm really sorry. Yeah, tell Amy I'm sorry too. I'll make it up to her, I promise. Can you come and take Peyton home please? OK, thanks, mate, I owe you one. Yeah, bye."

He hangs up the phone and looks at me.

REVELATIONS TATTOOS AND TEARS BOOK 2

"Why are you doing this? Just tell me what you were dreaming about, please?"

He scrubs his hands down his face.

"I dreamt that you were gone, that you died in that car accident. Are you happy now?" His voice is hoarse as he continues, "I was trying to save you, but every time I got close, I got pushed further and further away from you. No matter how close I got, you were always out of my reach, I couldn't get to you in time."

He is sobbing uncontrollably now, and I move closer to him. I want to throw my arms around him and reassure him, but he steps back. He wipes his eyes with the back of his hand and sniffs.

"It's all my fucking fault. I'm no good for you, Peyton, you deserve so much more than what I can give you. You should run screaming in the other direction."

I shake my head and tell him, "I love you so much, Sam, I couldn't run even if I wanted to."

He puts his hands to his head and laughs bitterly.

"You should, I hurt you, and I hit you in my sleep. What if I hadn't woken up? What if I had gone further? God, it doesn't bear thinking about, anything could have fucking happened."

I look up at him, and a tap on the door interrupts us. Sam paces out of the kitchen and opens the apartment door. I follow him and Cole steps into the living area. He is wearing blue-plaid pyjama bottoms, slippers, and a white t-shirt, and he looks the most casual I have seen him since I met him. He looks between us.

"Sam, mate, talk to me, what's going on?" he asks, his voice soft and calming. Sam walks over to the window with his back to us both.

"Just take her home, mate, please." His voice is barely a whisper and Cole keeps his eyes trained on me.

"Peyton, come on, sugar, let me take you home."

He takes me by the elbow. I shrug him off and walk over to Sam, spinning him around to face me. I am not about to watch the man I love push me away.

"I'm not fucking walking out of here, not until you talk to me, Sam."

He towers over me and closes his eyes.

"Look at me," I raise my voice; he complies, and he looks at me. "This isn't just over some nightmare."

He shakes his head.

"I hit you, angel, how can you even stand to be near me? You don't get it, you're too good for me, all I do is hurt you, the drugs, the accident... All of it is my fucking fault."

I daringly decide to change my tactics. I move closer to him, and when he starts to move backwards from me, I grab his arm and pull him closer to me until we are nose to nose.

"Baby, take me to bed and fuck me until I can't remember my own name," I whisper seductively in his ear and his breathing hitches. Cole continues to look from Sam to me and back again, observing our exchange and gauging Sam's reaction.

"Do you need me to take her home, Sam?"

Sam doesn't take his eyes off me and silently shakes his head.

"OK, mate, call me if you need anything else, goodnight," he says, shutting the door of the apartment behind him.

"Fuck me, Sam." I nip his earlobe and crash my lips against his. I suck his tongue until I feel him yield against my touch. Sam lifts me up in one rapid move and I lock my legs tightly around his waist. "I need you, Sam."

He doesn't say a word; he just loosens his grip and pushes my hair back from my shoulder. He kisses a trail from behind my ear to my collarbone, my favourite turn-on spot. He walks with me in his arms to the kitchen and sits me down on the worktop. The coldness of the marble makes me shiver. He takes his t-shirt off me in one lithe move, and then I am completely naked and at his mercy. He lowers his head to suck my nipple into his mouth. I moan softly, and he looks into my eyes, the pain from earlier replaced with pure lust. The corner of Sam's mouth twitches into the curve of a smile.

"Tell me what you want."

His voice is back to its usual husky orgasmic best, and it is the first time he has spoken. I shake my head and smirk.

"I'm the one in control now, Newbolt," I whisper.

"Is that so?" I nod and bite my lip seductively. I push him backwards and he holds his hands out to the side. "I'm all yours, beautiful."

He chuckles softly and lifts me down from the worktop. I push his boxer briefs down his muscular thighs and he steps out of them. His length is standing to attention and I lick my lips. I sink down to my knees and take his hardness into my mouth. He closes his eyes and groans softly.

"*Jesus*, what are you doing to me?"

I take him deep in my throat and run my tongue over the bell-shaped tip.

"You have a rather beautiful cock, Mr Newbolt."

He chuckles softly. I bob my head up and down as I take him further into my mouth, licking and sucking as I go. I can feel his cock twitching as I cup his balls.

"*Fuck,* that feels so good."

I keep sucking and open my throat to take him as far into my mouth as I can go.

"*Shit!* I'm going to come."

He spurts his seed into my mouth yelling as he finds his release, "Oh, *fuck*, Peyton."

I swallow and look up at him with a satisfied grin plastered on my face. He helps me to my feet and pulls me close to him.

"*Jesus,* that was a fucking awesome blow job," he says, causing us both to erupt into a fit of giggles.

"My turn," he says with a wink. "Lean back on your elbows for me, baby."

I do as he says, and a devilish grin spreads across his face.

"Who's in control now?"

I bite my lip.

"I said, who's in control?" His voice is commanding, and he sounds hot as hell. Our eyes lock.

"You are."

He nods, and I am panting with anticipation.

"Good girl, see how easily you submit to me?" He lifts my leg over his shoulder burying his face between my legs as his expert tongue licks my clit. "*Christ*, you're fucking soaking."

He laps at my pussy and I writhe underneath him.

"I need you to stay still," he whispers against me, and I do as he says. He pushes his long finger into me, and I moan softly.

"Oh, Sam."

He introduces a second finger. He lazily pushes it in and out while still licking my wetness. My breathing is laboured, and I bite my lip. I bite so hard I'm sure I can taste blood. I can feel my orgasm cresting like a wave. With one, long, lazy move of his tongue, I am lost in a ripple of pure ecstasy as I erupt, screaming his name.

"Sam, Sam, *Sam*. Fuck, *Sam*."

He lifts his head up and a wide grin crosses his face. He pulls me to a sitting position and plants a long lingering kiss on my lips.

"I'm sorry, angel."

I shake my head and put my finger to his lips. "Shhh, please just fuck me Sam; I'm not finished with you yet."

"I actually quite like it when you take control, no woman has ever done that before, and it's so fucking hot."

He lifts me down from the kitchen island and I lead him out onto the balcony where there is a dark-brown wicker table, two matching chairs and a black sun lounger. He raises his eyebrow.

"Outdoor fucking? Someone's feeling brave."

He chuckles softly and lifts me weightlessly in his strong arms. He lays me down on the sun lounger and straddles me, his muscular thighs on either side of me. He takes both of my wrists in one of his hands and pins them above my head. He presses his body against mine, and I love the feel of his skin on mine. He kisses my neck, and I wrap my leg around his waist. He moves his head down my chest, nips my breast with his teeth, and kisses a trail from my breasts to my navel. I am writhing underneath him as he touches every part of me. I can feel his erection pressing against my stomach.

"See how hard you make me?" he whispers against me.

"Fuck me hard, Sam."

He shakes his head. "I don't want to fuck, angel."

The tip of his erection finds my entrance and he pushes himself inside me. I let out a scream; he crashes his lips against mine to silence me.

"Shhh, I've got you, my lovely."

He takes my nipple in his mouth and gently laps it with his tongue. He moves in and out at a pace somewhere between slow and frantic, driving me higher and higher towards my second orgasm. He increases his thrusts, expertly swivelling his hips, he is so deep it feels like he is hitting my womb with every drive. We both explode at the same time yelling out incoherent cries of ecstasy. Sam is on top of me with his head nuzzled into my neck.

"Baby, that was ... *fuck*."

I chuckle softly. We lie like that in silence for a while, listening to the sound of our pounding heartbeats. He slowly pulls out of me, gets to his feet, and pulls me to mine. He picks me up and carries me inside.

"Come on, baby, I'm taking you back to bed."

With those words, the nightmare and the events of the night are forgotten.

3

Peyton

I am getting stronger and healing as the day's progress. I have been staying at Sam's since I left hospital and my possessive, mercurial rocker has been visiting more frequently. I am starting to feel a little suffocated by his constant need to keep me safe.

I am back at the shop working on reception to gently ease me back into things. Cole is driving me to work every morning; Sam has Skip sitting in his car outside the shop watching my every move. It is actually really starting to freak me out. I understand his need to keep me safe, but it seems a little unnecessary and excessive.

I wake up one morning with Sam's body wrapped around me like a vine; he looks so peaceful and carefree when he is sleeping. I pull myself from his vice grip and shower ready for the day ahead. I am so glad it's Friday. I am rinsing the shampoo from my hair when I feel Sam's large frame fold in behind me.

"Good morning, angel."

His voice is raspy and causes that familiar ache between my legs. He kisses my neck as the water cascades between our bodies. He takes my purple shower puff and puts my favourite strawberry shower gel on it, washing my body so gently as if I am made of glass. I love it when he is in this mood and he is tending to my every need. He finishes washing my body, and I repeat the action for him, washing every inch of his large tattooed body in a comfortable silence. We both step out of the shower at the same time and wrap ourselves in warm towels to dry off. We get dressed for work, moving fluidly around each other. He is in the mirror styling his hair when I break the silence.

"I think I'm going to move back to the flat today, babe."

He pulls on a black vest and layers it with a blue, black, and white checked shirt. He nods, as he buttons it up.

That was relatively easy.

"I'll call Diego and have his security team fit some CCTV cameras and station a guard permanently in your building."

I roll my eyes. *Here we go again.*

"Don't you think you're being a little too cautious, honey?" I try to placate him, but he looks at me as if to say '*are-you-joking*.'

"I'm just trying to keep you safe. The person who cut your brakes is still out there, and until they're caught, security measures are necessary." He pulls on his jeans then says, "Move in with me, angel."

I look at him as I pull the zip up on my denim shorts. My eyes widen at his sudden proposition, feeling suddenly exasperated.

"I didn't mean to just blurt it out like that, it's not how I planned on asking, but it makes perfect sense. You already practically live here anyway."

I shake my head, suddenly angry with him.

"No, you can't bloody do this, Sam! I like living with Ruby. I thought we were meant to be taking things slow. One step at a time, babe, we agreed I need my own space and you're fucking suffocating me." I raise my voice and he moves closer to me.

"I'm so sorry, it's because I love you, I want to protect you, and the thought of someone hurting you makes me feel ... violent and ..."

He doesn't finish his sentence and my eyes glaze over. *Stand your ground, Harper.*

"This is all too much, Sam, all of it. I feel uncomfortable and on edge all the time having people guarding me. You can't constantly monitor me. It's unhealthy. I'm terrified enough as it is."

I move back from him, needing some distance from him, and walk out into the living area. Cole is standing by the door with his hands in his pockets. I wonder how long he has been standing there and if he heard Sam and me arguing. I feel like I actually want to scream out in frustration, but I don't.

"Good morning, Peyton," he says with a nod, and I paint on a fake smile.

"Morning, Cole."

The door to Sam's apartment opens, and a young woman walks in, holding a little girl in her arms. The woman has black curly hair, flawless, coffee-coloured skin, and she is very beautiful. Her eyes are wide and almost black in colour and she has a friendly, warm smile. The little girl is equally as beautiful with a matching skin tone, bright, wide, inquisitive eyes and her curly black hair framing her face. She is adorable. I smile at her, and she blows a raspberry at me.

"Where's Sam, sugar?"

She looks at Cole and kisses his cheek. Cole wraps his arm around her slender waist.

"You know by now, babe, that boy always takes forever to get ready in the mornings. He's worse than a woman!"

They both laugh.

"I'm sorry, Peyton. This is my fiancée, Amy, and our beautiful daughter, Addison."

Amy reaches her hand out and I shake it.

"It's so good to finally meet you, hon, I feel like I know you already!"

She smiles brightly, and I find myself smiling back just as brightly.

"It's good to meet you too, Amy."

Sam walks out of the bedroom, rolling up the sleeves of his shirt.

"Amy."

Amy looks at him. "Thank you so much for the spa day, sweetie; it was just what I needed. You didn't have to."

Sam smiles. "You're welcome, Aims, and yes I did, I had to make it up to you somehow."

I think back to what he had to make up for. Then I remember the nightmare last week when Sam called Cole at three in the morning. She gives Sam a one-armed hug and kisses him on the cheek. Sam plucks the toddler from Amy's arms, her face lights up, and she plants a sloppy kiss on Sam's cheek.

"Hey, Princess Addie."

His eyes dance with laughter. He blows a raspberry on her neck and she giggles.

"Uncle Sammy!"

Seeing Sam with Addison makes my heart melt.

"Uncle Sammy has missed you lots, beautiful."

He swings the little girl around and throws her in the air. Amy rolls her eyes and turns to me.

"I swear he turns into an even bigger kid every time he's around her."

I laugh, and it is a welcome change to see Sam so happy and cheerful. I instantly get to thinking that one day he will make a brilliant dad. *Jesus, where did that come from? Baby steps, Harper.* I grab my coat and my bag, ready for work, and kiss Sam gently on the lips.

"I'll see you at lunch, I'll text you." He winks. "I love you."

Cole gestures for me to step out of the apartment before him. But I spin around, suddenly feeling more than a little rebellious.

"I-I've forgotten my phone, sorry, just give me a sec."

Cole nods and I go back into the apartment. I rush into the kitchen, grab a set of Sam's car keys from the magnetic rack not knowing which car they are for, and I quickly shove them into my coat pocket. I go back into the apartment, kiss Sam goodbye, and go out of the door. I silently follow Cole into the waiting lift and we go down to the parking garage. We step out of the lift, and Cole's phone starts ringing.

"Yeah, all clear, mate."

I take advantage of Cole's distraction and push the key fob—the lights of an electric-blue Dodge sport flash. I rush over, quickly open the door, and jump into the driver's seat. I see Cole sprint across the parking garage; I start the engine and pull out of the space at a speed.

"Peyton!" Cole's face is panicked, and he puts his hand to his head. "*Fuck!*" I hear him curse and I look at him with sympathetic eyes, mouthing the word 'sorry,' as I drive out of the parking garage.

I push the black button on the dashboard and the security gate opens. I pull out of the parking garage and almost instantly my phone starts ringing, Sam's name flashes up on the screen. I ignore the phone and begin my journey to work.

I am more than happy to have gained some of my independence back, and it is the first time I have been behind the wheel of a car since my accident. I could get used to this car; it is sleek, modern and drives like a dream. My phone rings constantly until I open the door to the shop. Seb's face lights up as I walk in.

"Mornin', honey." He gets up from his seat and walks over to me. He pulls me in for a bear hug.

"Morning, sweetie."

"It's so good to have you back, babe, I've missed ya."

Seb has been in America for two weeks finalising the details on his new shop, this is the first time I have seen him since he visited me in hospital.

"You're looking so much better."

I smile. "Thanks, I feel much better, actually."

My phone starts ringing again, and I silence it.

"Is everything all right, babe?"

I nod. "Yeah, everything's fine, nothing I can't handle, sweetie."

I go to the back of the shop to stow my stuff away and my phone starts ringing again. I see Ruby's name flash up on the screen.

"Hey, babe."

She lets out a breath. "Thank God you're all right. Sam called, he's been trying to get hold of you, he sounds really pissed. He says you dodged his security and took off in one of his cars." I hear the smile in her voice.

"I might have dodged Cole and drove to work in one of his sports cars! He has me constantly monitored. Fucking hell, Ruby, there's a guard sitting in a four by four right outside the shop. He is being ridiculous," I say, exasperated.

"I know you were trying to teach him a lesson, and I think you succeeded, but please call him back, babe. Let him know you're all right, he is going postal back there."

"OK, I'll call him, Rubes. I'll see you back at the flat, later."

"Bye, sweetie."

I hang up, switch my phone to silent, and put it in my bag. I need to teach Sam not to be so possessive. I go back into the shop and Harley has arrived. Harley Hernandez is a close friend of Seb's who runs Black Tiger Ink and guest spots for Seb from time to time. Harley is half-Spanish, medium height, very muscular, and with a medium build. He has long black hair pulled into a ponytail, with a black and white skull bandana around his head. He has a dark, trimmed goatee and light-brown eyes. We have a history; we went out on a few dates and he was one of the men I slept with while I was trying to get over Callum. He smiles as he sees me.

"Beautiful, *Chica*. Peyton, looking ravishing as ever."

He kisses me on both cheeks and Seb rolls his eyes.

"Do you mind not harassing my shop manager, Harley. Cheers, mate."

Seb and Harley both laugh. I go over to the reception desk and sit down. I take the lid off my Starbucks cup and take a long sip, relishing the caffeine as the warm liquid slides down my throat. I sink back into the leather chair and put my feet up on the desk, but I am startled, as I look up and see Sam's large frame in the shop doorway. His stance is loose, and he is breathing heavily; he looks positively murderous. He opens the door and strides in, his eyes locking with mine. Seb sees the look on his face and comes over.

"What the fuck do you think you're playing at, Peyton?"

I stand up defiantly and move towards him.

"What's going on honey? Is everything OK?"

Sam looks at Seb. "This isn't your concern, Seb." Sam's voice is cold and Seb folds his arms, his muscles bulging.

"I think it is when you're quite clearly upsetting her."

Sam takes a deep breath, and I can see he is counting to ten to try to calm himself down.

"You were suffocating me; you won't let me out of your sight since the accident. You've got a guard sitting outside the place where I work, for fuck's sake. What was I supposed to do? Humour you? Do as you tell me like a good little girl? I don't fucking think so, Sam," I spit out angrily and Sam growls. His stance is predatory, and his fists are clenched tightly at his sides. I can feel the anger radiating off him in large tsunami-like waves.

"Don't test me, Peyton. I'm trying to protect you; don't you get that? You dodged Cole and you took my goddamn car. I was going out of my fucking mind!" His raised voice is raspy, and he frantically runs his hands through his hair. "Anything could have happened—"

I hold up my finger to stop him. "But it didn't. There's a fine line between protecting me and suffocating me, Sam. You're being irrational."

Sam goes to step closer to me, but Seb moves in front of me, his large frame shielding me from Sam.

"Back the fuck up, mate. I think you've said enough, you need to calm down," Seb says in a calm voice.

They are toe to toe, and the way they are sizing each other up, I think they might start fighting in the middle of the shop floor. I side-step Seb and get in-between both of them.

"Sam, Seb, please stop."

Their eyes are still locked, and I try to push both of them back to no avail, due to their sheer size and strength compared to my small frame.

"Please, just stop!" I plead with both of them.

"It's all right, honey. Harley, get her out of here, mate, please. Sam and I need to have a little chat," Seb says calmly. Harley comes over and takes me by the wrist. As Harley's hand makes contact with my wrist, I hear Sam snarl and I roll my eyes.

"Come on, mi Amor, there's no appointments for an hour or so. I'll make us some coffee. I think there's some chocolate biscuits tucked away somewhere."

He smiles and takes me into the back of the shop. He switches the kettle on and I put my hand to my head.

"That was ... how you say? Intense?"

I nod and Harley smiles.

"The two men in your life fighting for your honour."

I shake my head and he hands me a chocolate biscuit. I bite into it; there is nothing like a hit of chocolate to calm the nerves.

"It's not like that at all. Since my accident, Sam's been acting strange. I can't help but think he is keeping something from me. Seb's just trying to protect me; he is like a brother to me. Sam can be intense and extremely pig-headed when it comes to protecting what's his."

I find myself strangely comfortable with telling Harley my troubles. It should be awkward that we had sex, but it isn't. He makes us both a cup of coffee and hands me the cup, regarding me intently.

"So you're *his* then? You're his property to do as he pleases and speak to how he pleases?"

Harley's brow furrows, and I shake my head, feeling the need to defend Sam.

"It's not like that at all, Harley."

I am leaning against the worktop biting my nails nervously when he brushes my arm.

"It will be OK, *miquerido.*"

I hear raised voices from the shop; I put my cup down and rush out. Harley is following close behind me, and I find Sam pinned to the wall with Seb's large hand closed around his throat. Seb is a few inches taller than Sam is and he looks positively menacing. Seb draws his fist back and Harley stops him, pushing him a few inches away from Sam.

"Seb, stop."

Seb drops his fist and lets go of Sam's throat. Sam goes to grab Seb, but I step in front of him and Seb jabs his finger at Sam, his jaw clenched tight.

"You ever fucking speak to her like that ever again, and I swear your pathetic rock star life won't be worth living." Seb's voice is cold and harsh. Sam's eyes harden.

"I can't fucking compete with you!" Sam runs his hands through his hair and his jaw is tense. I move closer to him until I am inches away from him.

Whoa! Where did that come from?

"Sam, I'm yours, you don't have to compete for my affections, but if you carry on behaving the way you are, you'll push me further away."

Sam takes a deep breath and his eyes start to soften.

"I'm so sorry, angel." His voice is hoarse and broken; I cup his face in my hands.

"I'm sorry I ran from Cole, I felt so ... trapped, but I understand that you were trying to protect me."

He envelopes me in his strong arms.

"Please don't run from me, angel, I can't bear it. Something happened way beyond my control and it ripped me open completely. I felt raw, like you could be taken away from me with a blink of an eye. I would die for you, Peyton, and I'm doing everything in my power to keep you safe. Everything I do is for you. Everything I own is yours. Everything I am is down to you, and I'm the man I am now because of you. If we hadn't met, I would still be that empty shell that used sex to forget how bad my life had become."

I squeeze him tightly and it is as if our argument is forgotten. Seb clears his throat. I let go of Sam and we both smirk.

"PDA in my shop is a hard limit for me, honey."

I raise my eyebrows. "Someone's been reading too many erotic novels about kinky billionaires."

"Touché!"

Sam kisses me gently on the lips. "I need to go, baby, I skipped out on a TV interview this morning, and the guys are pretty pissed with me. We've got a bunch of interviews, photo shoots, appearances, and signings today, but I'll call you as soon as I'm free."

I nod. He smiles that dazzling smile and leaves the shop, saluting to Seb and Harley as he leaves.

"Well, that was ... eventful!"

"I'm so sorry, Seb, I shouldn't bring my domestic shit to work with me, it's unprofessional."

"Don't worry, honey, it's fine, honestly."

He kisses the top of my head and with that, the dramatic events of the morning are soon forgotten as we lose ourselves in our work. The day is busy even just sitting behind a desk and I am glad when the closed sign goes up.

"Do you fancy coming for a drink to start the weekend, honey?" Seb says as I'm getting my coat on and I nod.

"Yeah, OK, why not. Just one, though."

"Of course." He winks.

"I'll call Ruby to see if she fancies joining us."

Seb nods. "The more the merrier, honey."

I call Ruby, and she agrees to meet us there. I re-apply my makeup and we lock up the shop. I link Seb's arm and walk to a bar near to the shop called Oscillo. It is a large bar with an urban bordello and a unique burlesque style with its ruby-red ceiling, tassel lampshades, and candelabras, with a solid Wild West saloon-style bar. It is one of my favourite bars and the food is to die for. It's just what I need to unwind after today. We walk in and Seb goes to the bar.

"What are you having to drink, honey?"

I don't hesitate, this place boasts the best cocktails. My favourite is called a Pont berry: vodka, cranberry, and cassis liqueur.

"A Pont berry, please, babe."

Seb raises his eyebrows. "Got it."

Harley gives Seb his drink order and we go to find a table. We grab a free booth and I scoot along the bench seat.

"So, you and the rock star. Is it serious?" Harley sits so close to me I can feel his warm spicy breath on my cheek.

"Do you mean are you still in with a chance?"

He laughs. *I have your card marked, Hernandez.*

"OK, you caught me, you can't blame a guy for trying, and you are more stunning every time I see you."

I am about to respond, when Seb comes over with the drinks followed by Ruby. He climbs in the opposite side of the booth.

"Hey, babe," she says.

"Hey, Rubes."

Harley moves out of the booth and leaves the table; Ruby scoots in next to me.

"What the fuck is his problem?"

I roll my eyes. "Long story, babe."

She raises her eyebrows. "Oooh, do tell."

Ruby takes a long pull on her glass of wine. I suddenly feel myself blushing and she eyes me carefully.

"Fuck me, you shagged him, didn't you?"

I take a sip of my drink and nod shamefully.

"It wasn't my finest hour, babe, believe me."

She narrows her eyes and asks, "Was he good?"

Seb almost chokes on his beer across the table.

"TMI, Ruby, I have to work with the guy. I don't want to be picturing him butt naked, thanks!"

Ruby smiles sweetly and blows him a kiss.

"So, details, was he good? Marks out of ten!"

"A lady never kisses and tells, babe," I say coyly, and she pouts.

More than a few drinks later, I get up to go to the toilet and I am more than a little bit drunk. I go to the ladies and am surprised that I don't have a thousand missed calls from Sam. I wash my hands and check my reflection in the mirror. I leave the toilet and see Harley in the corridor talking to another man. He has long blonde hair and looks almost European with pale-blue eyes. I listen to their conversation in the shadows.

"She was a tiger in the bedroom, she loved to be tied up and blindfolded. She was a ... how you say ... kinky bitch!" The other man starts laughing, and Harely continues,

"I swear that rock star she is dating, he is one lucky son-of-a-bitch. He has no clue what he is letting himself in for."

My heart drops when I realise he is talking about me.

"She loved it when I pulled her hair, she liked it rough, and it was the biggest turn on ever. I have never met anyone like her, she is a sexual goddess. It's always the quiet ones, man, I'm telling you, and we Spanish know how to give a woman an orgasm."

They both laugh, and I can't believe what I am hearing. *What a fucking prick!* I knew he was a slimy bastard but not to this extent. It's not even as if it's true; men fucking embellishing their sexual encounters to make themselves look good. I am so fucking angry right now. I take a deep breath and walk confidently down the corridor, smiling sweetly at Harley, halting his conversation, and walk straight past him. I sit down with Ruby; Seb is nowhere to be seen. Her brow furrows when she sees the look on my face.

"What's happened, babe? You were gone for ages. I was about to send out a search party." I shake my head and she strokes my hand. "Tell me, babe, someone's upset you."

"Fucking Harley Hernandez, that's who. I came out of the toilet and he was bragging to some guy in the corridor about having sex with me. It might be my paranoid brain playing tricks, but I'm certain the guy he was chatting to was a reporter."

She raises her eyebrow. "What a little *prick*. He is not going to get away with this, babe."

She gets up, and before I can stop her, she is striding off. Seb comes back over with more drinks.

"Where's Ruby going?"

I shake my head, exasperated. "Are you sure you're OK, babe?"

I nod. "Yeah, I'm fine."

I plaster a fake smile on my face, and Seb narrows his eyes at me.

"I've known you long enough to tell when you're lying to me, honey."

I am about to speak when I see Sam stride into the bar. The bar goes silent for a few seconds with people recognising him and then they resume their conversations. He looks positively pissed for the second time today. His green eyes lock with mine and he walks over to me. He crouches down in front of me, cupping my face in his hands, his face marred with worry.

"Are you OK, angel?"

I nod and automatically know that this has something to do with Ruby. My suspicions are soon confirmed.

"I came as soon as Ruby called; I was literally right around the corner at a photo shoot. I'm going to fucking kill him."

I look into his eyes and plead, "Please don't do anything stupid, babe, I can't bear to see you angry."

He smirks. "I'm not just angry, angel, I'm fucking *murderous,*" he seethes, his voice laced with disdain. He stands up and I grab his hand.

"Baby," I beg.

He kisses my forehead. "Trust me; I'll be right back, angel. I promise."

He strides off across the bar, passing Ruby on the way, and they exchange a few words. Ruby comes back over and sits down.

"Why the fuck did you have to call Sam for?" I spit angrily.

"Babe, you need to chill your beans and be grateful that he didn't come sooner. When you asked me to meet you earlier, I called Sam straight away. There was no way he would let you out without security. So when he found out I was meeting you, he relaxed a little bit. He's a pussy cat, really."

She smiles innocently. *Typical Ruby, she has Sam wrapped around her little finger.* I down my drink, and Seb watches us silently. I hear a commotion across the bar, so I go to stand up and Seb gets up right after.

"Stay here," Seb says to me. "I've got this, honey."

He walks across the bar and I put my hand to my head. I hear smashing glass, and I quickly get to my feet. I walk quickly across the floor closely followed by Ruby. Sam has Harley pinned to the floor and he is bleeding. He is about to punch him again and Seb holds him back.

"Mate, stop, not in front of Peyton, please. It's not worth it, he's not worth it."

Seb's calming voice seems to work and Sam goes lax in Seb's grip. I stand over Harley.

"*Mi Chica,* it was just a stupid joke. What is it you English say? Banter between the boys? I'm sorry, I meant no harm."

A look of disgust passes between us, and I kick him between his legs. Ruby whoops and claps her hands.

"That's for fucking bragging and bullshitting about having sex with me. For the record, you weren't that good anyway, dick," I spit angrily and Ruby bursts out laughing. Seb lets go of Sam and he wraps his arms around me. Harley gingerly gets up and rushes out of the bar at breakneck speed.

"Are you OK, baby?"

I nod and look up at him. His lip is cut, and his nose is bloody.

"You're bleeding."

He touches his nose.

"It's nothing, babe, don't worry about me. Look, I need to clean this mess up before the manager either calls the police or alerts the press."

He kisses me gently on the lips and pulls away from our embrace. I see him whispering to Seb and a look passes between them. They shake hands and Sam winks at me.

"I'll be as quick as I can, baby, then I'm taking you home with me."

I smile, and Sam strides off with his phone to his ear. Ruby links my arm and we go to the bar. We get another round of drinks and do copious amounts of Cherry Sourz while we wait for the boys. We are perched on two bar stools, and I'm feeling very drunk now, struggling to focus on my surroundings. Ruby giggles.

"Peyton is w-a-s-t-e-d!" she sings in my ear and I laugh hard. Her gaze shifts across the bar and she puts her finger to her lips.

"Shhh, Mr. Wonderful is coming," she slurs and closes one eye to focus. I follow her gaze and see Sam striding over to us. I grin widely, and in that moment, I am even more in love with him than I have ever been. He stops in front of me.

"Sammy, baby," I sing to him and he laughs.

"Has someone had a little too much to drink, angel?"

I nod.

"I'm going to take her home, Ruby. Cole's outside. He's taking you back to the flat."

Ruby narrows her eyes over the rim of her glass at him and I shake my head.

"Possessive rockers *always* get what they want, Rubes, don't argue with him or he'll go Christian Grey on your arse and spank the living shit out of you!"

Ruby laughs hysterically while I pull a face and salute. Sam throws his head back and laughs.

"Come on, gorgeous, I'm taking you home."

He lifts me into his arms easily as if he is carrying a feather and carries me out of the bar and Ruby follows us. We get outside, and I suddenly feel dizzy.

"Sammy, I feel sick."

He sets me down on my feet and I lean against the wall. I throw up on the pavement with Sam holding my hair out of my face and rubbing my back soothingly.

"Should I take the lady home, Sam?" I hear Cole's deep voice.

"Yeah, I've got her, mate, it's fine. I'll drive to my place, and Ruby's address is programmed in the sat nav."

"OK, give me a call if you need anything, mate."

I stumble as I try to regain my balance, and like lightning, Sam steadies me. He grips me around my waist.

"*Jesus Christ*, are you OK, baby?"

I giggle. "I'm Yankee doodle dandy!"

He laughs. I see two Sams in front of me and close one eye to try to focus. He carries me to his Porsche Cayenne 4x4 and sits me in the passenger seat. He buckles my seatbelt, goes around to the driver's side, and gets into the car.

"If you need to throw up, let me know, and I'll pull over."

I lean my head back in the seat to try and stop my world from spinning. I watch as Sam pulls smoothly away from the kerb. Even in the moonlight his profile is striking. I sigh, and he looks at me from the corner of his eye, chuckling softly.

"You're adorable when you're drunk, angel."

I look at him and sigh. "You're beautiful all the time. I love you, Sammy."

He moves his hand from the gear stick and strokes my leg.

"I love you more than life itself, angel."

I lean my head back in the seat and the next thing I know, I am being lifted and carried from Sam's car. He walks into his building and into the lift. I snuggle closer to his chest and grip the neck of his t-shirt. He plants a kiss on my forehead. I feel the lift stop and he steps out with me in his strong arms. He lays me down on the bed and before I know it, I am drifting off into a drink-induced sleep.

4

Peyton

I wake the next morning with the worse hangover ever. My head is pounding, and I suddenly don't remember getting home. I am in my underwear and I sit up to look around the room. I'm relieved to find myself in Sam's bed. He stands in the doorway of the en-suite bathroom with a towel slung low on his hips. He looks delicious with beads of water running down his abs.

"Good morning, angel."

He smiles his panty-dropping smile, but I am too hungover to appreciate the sight of his half-naked body.

"How are you feeling?" I clutch my head and he chuckles softly. "There's two aspirin and a pint of water by the bed, baby. Trust me, you'll feel better."

"Did I do anything to embarrass myself?"

"No, you just threw up and I brought you back here. You fell asleep in my car. I undressed you and carried you to bed."

I close my eyes, and apologize, "I'm so sorry, I don't usually get that drunk."

"It's fine, honestly, don't worry about it. You're adorable when you're drunk, and I didn't mind taking care of you."

I take the aspirin from the table beside the bed and polish off the glass of water in one long pull.

"You grab a shower, babe. I'll go and make breakfast."

I raise my eyebrows. "Do you even know how to cook?"

He throws his head back and laughs. I decide there and then that his laughter is my favourite sound in the world.

"I get by. I'm in-between housekeepers at the moment so I've either been living on takeaway, or my mum's been leaving already prepared food in my fridge."

I laugh. "Does your mum do everything for you?"

He smirks. "Just my washing and my cooking right now. Amy helps when she can too. I need to start interviewing for a new housekeeper as soon as."

I roll my eyes and get up from the bed, feeling a little steadier on my feet. I go over to the bathroom and he kisses me on the cheek, avoiding my morning breath.

"I'll go and make breakfast. Take as long as you need, angel."

I step into the bathroom, strip out of my underwear, and turn on the shower. I catch sight of myself in the mirror, and I look like shit. I didn't take my make-up off last night; I have panda eyes and my hair is dishevelled. I step in the shower, welcoming the feel of the hot water cascading over my body. I spend longer than my usual twenty minutes under the shower washing my hair and trying to get back to something that resembles human. When I emerge from the shower I'm feeling refreshed and ready to face the day.

My outfit for the day consists of black skinny jeans and an off-black distressed *Rolling Stones* t-shirt. I make my way to the kitchen; Sam is on the phone, he has the phone resting between his ear and his shoulder. He is cooking breakfast at the same time. *A man who knows how to multi-task, I'm impressed!*

"Yeah, we leave first thing Monday morning, mate. I need to speak with her first. We're going on tour, not leaving the fucking country. Last night, yeah, you buried it? Thanks, you are a total legend, mate, I appreciate it. I need to go, I'm making breakfast. You funny bastard. I'll make sure I don't poison her. Speak soon, bye."

He hangs up the phone and I am curious as to what he needs to speak to me about. I perch myself on a stool at the kitchen island and lean on my hands.

"Feeling better, angel?"

I nod. "Much. Thanks, babe."

He smiles, and he serves us both breakfast consisting of ham, poached eggs, and mushrooms on brown toast—it looks delicious. He takes a seat on the opposite side of the island and we both tuck into our breakfast.

"That was Tate on the phone. He sorted last night out, and he purchased the bar for me. He made sure all evidence of the fight was buried to stop it leaking to the press and wiped all CCTV evidence. That bloke is a total bloody legend."

I look wide-eyed at him. "You bought the bar? That's a bit excessive."

"It's no use having money when you don't spend it, babe. I told you before, it's nothing to me, I own this building, I own a few other bars, I have an apartment in New York, a penthouse apartment in Vegas overlooking the strip, I have a mansion in Dublin, beach houses in Hawaii and Florida, and a few other properties. I intend on taking you to all of them, but it's all irrelevant, really," he says nonchalantly whilst taking a bite of his breakfast. "Look, I need to speak to you about a few things."

I nod for him to go on.

"We're going on a three month UK tour on Monday; I want you to come on tour with us. Before you start arguing, I need you with me, baby. I hate the thought of you being here without me. I want you to let me protect you. We've got a double-deck tour bus, and there's a double bedroom."

My mouth forms an O shape. I can't believe he is asking me to go on tour with him. *Three months on a tour bus with a bunch of rockers?* It sounds like my worst nightmare, but it also sounds like it could be fun. He regards me intently, waiting for my response.

"A double bedroom?"

"Yep, there's two double bedrooms on the top deck, a small kitchen, TV, and seating area, a bunch of sleeper pods on both decks, a bathroom and a small office—it's basically a house on wheels."

I am suitably impressed by his description.

"I need to clear it with Seb. He owes me some time. But I'm not sure I can do the whole three months, but certainly a few weeks, to a month or so."

His face breaks out into an ear-splitting grin. "So is that a yes?"

I smile. "Yes."

He comes over to me and lifts me from the stool, enveloping me in a big bear hug.

"Being on a bus with a bunch of rockers isn't as bad as it sounds, I promise."

He pulls away. "There's something else too, baby." I look up at him, unsure of what he's about to say, "My parents have invited us for dinner tonight; I sort of said we would go."

"So I'm finally going to get to meet the rest of your family?"

"Yep, plus my dad's band is going too. They're having some sort of reunion, so my mum decided to make it into a dinner party."

I am suddenly struck with nerves at meeting the rest of Sam's family. Panic sets in, and he seems to sense it immediately.

"They're going to love you, angel, I promise. My dad was quite taken with you, you know Willow already, so it's just my brothers and my mum."

I start to relax a little. *What could possibly go wrong?*

We spend the day together, working out, shopping, and preparing for the night ahead. I get my hair done and call Seb and explain about going on tour with Sam. He agrees that I deserve a break, time to fully recover from the accident, and time to adjust in my role as shop manager. Although I am nervous and apprehensive of what to expect, I am feeling in such a good mood as we shower and get ready for dinner at Sam's parents.

I want to make a good impression, so I opt for a red and black maxi dress and as a surprise for Sam; I'm not wearing any underwear. I team my dress with black diamante flip-flops and tousle my hair in loose waves. I feel relaxed and comfortable.

"You always look beautiful, angel. You make it look so effortless. You could even make wearing a bin liner sexy."

Laughing, I say, "Hardly. When we first met, I couldn't look directly at you because I found you so handsome and devastating. I was so affected by you, no man has ever affected me the way you did, and I was a total mess. I was trying so hard to be indifferent to you, but you made it so god damn hard."

He raises his eyebrow and grins. "As soon as I saw you, I was instantly smitten." He puffs out his cheeks at the memory. "You were so feisty and fiercely independent. You weren't afraid to say no to me and I loved that. When Ruby took you to lunch that day I felt like a caged animal waiting for my next encounter with you. Last night when she called and told me that Harley had been bragging and saying shit about you, the thought of his hands all over you made me feel physically violent. I know we weren't together then, but I can't stand it. The only guy I trust around you is Seb. We had a long chat after you fell asleep, he made his feelings clear, and I apologised for being such a dick."

If only you knew. I quickly push that thought to the back of my mind and smile. I am glad that the two men in my life are at least on friendly terms. I finish getting ready and jab my finger in Sam's chest.

"You need to stop being so handsome and distracting. You need to get dressed."

I kiss him on the lips and he pulls me down on the bed. I don't know how he does it, but he has me pinned beneath him, and before I know it, he is straddling me with his muscular thighs on either side of my waist.

"What if I don't want to get dressed?" he asks huskily, and I instantly feel liquid heat between my legs.

"We're going to be late, baby."

He chuckles softly and nuzzles his face in my hair.

"I like your hair. You look spectacular," he whispers huskily in my ear as he cups my breast in his large hand. "Is this distracting enough for you, angel?"

I bite my lip, and he rolls my nipple between his fingers causing me to moan softly.

"Mmm, Sam."

He moves his hand under my dress and between my legs and he strokes my bare sex.

"Mmm, no underwear. Are you deliberately trying to tease me, angel?"

The sound of his voice twinned with the feel of his fingers stroking me is making me desperate to feel his cock inside me.

"I can feel how turned on you are baby and it's all for me. No other man can make you come like I can."

His voice is dripping with seduction and I am a slave to his touch. He pushes his middle finger inside me, finds my sensitive nub with his thumb, and strokes gentle circles. I am writhing and panting beneath him, desperate for his touch, fraught for my release.

"Look how you respond to me, angel."

I can see his thick erection straining through his boxer briefs.

"Sam, fuck me please," I whine, breathless and desperate. He smiles wickedly and winks.

"Not until later, baby. I need to get dressed or we're going to be late."

He climbs off the bed, leaving me panting and craving my release. *Fucking tease!*

He moves over to the walk-in wardrobe and I shout, *"Fine!* I'll finish myself off then!"

Like lightning, he sprints back over to me and pins both of my hands above my head in one of his hands, pressing his muscled chest against me.

"Do not touch yourself; you're going to trust that I'll take care of you later, angel."

He winks and knows he has me right where he wants me. *Bastard!* He plants a chaste kiss on my lips, pulls me to my feet, and goes back over to the walk-in wardrobe. He emerges wearing black skinny jeans, a white skull vest, a fitted, black, suit jacket and black Doc Marten boots. He looks mouth-wateringly attractive. I watch as he gets ready and lick my lips—he catches me watching him and laughs.

"See something you like, my lovely?" I bite my lip. "Now, you know what biting your lip does to me. Play nice, baby."

He checks his reflection, runs his hand through his freshly-spiked hair and straightens his jacket. I pick up my black clutch bag and he offers me his hand. I take it and we walk into the living area. Cole is waiting for us; he looks at his watch.

"Someone's cutting it fine, mate."

Sam laughs and says, "Blame this one. Bloody women."

He swats my bum, then Cole and he both laugh. We go down to the parking garage and Cole is driving Sam's white Porsche Cayenne 4x4. We make our way to Sam's parents' house in Ashford in Kent. It takes us over an hour to get there, and when we pull up outside, I am awestruck by the property in front of me. We get out of the car, and Sam laughs at my reaction. He explains to me that it is a detached five-bedroom house with a double garage, stables, and around three acres of land. It has been built in the style of a traditional Kent barn.

Sam leads me over to the door and pushes it open. A striking older woman greets us. She is tall, slender, has dark-brown, jaw-length hair, blue-green eyes, and a bright-red-lipsticked smile.

"Sam, darling," she croons. She hugs Sam and kisses his cheek. I notice that her accent is soft and American. "It's so good to see you."

She pulls away from Sam's embrace.

"It's good to see you too, Mum. Looking stunning as ever. I've missed you."

"Charming as ever, sweetie, just like your father," she says with a laugh. She turns to me and takes both of my hands in hers. "You must be Peyton; it's so lovely to finally meet the woman who's turned my boy into a monogamous man."

I laugh and clear my throat. "It's so good to meet you too, Mrs. Newbolt."

"Please call me Lori. I've heard nothing but great things about you, Peyton, can I get you a drink?"

I nod. "Yes, please, rose wine would be fantastic."

"A girl after my own heart. Coming right up. There's some beers in the refrigerator, darling, help yourself."

Lori goes off into the kitchen and Willow comes bounding down the wooden staircase. She is as lively as ever with her short-cropped dark hair, quirky dress sense, and enthusiastic personality.

"Peyton! Sam!"

She jumps into Sam's arms, and I laugh at their brotherly-sisterly exchange. She pulls away from Sam and comes over to me; she throws her arms around me, squeezing me tightly.

"Oh, my God, Peyton, I heard about the accident. I'm so glad you're OK, why didn't you call me?"

She pulls away and I go to speak, but Sam stops her.

"Don't crowd her, Wills."

She smiles sweetly. "Sorry, it's just so good to see you guys. It's been forever," she says dramatically and Marlowe strolls into the room.

"Son." Sam smiles and they hug. "Peyton, it's so good to see you again, looking beautiful as ever."

Marlowe smiles and kisses my hand. Lori comes back into the room with our drinks.

"Let me give you the tour, Peyton."

I take my drink from her and follow her out of the room. We step into the large open-plan kitchen.

"When I heard my boy had met a girl, I was hoping it wasn't one of those god awful groupies him and that band of his surround themselves with. I was pleasantly surprised. You seem to ground him, and with Sam, that's always a good thing, believe me, honey."

I nod and smile, suddenly feeling nervous. I take large gulp of my wine.

"Relax, Peyton, first impressions? I really like you, I haven't seen him this happy in such a long time. He has his old sparkle back."

I take a sip of my drink and she brushes my arm.

"Do you want my advice, sweetie? Don't let the rock star thing taint your views. I've been a rock star wife for almost thirty years now and I know how it is, tour buses, groupies, and that vile man J.D." She shudders as she says his name and I am curious to what she means. Before I can ask, we are interrupted by the arrival of two young men. The one is a paler, thinner version of Sam with dark spiky hair and friendly green eyes; the other is tall with shoulder-length, dark-brown hair, muscular with bronzed skin, blue-green eyes, and a bright casual smile.

"Peyton, these are my other two sons, Elijah and Brandon."

The shorter one smiles. "You can call me Eli if you like?"

I find myself smiling back and nod before saying, "I'm Peyton."

The taller one salutes coolly, and it reminds me so much of Sam.

"Brandon." His voice is husky like Sam's and a mixture between English and American, just like Savannah.

"Brandon is also in a band called The Iron Warriors and Elijah is studying medicine," Lori informs me, and I nod, impressed at the diversity of their lives.

"Do you need a hand in the kitchen, Mum?" Elijah offers.

"No, thank you, sweetie. Could you and your brother go and lay the table please?"

Elijah and Brandon leave the room. A few minutes later, Sam, Marlowe, and two other older men join us. I recognise them from the picture on Sam's fridge—the other two members of Marlowe's band The Lightning Bolts.

"I'm Milo Lightman. You must be the very beautiful Peyton."

He kisses my hand. His voice is deep, raspy, and has a prominent East London accent.

The other man nods and says, "I'm Seth Jones, pleasure to meet you, my love."

"Sam tells me you're a tattoo artist, Peyton." Milo regards me intently and takes a sip of his beer.

"Yes, for my sins!" I joke and we both laugh.

"You're way past the mid-life crisis mark, Milo," Marlowe quips. We spend an hour or so chatting between ourselves easily. The conversation and the booze are flowing freely.

"Dinner is served," Lori calls from the dining room, and we all make our way into the large open-plan dining room with a large table and a large, impressive, white calla lily centrepiece. Sam hangs back and places his hand at the small of my back.

"Are you having a good time so far, angel?"

I nod; he kisses the top of my head and smiles warmly. We make our way into the dining room and already sat at the table are Savannah and Callum. *Fuck.*

My face drops as I catch sight of Savannah's smug face and Callum's mouth forms a perfect O shape as his eyes lock with mine. Sam grips my waist so tight it verges on pain.

"I'm so sorry. I didn't know they were going to be here, angel, I swear," he whispers in my ear and I shake my head.

"It's fine," I say tightly, and we take our seats around the table. I am sat between Sam and Willow and I'm grateful for the seating arrangement.

"I take it you, Savannah, and Callum are already acquainted?" Lori looks at me questioningly and I nod. I look in their direction and smile as politely as I can manage.

We eat a three-course meal of seared scallops with salad for starters, grilled rib-eye steak with sweet potato mash and green beans for our main course, and vanilla cheesecake for our dessert. The whole meal is delicious, and I didn't realise how hungry I was until I tucked in.

The conversation around the table is happy and flowing with the exception of the death stares I am getting from Savannah. After we finish dessert, we are moved into the large living area with open fire, large sofas, and exquisite artwork adorning the walls. I excuse myself to use the bathroom. I use the facilities, wash my hands, and as I leave the bathroom, Callum is leaning casually against the wall with his hands in his pockets waiting for me.

"Peyton, I'm so sorry, I didn't know you were going to be here, or I would never have agreed to come."

"How shocked do you think I was when I saw the two of you just sitting there? Acting like it's the most natural thing in the world. Everyone knows we dated, Callum, you've got no idea how awkward and uncomfortable it is for me to be here."

"Please don't be like that, baby cakes, I had no idea."

I recoil at his pet name for me. He takes my hand, but I snatch it away from him.

"Don't fucking touch me, don't act like this is normal, Cal, you had to have known we would be here, she's Sam's sister, for fucks sake."

He puts his hand to his head and says, "I swear I didn't have a clue. I can't apologise enough. I thought we agreed to put the past behind us; we were supposed to be friends."

"That was before you decided you were going to change the goal posts Callum. I don't know why I didn't see it coming. You do it every fucking time," I say through clenched teeth. He looks at me and changes his tactics. *Typical Callum.*

"So, it's definitely serious between you and Sam then? A little bird tells me you're going on tour with him and his band? That should be interesting. You on a tour bus with a bunch of rock stars. I just can't imagine it, baby cakes."

He has the cheek to look amused.

"I know about you and Eden, Callum," I spit angrily in a moment of madness and his face drops. He is silent, and in the silence, I am instantly transported back to the day I caught Callum cheating on me.

5

Peyton

Past

I had been wandering around in a daze for two solid weeks. Ever since I lost our baby, I have felt like I have lost my purpose in life. I have felt useless and responsible. Callum had just completely closed himself off from me; he wouldn't even come near me. I walked into a room, he walked out. It was if he couldn't bear to be within a hundred yards of me. He was always working late at the gym and was spending less and less time with me. I had fallen into a deep depression, choosing to sit in the flat day and night with the curtains closed because I couldn't face anyone. I had lost weight, and when I looked in the mirror, there was a stranger staring back at me. Pale, hollow, drawn, and dark circles under my eyes. I hadn't slept in two solid weeks because every time I closed my eyes I relive the moment over and over again. I'd wake up screaming, drenched in sweat, sobbing and alone. Some nights I noticed that Callum didn't bother coming home at all, and I didn't know what I was going to do. Maybe Ruby was right, maybe we should have just called it a day and ended it.

It was Saturday and I was lying on the sofa in my robe staring into space when Ruby stood in front of me with her hands on her hips, frowning.

"Right, Harper. Up now."

I looked up at her with wide watery eyes and shook my head.

"I can't, Ruby, please."

She grabbed me and pulled me to my feet.

"Get in the shower and get dressed; we're going out. If you're adamant you're staying with that prick, then we're going shopping. Retail therapy always works. You're buying some sexy underwear, and then I'm dropping you off at Callum's place. You're going to order his favourite takeaway, surprise him, and get your relationship back on track."

I hated to admit it, but she was right. She was always bloody right. Reluctantly, I got off the sofa and I was surprised there wasn't a Peyton Harper shape embedded into the sofa. I got dressed and my clothes were literally falling off me because I had lost so much weight from lack of eating. I tied my hair up in a loose bun, put on some lip-gloss and mascara, and pulled on my jacket. I got out into the living room of our flat and Ruby looked me up and down.

"You'll do, you skinny bitch! Come on."

Ruby laughed and dragged me out of the flat. We spent a couple of hours in town, getting our nails, hair, and makeup done. I felt better than I had in a couple of weeks and I was feeling a little more positive about things. I actually had a smile back on my face. Ruby grinned at me.

"You look fabulous, almost back to your usual self, babe."

We both smiled and climbed back into Ruby's pink Mini Cooper. She drove me to Callum's flat and I was surprised to see Callum's silver Audi TT parked outside. Ruby pulled up and cut the engine. She turned to face me.

"You look absolutely gorgeous; you'll definitely knock him dead." She kissed me on the cheek. "Go get him tiger!"

She laughed, and I got out of the car, feeling nervous at facing Callum. After being in my own bubble for the past two weeks, it felt good to be me again. I used my key to let myself into Callum's flat and I was greeted with clothes strewn all over the living room floor. I heard low grunts coming from the kitchen.

"Cal, babe, it's me."

My voice echoed through the flat. As I walked into the kitchen, I was not prepared for the sight in front of me. I saw Callum naked, shamelessly fucking another woman on the kitchen worktop. I stood there, open-mouthed, rooted to the spot at what I was seeing. Callum was grunting with pleasure and his hands were all over her—she was screaming like a porn star and clawing at his back. I felt like I was going to throw up. *Fuck, fuck, fuck, this was not happening.*

"What the fuck, Callum!" I screamed, and he didn't stop.

He carried on, regardless of my interruption, and I felt like I was watching a live porn film in Callum's kitchen. My nausea passed, and an overwhelming fit of rage boiled up inside me. I grabbed the nearest thing to me, which happened to be a plate, and threw it at him. It missed and smashed all over the floor. He growled as his orgasm took him and practically shoved the girl off the worktop as he spun around to face me. He had no remorse on his face at all and the Callum I once loved had gone. I was looking into the deep hazel eyes of a stranger and I launched myself at him. I hit him, and I punched him with everything I had in me.

"How could you do this, Callum? Why?" I screamed. He stood there stock-still and let me hit him. "You're a fucking prick, Callum."

He grabbed my wrists in silence and looked me in the eyes.

"We're over, Peyton, I can't fucking do this anymore."

The girl, who was a tall, slim, brunette with wide jade green eyes. She was wearing Callum's t-shirt and she brushed his arm.

"Baby, I can go. It's obvious you two have a lot to chat about, I'll call you," she said in husky American lilt.

She called him 'baby', what the fuck?

"No, don't go on my account," I snapped. "How long, Callum?"

He hung his head as he pulled on his jeans.

"Don't fucking do this babe, please? Look, Sav, I'll call you, OK?"

He cupped her face in his hands and I couldn't remember when he looked at me that way. My heart felt like it had been completely ripped out of my chest and it was taking all I had not to break down in tears. She kissed him and then she left, leaving Callum shirtless and running his hands through his messy blonde hair. Something inside me told me I should go after her, drag her around the room by her hair, call her a 'fucking home wrecker' but I didn't have the strength.

"How fucking long?" I asked coldly.

"Jesus Peyton, is it really that fucking important?" he shouted.

"How long?" My voice was shaky. Come on, Harper, don't let him see you cry, don't give him the satisfaction. Get it together.

"Not long, a few weeks. You told me you were pregnant, I freaked out, and I shagged her."

He shrugged nonchalantly as if it was nothing. I couldn't believe what I was hearing, and it was like my heart was being ripped out all over again.

6

Peyton

Present

I am jolted back to the present by Callum's voice.

"Peyton, please, it's not like that, she is nothing to me, and it was just one night a long time ago. We were both drunk; it was a stupid mistake, I swear. You have to believe me. It's always been you, baby cakes, I've never loved anyone the way I love you."

He strokes my hair and puts his hands on either side of my head, trapping me. He is so close I can feel his breath on my cheek and the smell of his aftershave. He leans in and kisses me on the lips. I push against him, but he is so strong. I slap him around the face and go to duck under his arm, but he grabs my wrist and pulls me back.

"The spark's still there, baby cakes."

I hear heavy footsteps coming up the stairs.

"Take your hand off her and get the fuck away from her, Kennedy. Now." Sam's voice is harsh and commanding. He grabs Callum and punches him in the face hard, Callum's nose is bleeding. The third time in as many days that he has got into some dispute because of me.

"If you know what's good for you, you'll make your excuses and fuck off." His stance is loose and predatory. Callum is about to speak, and Sam stops him. "I don't want to hear your fucking bullshit excuses. I just want you to leave my girl alone. She was done with you a long time ago," he spits out.

Callum smirks and holds his hands up in surrender. Sam lunges at him and pins him to the wall by his throat.

"Don't get fucking smart with me, you smug little bastard. I saw you try to kiss her; if I ever catch you near her again, if you even look at her, I swear to God, I will fucking end you." Sam's voice is so low and threatening, it makes my blood run cold. He tightens his grip, and I can see Callum struggling to breathe. He punches him hard in the ribs, and I touch Sam's arm gently.

"Sam, baby, stop now, you've made your point," I say softly. He complies and lets go of Callum's throat. Callum is coughing and spluttering. He looks back at me.

"Baby cakes, this is far from over."

Sam goes for him again, but I grab his corded wrist tight. Callum makes his exit down the staircase.

"What the fuck was that?" I raise my voice. "You can't keep behaving like some fucking Neanderthal, throwing your fists around left, right, and centre. I was handling it!"

Sam looks at me and backs me against the wall. He strokes my face with the back of his hand.

"I was watching. He kissed you, and he had his fucking filthy hands on you. Him even breathing the same air as you makes me ... *murderous*. I've never felt this protective over a woman before, and it's scaring the shit out of me. I don't know how to deal with these kind of emotions, I didn't feel anything before you, and I couldn't care about anyone or anything, because I just didn't give a fuck. You've awakened something in me, Peyton. I saw red as soon as I saw him within an inch of you. You make me feel exposed. I fucking hate feeling that way."

I find myself softening towards him. Him truly opening up to me is a rarity, and I love seeing his vulnerable side. It makes me love him that bit more with every titbit and every snippet of himself he decides to share with me.

"Every part of me, every inch is yours, Sam, when are you going to get that into that beautiful fucked up head of yours?" I touch his temple with my finger gently. He scoops up my hand and brings my fingers to his lips.

"I'm trying, angel, I'm trying so hard not to push you away. I fuck it up every time, and for that, I'm truly sorry. I'll spend my life trying to be enough for you, to be the man you deserve."

"You're everything to me, Sam. I love you so much, hold onto that."

I press my lips to his and kiss him gently. He smiles that heart-stopping smile.

"Let's go back and join the party."

I clasp Sam's hand in mine and we go back downstairs to re-join the party. The conversation is in full swing and there is soft jazz music playing in the background.

"There you both are. We were wondering where you got to. Callum and Savannah had to leave."

"I was just giving Peyton the tour of the upstairs."

Milo, Seth, and Marlowe all laugh aloud at the same time.

"Is that what you kids are calling it these days?" Seth raises his eyebrows suggestively, and I feel my face flush. Sam kisses my forehead.

"Don't sweat it, angel, they're just winding you up because they're not getting any hot loving at home!" Sam chuckles and they all laugh.

"Can I get you both another drink, sweetie?" Lori cuts in and I am glad of her intervention. I smile gratefully, and Sam jumps in.

"Actually, mum, we were going to head home."

"OK sweetie, it was so good to see you, and it was fabulous to finally meet you, Peyton. You should definitely come over again soon."

I nod. "Yeah, of course, I've had a really nice night; it was so great to meet you all at last."

Lori hugs Sam tight. "Call me soon, darling." She hugs me and kisses me on both cheeks. "Don't be a stranger, Peyton, and remember what I said?"

She winks and pulls away. We say our goodbyes to everyone and we step outside into the cool night air. Cole is in the driveway waiting by the car.

"Sam, Peyton."

He nods to us both and opens the door of the Porsche. We both get in, and I lean on Sam's shoulder. We make the journey back to Sam's place in just over an hour. The night-time traffic is light, and I am glad to sit watching the world go by in a blur wrapped in Sam's safe arms.

We get back to Sam's apartment, and as soon as he closes the door, he pins me against the wall.

"I promised you I'd take care of you, angel, I'm making sure I keep my promise," he says huskily as he pushes the straps of my dress down my shoulders. He kisses a trail from my neck to my shoulder. I am burning for him; no man has ever made love to me the way Sam does. He takes his time, he is gentle yet commanding, and every time he touches me, every nerve in my body stands to complete attention. He takes off my dress, and it pools at my feet.

"Fuck me, you're beautiful."

I kick off my shoes and he lifts me off the floor.

"Wrap those delicious legs around me, angel."

I wrap my legs around his waist and he claims my mouth hungrily. I am vaguely aware of my surroundings, as he carries me through his apartment, his lips never leaving mine. He kicks the door open and we are in his recording studio. He doesn't let me go; he just sits down on the large leather office chair with me in my bra straddling his lap. He leans back and looks me in the eyes.

"God, how did I get so lucky?" he whispers, and I smile.

"This is highly unfair; I'm the only one who's naked," I pout, and he chuckles softly. He holds his hands out to the side.

"I'm all yours, angel."

I get up, unbuckle his belt and unzip his trousers. He lifts his hips off the chair and I manoeuvre them down his legs. I throw them across the room and his cock is straining against the material of his boxer briefs. He shrugs off his jacket and strips off his vest in one lithe move until he is gloriously naked. I lick my lips; I will never get tired of seeing him naked.

"Better?" He smirks, and I nod.

"Much."

I smile with satisfaction. He stands up and his tall frame towers over me.

"You're still wearing your bra, that's highly unacceptable," he tuts. He unclasps my bra with one hand, looks cockily at me, and smirks.

"Years of practise, my lovely!" He winks and hangs my bra on the microphone stand near the desk. "Let's call that a souvenir! Every time I come in here I'll think of you. I won't be able to hide my erection, seeing your beautiful pussy spread out for me." He moves me over to the desk. "Lean down on the desk and grip it tight. Don't let go unless I tell you, angel."

I do as he says and lean down on the smooth wooden desk. I grip it and he runs his fingers down my spine, causing my body to shiver and goose bump at his touch.

"I'm going to take you from behind, baby."

He runs his fingers down my soaking wet folds and pushes two fingers into my pussy. I mewl softly.

"You're always so wet and ready for me, angel."

He removes his fingers and replaces them with his erect cock. He pushes roughly into me, and I shriek at the force.

"Oh, fuck, baby," he growls. He plunges in and out at a fast pace driving me towards the release I have been desperately craving since he teased me earlier.

"Mmm, Sam!" I let out a scream. He increases his momentum and we both detonate at the same time with strangled cries of pure sexual bliss. He grips my waist and collapses on top of me. We are both left panting and breathless on the desk.

"I never get tired of being inside you, baby. You're so beautiful, I love you so much," he whispers in my ear and pulls out of me. He lifts me off the desk and sits me on the edge. He nudges himself between my legs and wraps his arms around me.

"I love you, Sam, so much."

I nuzzle into his chest and he holds me tightly.

"Move in with me, angel, I want to wake up next to you every single morning and go to sleep with you every night for as long as I'm breathing."

"Maybe after the tour? I need some time to think, baby."

He seems to understand and nods. He lifts me off the desk and carries me down the corridor into his bedroom, deposits me on the bed, and lies down next to me. We say goodnight, and I fall into a restful sleep.

We spend the whole of Sunday being a normal couple—breakfast in bed, packing, and preparing for the tour. We go out for farewell drinks at a local bar with Seb and Ruby; we have a good time drinking, chatting, laughing and hanging out with our friends. We get back to Sam's apartment, make slow passionate love on the sofa, and for the first time in a long time, I am so blissfully happy I don't ever want this feeling to end.

Before we know it, Monday morning has rolled around, and today is the day I go on a tour bus with a bunch of rockers. I am nervous and apprehensive as to what I am letting myself in for, but I am also excited. Cole drives us to the tour bus, and when we get out of the car, I am stunned to see the tour bus in front of me. It is a black and silver, sleek, double-deck bus, with tinted windows, and the band's logo down the side. It is very large and impressive from the outside.

"This is our home for the next three months, baby," Sam tells me.

He smiles his dazzling smile and I am temporarily disarmed. I love his smile—it is one of my favourite features of his. The other guys arrive a few minutes after us, and Jax comes bounding over to me.

"Peyton!"

I love his child-like manner; it never fails to make me smile. He picks me up and spins me around.

"We'll look after you, love, I promise."

He winks and puts me down. Brody salutes coolly, and Lucas gives me a one-armed hug. J.D. is talking to a tall, muscular, middle-aged man with a dark-haired buzz cut. The guys make their way up the stairs of the bus, and Sam swats my bum playfully as I walk up in front of him. We all get onto the bus and I am again amazed by the interior. I walk around to get acquainted with my new home on wheels.

"Let me show you the upstairs," Sam says, raising his eyebrows suggestively.

Men and their filthy minds!

I follow him up to the upper deck. It is equally as impressive as the lower deck. Sam swings the door to the bedroom open. It is decorated in masculine black, turquoise, and silver tones. However, it is cosy, and I instantly feel at home.

"You like?" Sam looks at me.

"It's cosy."

He smiles at my reaction and says, "The first gig is tonight up in Glasgow. It takes around seven hours to get to Glasgow from London depending on traffic, but we'll have a few stops along the way. Come on, I'll introduce you to our tour bus driver, Lex."

He takes my hand and we go back downstairs to the lower deck. The other guys have settled in—Brody is lounging on the sofa with his headphones on reading a rock magazine; Lucas and Jax are having some sort of Xbox duel on Forza Horizon 5, their faces full of concentration. I smile at the sight. *Boys and their toys.*

"There's someone I want you to meet, babe." Sam pulls me towards the driver's cab. "Lex."

He turns around and smiles a crooked smile. He looks to be in his mid-forties, has a dark buzz cut, dark, steel-blue eyes, and stubble across his square jaw. Lex shakes hands with Sam.

"Good to see you, Sam."

Sam smiles and says, "You too, mate. Lex, this is my girlfriend, Peyton; she is coming on tour with us for a few weeks. Peyton this is our driver, Lex."

I smile, and Lex shakes my hand.

"I hope you know what you're letting yourself in for, darlin'. These boys can be a handful. Lucky for me, I know their tricks, so I can handle them just fine. Stick with me, kid, I'll show you the tricks."

"Let's not scare her to death, man."

Lex laughs. I instantly like him; he seems like a really nice person with his humorous personality, and he seems like a sort of father figure.

"I'm just joking, darlin', but if you ever need to get away from the boys for a bit, you can always come and chill with me up here, anytime."

I smile at the sentiment and nod, saying, "Thank you, Lex, I appreciate that. I'll definitely bear it in mind."

"We're going to get on the road in the next ten minutes, if you need me to pull over at any time for rest stops just give me a shout."

"Nice to meet you, Lex."

Sam and I go into the living area of the bus. We settle down on the sofa and I can't believe I am on a tour bus with a rock band—it's all so surreal. Let the madness of Rancid Vengeance commence!

7

Peyton

It feels like we have been on the road for ages. I have been alternating between listening to my Spotify playlist, reading my Kindle, and surfing the internet on my laptop to pass the time. I have no idea where we are but figure that we must be in Glasgow by now. Sam is taking a shower and Lucas and Brody are playing Xbox. The bus suddenly pulls to a halt, but the engine is still running. Jax gets up and looks through the bus window. He strides to the driver's cab.

"Lex, we're in the middle of bum fuck nowhere! It's a fair assumption to say we're bloody lost!"

Brody and Lucas put their Xbox controllers down on the table. They are on the sofa laughing hysterically at Jax's sudden outburst at Lex.

"And just because the sat-nav is a bird doesn't mean you have to ignore her and argue with her, because frankly, mate, it's really fucking weird!"

Lex cuts the engine on the bus and storms down the bus aisle.

"I've been awake for thirty-six fucking hours so I'm sorry that we're bloody lost. I'm knackered, and I need to get some sleep, so one of you ungrateful motherfuckers is going to have to drive the god damn bus!"

Lex throws the keys at Jax and stomps off the bus, bumping into Sam as he leaves. Sam has just stepped out of the shower and he has a towel wrapped around his lean waist. He looks gorgeous and glorious with beads of water running down his tattooed torso. I lick my lips as I catch sight of him and his dazzling smile turns to a puzzled look.

"What's up with Lex? Have you been winding him up again, Jax?"

Jax holds his hands up innocently. "We're in the middle of fucking nowhere because of him, it's like the beginning of a bad horror movie out there. I'm too young and pretty to die. I've seen Deliverance, and that shit ain't happening to me, dude!"

Sam rolls his eyes and laughs. "You need to go and apologise to Lex, man."

Jax folds his arms and pouts, "I'm not apologising, it's his fault we're lost! Why should I be the one to say sorry?"

Sam shakes his head, exasperated. "Because he's going through a rough time at the moment. He's going through a divorce. He has worked for us for years, he doesn't have to drive for us, but he does because he's a good bloke. You treating him like shit and being a total arse isn't helping things, Jax. Lost or not, who else is going to drive the bus?"

Jax rolls his eyes. "For fuck's sake!"

Jax sounds like a stroppy teenager and we all burst out laughing. Maybe being on a tour bus with a bunch of rockers won't be so bad after all. Sam goes up to the top deck.

"Baby, could you come and give me a hand with something, please?"

Brody sniggers and winks at me. I feel my face flush and go up the stairs. I push the bedroom door open; Sam is freshly showered and sprawled out naked on the bed. I lick my lips at the sight of his muscular body.

"I thought we could christen the bed, angel." His voice is laced with promise. "Strip for me, baby, I need you ready for when I take you. I want you wet, naked, and at my mercy." When all I do is chuckle, he says, "Are you going to do as I tell you, or am I going to have to take you over my knee and spank you?"

My heart beat increases. *Take me over his knee and spank me?* I didn't know he was into that. But something about being taken over his knee and being spanked oddly turns me on. He regards me intently and I take off my t-shirt. He smiles.

"God, you have such an impressive rack."

I laugh and continue my slow strip tease. Suddenly, I hear a blood-curdling scream. Sam and I look at each other, before he dives off the bed and starts to pull on a pair of loose-fitting jogging bottoms, trying to hide his raging hard on. I pull my t-shirt back on and we both go down to the lower deck. Sam nuzzles his face in my hair.

"To be continued!" he whispers, and I bite my lip. "What the fuck is going on?" Sam shouts. Brody and Lucas are rolling around on the floor in fits of hysterical laughter. Jax is running his hands through his hair frantically, he looks rather pale.

"Jax, what's going on, dude?"

Jax looks at Sam. "I swear I saw someone in the woods wearing a ski mask with a big fucking knife. Sam, we're all going to die!" Jax says dramatically and panicked. Sam bites his lip to stifle his laughter; I go over to Jax and brush his arm.

"Are you OK, sweetie? Are you sure that's what you saw?" I try to comfort him, and Brody rolls his eyes.

"Don't encourage him, darlin'."

Sam looks at Brody and Lucas.

"Has this got anything to do with you two?"

Lucas and Brody look at each other feigning ignorance.

"Don't know what you're talking about, mate"

They both continue their hysterical laughter.

"You pair of complete and utter wankers!" Jax shouts. "I actually thought someone was out there, you bastards."

He stalks off down the bus aisle and I shake my head. Brody rolls his eyes. I get the feeling that he doesn't like me very much.

"He had it coming. He's being such a baby, and we were just ... teaching him a lesson."

It's my turn to roll my eyes. Sam looks at Brody and Lucas. Sam seems to be the bandleader, the voice of reason and the sensible one.

"One of you fuckers is going to have to drive the bus, because it sure as shit isn't going to be me again."

They go to protest and J.D comes down the bus aisle.

"Right, you bunch of fucking reprobates! The itinerary when we eventually get to Glasgow is as follows. We're checking into the hotel then you're scheduled for a magazine interview and photo shoot. The gig is at the o2 academy; it's a sold out venue and it's an intimate gig. There will be an after show party, which has been organised by the venue, so enjoy, boys."

J.D. smiles and goes back down the bus aisle. He seems unusually friendly and polite. It actually unnerves me; I can't help but think he is plotting something. Sam looks at me and shrugs. I wrap my arms around him and he kisses my forehead.

"It's a blessing that we've got a hotel for the night; we normally just have to make do with the bus." He smiles. "Lucky for us, baby, I'm going to make you come a thousand different ways and I'm going to fuck you until we both pass out," he whispers seductively, and I melt at his words. "Starting now."

He winks, and he goes up the stairs to the top deck. I follow him, and Sam is once again sprawled out naked on the bed leaning on his elbow. His eyes are dark and hooded with lust.

"Now where were we, angel?"

He bites his lip and smiles devilishly.

"Oh, yeah, you were stripping for me."

He winks. I pull off my t-shirt and throw it on the floor, shaking my hair, as I reach around to unclasp my bra.

"Slower, baby, I want to savour every part of you, I want to commit every inch of you to memory so when we're apart I can imagine your beautiful body just like this."

He really knows how to make me feel special, as if I'm the only woman for him. I throw my bra on top of my t-shirt and start to slowly unzip my jeans. I wiggle my hips and Sam raises his eyebrows.

"You're such a beautiful tease."

I shimmy out of my jeans and kick off my shoes and throw them onto the pile of discarded clothes. I am standing in just my knickers in front of him. Suddenly feeling conscious of my body, Sam senses my unease.

"Please don't hide yourself from me, you're absolutely stunning. Come and lie down, baby, I want to try something we haven't tried before. Please don't freak out, if it's too much let me know and we can stop."

I feel nervous and anxious of what he has in store for me. I do as he says and lie down on the bed. He moves me with ease to the middle of the bed and reaches into the drawer next to the bed. He takes out a pair of leather cuffs and a soft silk blindfold. My stomach rolls with apprehension.

"Don't look so worried, angel. I'm going to make you feel so good, I promise."

I nod for him to proceed.

"Lift your arms above your head."

I do as he says, and he starts to fasten the cuffs to my wrists, binding me to the metal bed frame. They feel comfortable around my wrists and the leather is soft. *This isn't so bad.* He wraps the blindfold around my eyes and I can't see anything. My heart beat kicks up a notch and every nerve is standing to attention at one of my senses being temporarily disabled.

"Does that feel OK, baby?" I nod, his voice instantly soothing me. "Good girl." He kisses the end of my nose. "You need to trust me, angel, do you trust me?"

I nod again.

"Say it, I need to hear you say the words."

I bite my lip.

"Don't bite your lip, please. It's taking everything I have for me not to just fuck you raw," he says gruffly, and I wriggle.

"I trust you, Sam, with my life."

"God, you're amazing, how did I get so lucky?"

I hear the smile in his voice. The bed dips and I hear his footsteps around the room then the click of the lock.

"Now we won't be disturbed."

I can sense him moving with grace around the room. I hear him open and shut the drawer.

"God, you look beautiful like that, I want to devour and worship every inch of you."

The bed dips, and he nudges my legs apart with his knees. He pushes his finger inside me then introduces a second.

"Does that feel good?"

I bite my lip and let out a moan as he hits my g-spot.

"So good, baby," I say breathlessly, and he chuckles softly. He pushes further into my wetness and I gasp.

"*Jesus*, you're soaking," he growls, and I writhe at the sensation. "God, you're killing me, angel."

He suddenly removes his fingers. I feel his body press against mine and his mouth latches onto my nipple. He sucks my nipple into his mouth and laps it until it becomes an erect bud. He moves his hands gently across my stomach and caresses every part.

"So beautiful," he whispers. He cups my breast in his hand and squeezes gently. He moves from my nipple and up to my neck. I can feel his hot breath on my skin. He nips my neck and earlobe.

"Tell me you're mine, baby."

I moan and bite my lip. "I'm yours, Sam."

He moves down my body and I feel his breath against my pink wet folds. He thrusts his tongue inside me, and I cry out.

"Shhh, I've got you, I'll take care of you, angel."

He continues his assault of pleasure on my wetness. I am handcuffed and at his mercy. He laps at my pussy and introduces a finger.

"Sam, please fuck me," I moan desperately, and I feel him shake his head.

"Not yet. Soon, I promise."

Bastard! He moves from his position between my legs and I feel bereft of his absence.

As if he senses my angst, he says, "I'm just here, angel. I'm not going anywhere, I promise."

How did he know just what I was thinking? It's at that point that I think he knows me better than I know myself. I hear him open and close the drawer again and the bed dips as he resumes his position.

"I need you to completely relax for me, baby."

I nod and bite my lip unconsciously.

"Sam," I whisper.

"I'm just here, angel," he repeats his earlier phrase in reassurance. He leans his body down and kisses me gently on the lips. I am brimming with trepidation, trying to anticipate his next move. The gorgeous man in front of me is an expert in the bedroom. He is an expert in the art of making love. He knows my body and he plays it like an instrument. Without warning, he flips me over onto my stomach and I shriek at the unexpectedness.

"I've got you, baby." His voice is barely a whisper as he parts my bum cheeks. I suddenly feel tense. "Shhh, just completely relax for me, angel. I want to be the first and the last person to be back here," he soothes, and I'm having an inner battle with myself.

Fuck, fuck, fuck. Just relax, Harper, and stop being such a girl. I take a deep breath and feel myself relax a little.

"Good girl."

I feel him smile against my skin and he plants a kiss on my shoulder blade. He parts my cheeks and I feel his lubricated finger push against my puckered hole.

"You need to let me in, angel, relax."

He pushes his finger in a little at a time and after the initial stinging invasion, I feel an intense pleasure wash over me, which causes me to scream out.

"Does that feel good?"

I moan, "God, yes. So good. Oh, fuck, Sam."

He chuckles softly as he pushes his hardness into my pussy. I gasp at the feeling of fullness. He moves in and out at a painfully slow pace, growling with each thrust. With each powerful plunge, he propels me further into sexual oblivion. He increases his relentless pounding grunting variations of my name. I can feel an intense orgasm building somewhere deep in my womb. I writhe underneath him.

"Peyton."

I let out a scream and explode around his throbbing hardness. My orgasm is so overwhelming I feel like the whole room is spinning and I see stars underneath my blindfold. A few seconds later. Sam finds his release and unleashes his seed deep inside me, yelling my name in garbled ecstasy.

"Fuck me. That was intense."

We are both sweaty and panting. He leans down and kisses my shoulder. He frees my wrists and takes off my blindfold. My eyes take a few minutes to adjust to the light in the room.

"Are you OK, angel?"

I swallow and don't think I can speak. He pulls out of me and removes his finger from my forbidden entrance. He lifts me into his arms and I rest my head on his chest.

"That was amazing."

"Good, I'm glad, baby."

He tenderly strokes my hair, and I am almost asleep on his shoulder when there is a gentle tap on the door.

"Sam, we're in Glasgow, mate," I hear Jax's muffled voice say outside the door.

"Cheers, man, we'll be out in a sec."

Sam kisses the top of my head rousing me from my sleep.

"We're in Glasgow now, angel."

I snuggle closer into his side. "Five more minutes, baby," I say sleepily, and he laughs.

"Come on, sleepy, let's get you to the hotel room. You can take a nap while we go to the interview."

Sam lifts me from his chest and gets up. He goes to the bathroom to wash his hands and he is completely naked. A few minutes pass, and he comes back into the bedroom. I watch as he gets dressed and I am suddenly very awake and very aware of his beautiful body in front of me. He really is the epitome of all the things a man should be. He is striking and very easy on the eye. He laughs again, and his green eyes dance with amusement.

"Ready for round two already, angel? You're insatiable," he says huskily, and I bite my lip. "I love you, but as much as I'd like to stay for round two, we need to get dressed."

He zips up his jeans. I reluctantly get up from the bed and start to get dressed too. Once we are fully dressed, we go down to the lower deck and the boys erupt in a round of applause. My face flushes with embarrassment. *They heard us? Shit! Note to self: Must be quieter next time!* Sam laughs, and he takes my hand. If you can't beat 'em, join 'em! We both bow gracefully, and the boys all whoop and cheer.

We all exit the bus, and it feels so good to finally stretch my legs. We are pulled up outside the Radisson Blu in Glasgow. It looks impressive from the outside with an aquamarine-tone-all-glass entrance. Sam takes my hand and a flashbulb suddenly goes off in our faces. Sam pulls me close to his side and tries to shield me. He tugs my hand and leads me into the foyer of the hotel.

"I'm so sorry about that, baby."

"You don't have to apologise every time someone takes my picture, baby, I accepted that the moment I met you."

"Have I ever told you how amazing you are?"

I put on my thinking face and Sam laughs. "Hmm, no, but I think I could get used to it."

He kisses me gently on the lips. "I'll make sure I tell you every day then, angel." He winks. The rest of the boys join us, and Brody rolls his eyes.

"Fucking hell, will you two get a room?"

"We're working on it, fuck face."

Brody shoots Sam a look and he strides over to the reception desk. J.D. walks over to us.

"Meet back here in half an hour, boys."

I get the feeling that it is more an order rather than a request. We all check into the hotel and go up to our suites. We occupy the whole fourth floor. We step into the room and it is modern and contemporary.

"I'm going to take a shower before the interview, baby, want to join me?"

I start to undress by taking my top off. "Please don't do that or I'm not going to make the interview."

I take off my bra with a defiant look on my face and giggle mischievously.

"You are going to be the death of me, woman!"

He carries me into the bathroom and we take a shower together. I feel refreshed and relaxed afterwards. I lie down on the bed wearing the white fluffy hotel robe and watch as Sam changes. I think watching him get dressed in front of me is my new favourite pastime.

"Enjoying the show, angel?"

I nod and laugh. He finishes getting dressed and presses his lips to mine.

"I have to go, but I'll see you later, baby. Feel free to order room service."

I nod. "I think I'm going to take a nap, I'm knackered."

I yawn and find it unusual that I'm tired during the day.

"Don't miss me too much," he says with a wink.

"I love you, Sam."

"Love you too, angel."

With those words, he leaves the room. I start to reflect on this bizarre situation of being on tour with one of the world's biggest rock bands. It is both surreal and exciting to be thrust into the world of Rancid Vengeance. I need to buckle up and enjoy the ride while it lasts.

I have no idea how long I have been asleep, but I am woken to the bed dipping next to me and Sam nuzzling my hair. His soft lips kiss the spot below my ear.

"Wakey, wakey, beautiful," he whispers. I sleepily turn over and his smiling face is the first thing I see. I instantly find myself smiling back.

"Hey, gorgeous, how long have I been asleep?"

He looks at his watch.

"Well, the interview and the photo shoot took a little longer than expected, so just over two hours I think, babe. We need to get ready for the gig, and we're on stage in an hour."

I nod and get up from the bed and get ready, complete with make-up and straightening my hair.

"You look beautiful as always, angel."

Sam kisses my neck and wraps his arms around my waist. He is looking especially delicious tonight in his stage outfit. He is wearing devilishly tight leather trousers to emphasise his crotch area, a black skull vest, which showcases his bulging muscles, black cowboy boots and his stage make-up consisting of black eyeliner. His hair is gelled and styled into soft spikes. It is taking all I have not run my fingers through his raven-black hair; he is a sight for sore eyes. We leave the room hand in hand and go down to reception in the lift. Once the lift doors close, we are alone. Sam backs me up against the wall and claims my mouth.

"I can't keep my hands to myself when you're around."

I laugh. "Well, good things come to those who wait, rock star."

I wink, and the doors slide open. Sam releases me, and we step out of the lift. He swats my bum.

"You're such a cock tease!"

I emphasise my walk and swing my hips suggestively.

"Now, play fair, angel, that's just going to get you fucked right here on the hotel floor in front of all these people," he whispers huskily, and I can't help getting turned on by his seductive words. He raises his eyebrows suggestively.

"You're shameless, Newbolt."

He comes up behind me and grips my waist pulling me flush against him. He nuzzles my neck and whispers in my ear, "Only where you're concerned, angel."

We all pile into a black limo driven by Cole and make our way to the gig. When we arrive at the o2 Academy Glasgow, I hear loud screams and the deafening chant, "Vengeance, Vengeance, Vengeance."

The screams seem to get louder as the bus pulls to a halt behind the venue. We prepare to exit the bus and Sam grabs my hand.

"Stick close to me, angel, it's going to get messy."

We get off the bus and are greeted by hundreds of excited fans and four, large, burly and muscular men in matching <u>Men in Black</u>-esque suits. Sam pulls me to his side, gripping my waist with his large hand.

"Bolt! Flash! Snake! Axeman! We love you! We want your babies!"

A fan pulls Sam's t-shirt and the security guard has to restrain her. We make our way through the hoard of fans and I get a few dirty looks from at least five different women. We finally get into the venue and walk down a short corridor.

"I told you it could get messy; some of our fans are a little crazy and obsessive!"

We both laugh, and I am again reminded of the difference in our lives. Sam can't go out without being recognised by his fans and his life is like an open book for people to peek into. Sam pulling me close to him and wrapping his strong arms around me interrupts my thoughts.

"I need you on the front row centre, baby; you're like my good luck charm."

I smile. "You don't need luck, babe, you're amazing."

He laughs and kisses me gently on the lips. Cole walks over to us.

"Cole, could you take care of my girl, please, mate? Make sure she's at the front, somewhere where I can see her." He winks and Cole nods.

"I want you to know that when I'm singing, I'm singing the words to you, angel, *just you,*" he whispers, and again I am disarmed by his sweet words. My insecure and vulnerable rocker is making a welcome appearance tonight. Sam kisses me passionately on the lips.

"Wish me luck."

"Not that you need it, but good luck, baby."

He sprints off down the corridor leaving Cole to escort me silently to the front row. Ever since our chat in the surveillance suite, he has hardly said a word to me.

The venue is intimate with just a two-and-a-half-thousand capacity. I take my place and fold my arms; I suddenly feel nervous with anticipation. There is a striking woman to the left of me with platinum blonde hair, dip dyed with pillar-box red streaks. She has a small nose stud and is tall, bronzed, and slim. She has wide blue eyes and a bow-shaped mouth. There is something about her that seems vaguely familiar. She is wearing a black leather pencil skirt, a black fur gilet with a white skull vest underneath and sky-high studded ankle boots. She looks me up and down, I smile, and she smiles back but it doesn't reach her eyes. She cocks her head and regards me intently.

"I have to say, you're not what I was expecting. I was expecting you to be ... I don't know. Blonde, and taller, maybe. You're definitely Sam's type, though; vulnerable, pretty. He's definitely excelled himself this time."

I look puzzled. *Who is this woman? What is she talking about?* She smiles sweetly.

"He gets you with the words at first, he makes you fall in love with him, and he makes you need him, that's the worst thing."

I glance away from her, suddenly uncomfortable in her presence.

"Oh, dear, he's already made you fall in love with him, hasn't he? Charming bastard. Now you can't walk away because he won't let you."

I look at her and clear my throat.

"I don't know what you're talking about. Who are you?"

She folds her arms, mirroring my body language, and she smirks.

"Of course you don't, darling, I'm just one in a long line of girls, just like you."

The screams of the crowd are making it hard for me to hear her properly. I go to speak but the lights go down. I look towards the stage, and when I turn around, she is gone. *How strange?* Being confronted by a mystery woman. I am confused and curious of who she was. How did she know I was Sam's girlfriend?

My thoughts are interrupted by Lucas' familiar drumbeat filling the venue. The stage is in darkness and the spotlight goes up, revealing Sam in all his tattooed glory. Jax's signature guitar riff accompanies Lucas' drumbeat. Brody moves next to Jax and they are standing back to back, playing their guitars effortlessly. Sam steps to the front of the stage and his face lights up as he looks out at his adoring fans. He looks in my direction and winks; he lifts the microphone to his lips.

"I am an enigma, a fucking inferno, a beautiful fucking disaster. I am an errant child, an inhuman wreck, a beautiful fucking disaster. I am a shell of the man I used to be, a robot, a meat suit for these bones in which I live, a beautiful fucking disaster."

I haven't heard this song before and I instantly like it. He completely loses himself in the music and lyrics.

"I wear a mask, I wear my scars, like a badge of honour, I am a beautiful fucking disaster. I am the man who cries invisible tears, ravaged with guilt and crimson coloured hues, I am a beautiful fucking disaster. I am a shadow, a soul so broken and torn, an avenging angel, a devil in disguise, a beautiful fucking disaster."

Jax steps out to the front of the stage; his guitar solo fills the venue, and the crowd goes crazy. I am amazed at his guitar skills; the way his fingers make love to the fret board. I watch as he closes his eyes and effortlessly strums his solo. After the song finishes, Sam steps to the front of the stage.

"Glasgow! How the fuck are we doing tonight?"

The crowd screams and stomps their feet.

"Please allow me to introduce you to the band."

Jax steps beside Sam and breaks out into a solo.

"This is Flash, the best fucking guitar player in the world."

The crowd whoops and cheer.

"Hello, Glasgow!"

Jax jumps up and down with excitement. Sam sweeps his arm out to the side and Brody steps to the other side of him. He strums a more elaborate solo and winks at a girl in the front row; she looks like she might faint.

"This is Snake, the craziest motherfucker on the planet."

Brody wiggles his split tongue suggestively and grins. "Ladies."

Lucas pounds his drums and does an impressive drum beat.

"Up in the back we have The Axeman, best fucking drummer I've ever seen."

Lucas finishes with a twirl of his drumsticks, salutes, and winks.

"And I'm Bolt," he growls into the microphone. "How are we all doing up in here tonight? All you crazy Glasgow people are you ready to take the roof off this fucking place?"

The crowd get wilder as he carries on speaking. I am mesmerized by his stage presence; I can't take my eyes off him. He is a true showman who knows how to work a crowd. The crowd is practically eating out of the palm of his hand.

"We all want to treat you to a brand new song we've been working on for our next album, how does that sound?"

The crowd gets louder, and I am almost convinced that I can feel the whole place vibrating with the noise.

"This one's for you." Sam looks at me and smiles warmly.

"Give me a beat, Axeman, one-two-three-four."

Lucas pounds a drumbeat. Brody takes centre stage and strums a complex solo, and then Sam steps forward bathed in a lone spotlight.

"You unlocked my soul and I let you in. I felt like my heart would burst through my chest. My self-control being judged, and you were the test. The voices in my head are screaming, run as fast as you can and don't, don't look back. Say you'll walk beside me, let me give you all that I am. When will you make that move and turn those words into bittersweet truths. My doubts drifted with the breeze, my soul took flight, and I couldn't run away if I tried."

Sam's voice is like pure liquid gold. The way he sings the lyrics, with such meaning and sincerity, I am hooked. Whoever the mystery woman was, she was right, I love this man with all that I am, and I couldn't walk away if I tried.

8

Peyton

After the gig is finished, Cole is instantly at my side to escort me to the backstage area.

"Did you recognise that woman who was standing next to me?"

Cole looks to the floor and avoids eye contact.

"You know her, don't you? Who is she?" I know my tone is accusatory, but I can't help myself.

"It's not my place to say, Peyton, just like any other bloke, Sam has a past."

I raise my eyebrows.

"That's bullshit, Cole, and you bloody well know it!" I shout and go to walk away, not wanting to be around him right now. I am sure I'm getting close to my period with the mood swings and tiredness. Cole grabs my arm.

"Peyton, he's a good bloke, please don't shoot him down until you've heard him out and please don't push him. If you need a chat afterwards, come and find me, sugar."

Now I am worried. *What would I need to speak to Cole about?* I vow to speak to Sam about it as soon as I can. Cole lets go of my arm and I walk ahead of him, making it clear that I'm pissed off and our conversation is far from finished. I see Sam's tall frame walking towards me with a white towel around his neck and drinking bottled water. He looks delicious covered in sweat. He smiles his dazzling panty-dropping smile and I run towards him. He catches me before I knock him off his feet and I wrap my legs around his waist.

"Hey, beautiful, someone's pleased to see me. Did you enjoy the show?"

I smile and kiss him on the lips.

"You were fantastic, baby, just like I knew you would be," I whisper, and he laughs.

"Thanks, did you like the song?"

I nod. "I loved it."

"You ready for the after party? We need to go back to the bus to get changed."

He plants a chaste kiss to my lips and sets me on the ground. Cole whispers to Sam, and his face drops. Sam brushes Cole's arm and winks.

"Cheers for letting me know, mate, I really appreciate it."

Cole smiles and leaves.

"What was that all about?"

Sam shakes his head. "Nothing for you to worry about, angel. Come on, let's go."

He kisses me gently on the end of my nose, clasps my hand in his, and we go to the backstage door. There are legions of fans waiting outside, screaming their familiar chant.

"Vengeance, Vengeance, Vengeance."

The other boys join us, and we make our way through the sea of bodies in the car park, flanked by at least five large security guards in matching black suits. Brody hangs back and pulls two girls from the crowd. He casually saunters across the car park with his arms around both of them. Lex is waiting by the bus with his hands tucked into his pockets and he salutes as we approach.

"Good show, boys?"

They all nod.

"All good, Lex."

Lucas winks, and we make our way up the bus steps. Sam kisses me on my forehead and runs up to the upper deck. I sit on the sofa and Lucas places a bottle of beer in front of me.

"Here you go, Peyton."

He takes the cap off his beer and takes a long pull. "God damn, I needed that."

I take a sip of my beer. Lucas is about to speak when Brody flops down on the sofa with the two women he pulled from the car park.

"This is Candy and Precious."

They both giggle from their positions perched on each of Brody's knees.

"My names Ke—"

Brody stops her by putting his finger to her lips. "Tonight you're whoever I want you to be, sweetheart."

A look of disgust passes over my face. Where does he get off treating women like that? I shake my head, get up, and go to the upper deck, not wanting to be in the same room as him right now. There is something about him that rubs me up the wrong way. J.D. stops me at the top of stairs and he grabs my arm.

"Tour buses can be dangerous places for sluts like you, Peyton. One false move."

He pushes me towards the stairs but then pulls me back roughly.

"Don't fucking test me, little girl, because I can make your life a living hell while you're on tour with us, just remember that."

He smiles maniacally, and I feel the colour drain from my cheeks. I swallow hard and summon up the courage to deliver a comeback.

"Like I said before, you don't fucking scare me, J.D.. You might be able to manipulate the boys, but you definitely can't manipulate me, make sure *you* remember that," I spit angrily. I jab my finger in his chest and snatch my hand away from him. I push past him and go into the bedroom. Sam has just got out of the shower with a towel around his waist.

"Is everything all right, angel?"

I nod, trying not to let the incident with J.D. show on my face, even though deep down I am a little unnerved by the whole thing.

"Brody's just bought two of his groupies back to the bus."

He rolls his eyes. "So it begins!" He says with a laugh. "It's kind of a first night tour tradition for Brody, he calls it his 'bag 'em and shag 'em routine'."

I roll my eyes and Sam goes into the bedroom. I lean in the doorway and watch as he gets dressed. He changes into a pair of ripped, faded, blue jeans that are slung low on his lean hips, a black *AC/DC* vest, New Rock boots, and he gels his hair into his signature spiky style before he pulls on a black leather jacket. He looks the epitome of what a bad boy rocker should look like. He catches me staring and he chuckles softly.

"Do you never get tired of ogling me, angel?"

He rolls his eyes dramatically and we both laugh.

"Never, I like to ogle! I'll never get tired of looking at you; I can't believe my luck sometimes, baby."

He smiles and pulls me into his chest. "I love you so much."

He kisses me gently and takes my hand in his as we walk down the stairs.

"It's about fucking time! I can see your vagina from here, Sammy!"

Jax laughs, and Sam hits him playfully. We all pile off the bus and get into the waiting limo driven by Cole. We make the ten-minute journey to a club called The Polo Lounge. Sam has his arm slung around my shoulders; the doorman nods to the boys and lets us through the velvet rope.

"What are you drinking, angel?"

I lean in to him.

"Vodka and cranberry, please, baby."

He nods, and he beckons Lucas over to him. He whispers to him and Sam winks. Lucas takes me by the elbow.

"Come on, sugar, let's go sit down."

I follow Lucas and we go into the V.I.P section. We sit down on a large, brown-leather seating area surrounded by glass tables. Lucas sits next to me. The music is pumping, and the club is packed with people. A few minutes later, Sam joins us; he puts the drinks down on the table and a waitress in skimpy shorts and a gold bikini top puts four buckets down with four bottles of Cristal champagne in. She smiles an all-too-bright white smile, and Brody shoves a bunch of twenty-pound notes in between her breasts. He winks, and he pats his lap. I swear that boy has no shame. Sam sits down on the other side of me; all of the bands entourage have joined us. Including Donovan, Caleb, Blu, Tate, Skip, Cole, and Lex. J.D also joins us, much to my dismay. I take a long sip of my drink and Sam wraps his arm around my shoulder.

"Is everything OK, angel?"

I nod and smile.

"Yeah, of course it is, baby, why wouldn't it be?" I say a little too enthusiastically.

Sam cocks his head and regards me intently. We spend most of the night chatting, laughing, and drinking. Halfway through the night, I get up and go to the toilet. As I approach the ladies, I see J.D with his back to me so I decide to hang back in the shadows and listen.

"I want her fucking gone, Lyla; I want you to make sure they split up for good this time."

The person he is talking to steps to the side. The woman from the gig. I put my hand to my mouth to stop myself from making a sound.

"I tried, J.D, I really tried."

J.D. shakes his head.

"No, you obviously didn't try hard enough. She's a manipulative little slut who's using Sam as her meal ticket; I've seen girls like her a million times."

"He really loves her, he's ... different. He's not the same Sam I fell in love with. He's grown up; as much as it hurts to see him with her, I can't do it to him."

My eyes glaze over at her words. *Why have I never heard of her?* Sam said his only serious relationship was years ago with some girl he grew up with. J.D holds his finger up.

"I'll make it worth your while. Five grand? Ten grand? How much is it going to take, Lyla? Name your price."

Lyla takes a breath.

"I don't need your money, but make it twenty grand, and I'll make sure she dumps him. This is the last time, J.D, the last fucking time."

She actually sounds angry which makes me wonder what her story is. J.D nods.

"Thank you so much, sweetness. You won't regret this, you know it makes sense, I'll be in touch."

He hugs Lyla, and they both stride off in opposite directions. I step out of the shadows and rush to the toilet. I quickly swing open a free cubicle door and step inside. As soon as I lock the door, I try to compose myself. A few minutes later, I unlock the door, wash my hands, and exit the toilet. I am in desperate need of a drink, so I go off to the bar. I order my drink and there is a guy standing next to me smiling.

"Grab your coat, sweetheart, you've pulled."

I cock my eyebrow at him. *Seriously? On what planet would that line actually work?*

"Pulled what, a muscle?"

He chuckles.

"I deserved that one. Can I buy you a drink, sweetheart?"

His accent is soft and Scottish. I look at him and shake my head.

"No, I'm good, thanks."

He shifts closer to me.

"Oh, go on, just one drink. You're gorgeous."

I move subtly away from him.

"I said no thank you, I'm fine. I'm actually here with my boyfriend."

He smirks and moves even closer; I can feel his alcohol breath on my cheek. He touches my arm.

"Come on, sweetheart. If you were my girl, I'd never let you out of my sight, not for a second."

I look up at him.

"Luckily, I'm not your girl then. Just fuck off and leave me alone," I snap, and I unexpectedly feel a presence behind me and Mr. Scottish is removed from my side.

"You heard the lady, I suggest you take your hand off my girl and fuck off if you know what's good for you." Mr. Scottish holds his hands up in defence and walks off. "Are you OK, angel?"

I nod, and his face is marred with worry.

"I'm fine, baby, honestly."

He plants a kiss on my cheek.

"When I saw him put his hand on you, I actually wanted to physically damage him," he says through clenched teeth.

My possessive rocker is back. I suddenly feel an overwhelming sense of anger towards him and I yank my arm free from his grasp.

"Stop fucking suffocating me, Sam!"

Even over the music, I can sense the eyes of the people in the club on us. He steps back, and his eyes widen.

"Angel, I'm just trying to protect you, please understand that," he says softly, and I shake my head.

"No, Sam, I don't, I just need to be on my own right now."

He goes to speak, but I back away and storm off towards the exit, leaving him with a truly dumbfounded look on his face. I am so angry with him for being so suffocating, overprotective, and possessive. I can't help but think that every time I think our relationship is moving forward, something comes along to push us back three steps.

I walk out of the club and into the cool night air, relishing the fresh air on my clammy skin. I feel an arm reach for me and grip my wrist gently.

"We should talk," she says softly and without an ounce of malice in her voice. The woman from the gig. *Lyla.* She pulls me into an alley beside the club. "I'm doing this because you seem like a really nice girl, but you can't trust him. He's good at acting, he's perfected the sincere rocker thing, but once you get to know him, once you break the surface, and once he's drawn you in, he's got you right where he wants you."

I cock my head and look up at her. Even in heels, she is at least a foot taller than I am and extremely beautiful.

"Who are you? He won't tell me."

She smiles. "I'm Lyla. Sam and me ... We go way back. We were together for a while; I was totally smitten with him."

She seems a little vague, which makes me more suspicious and I fold my arms.

"Why are you doing this? I don't know you."

She brushes my arm.

"I know that he's serious about you and I can see it going the same way as me and him did. I don't want to see you get hurt, and don't get me wrong we'll never be best friends not by a long shot, but I'd like to think I care enough to at least try to prevent what happened between Sam and me."

I smile. "I saw you with J.D..."

Her face drops.

"It wasn't what it looked like; you need to watch out for him," she warns. "Promise me you'll be careful around him?"

Her voice is full of concern, and I begin to wonder what she could mean. I am about to ask her when I hear a male voice call my name, "Peyton."

I recognise the voice as Jax. I peek around the corner and when I turn around again, Lyla is gone. *Strange.* I have all these thoughts rushing around my mind and my head is spinning. I step out from the alley and Jax rushes over to me.

"There you are. Sam is about to tear the walls down in there looking for you."

I take a breath.

"Take me back to the hotel, Jax, please. I really can't be around him right now, please."

He sees the pained look on my face and he nods, brushing my arm reassuringly.

"I'll be right back, babe, I need to get my phone, and I'll make sure he doesn't follow. Trust me."

He winks and goes back inside. The large doorman steps to my side.

"Do you need a taxi, darlin'?" he asks in a soft Scottish lilt and smiles cordially. I nod and smile as he flags a taxi down and it pulls up at the kerb.

"Thank you so much."

I open the car door, and a few minutes later, Jax joins me in the back seat as we make our way back to the hotel. I lean my head on his shoulder.

"Hey, do you want to tell me what that fuck-wit did this time?"

A tear rolls down my cheek. "A girl called Lyla showed up."

Jax's eyes widen.

"Lyla? Lyla was here? Are you sure, babe?"

I nod. "She was at the gig as well, she kept telling me not to trust him. What's he hiding, Jax? Who is she?"

He puts his hand to his head. *"Fuck,"* he curses and takes out his phone.

"Jax, don't call him, please," I plead. Jax looks at me and puts his arm around me.

"He needs to know she's here, babe."

Defeated, I lean my head back on his shoulder and nod as he carries on texting Sam. Ten minutes later, we are pulling up outside the hotel. Jax pays the driver and I stride into the hotel foyer. I press the button for the lift, and Jax runs to catch up with me.

"This isn't his fault, babe, at least hear him out, he deserves that. I have never seen him the way he is with you ever. It's a first for him, he is ... happy."

We both step into the lift, I push the button for the fourth floor, and the doors slide shut.

"What's going on with you and Ruby?"

I swiftly change the subject, and he smiles, leaning back against the wall with his hands in his pockets.

"I'm falling for her, Peyton, she's ... incredible. She doesn't stand for my bullshit. She doesn't expect anything from me, I know I slept with someone behind her back, and I'm so fucking sorry for that. We never made promises to each other, I thought we were clear on that. Now she keeps blowing hot and cold, I can't keep up with her. Her mood swings are literally giving me whiplash."

I definitely know that feeling all too well.

He sighs. The lift stops at our floor and we step out into the corridor.

"Do you want me to talk to her?"

He smiles. "Thanks, Peyton, that's really sweet, but I'm a bit old for the whole my friend fancies your friend!"

"She's been hurt so many times, Jax, but she must have some feelings for you; show her how much she means to you. I see how she is around you, she plays down her feelings, and she hides behind the tough girl act."

"Just like you, you're more alike than you realise, babe."

I smile shyly and fidget with my hands. "Maybe, but this isn't about me."

He stops outside mine and Sam's room.

"But it was about you; until you changed the subject, remember?"

He raises his eyebrows, and I hold my hands up. "OK, you caught me!"

"Look, I've seen Sam at his lowest points, he has bounced back every single time, but I don't think he'll bounce back so easily if you run from him again. You were the reason he got up on that stage tonight. Talk to him, he is ... fragile right now. Please don't break his heart, babe."

Jax's voice is pleading and I nod. There are so many things I want to say and ask Jax about Sam's past because he seems to be the person who knows him best. But a part of me is terrified of the answers, so I decide to keep my mouth firmly shut.

"I won't."

He brushes my arm. "I'm going back to the boys at the club, text me if you need anything, love," he says softly, and I nod.

"Thanks, Jax."

I kiss him on the cheek and he smiles. He salutes and turns to walk back down the corridor. I insert the key card and push the door open. The door clicks shut behind me and I turn on the light. I kick off my shoes and go straight into the bathroom to take off my make-up. I pull out a baby wipe and look at my reflection in the mirror. I look so different to the way I looked a few short weeks ago before Sam breezed into my life with his leather and his tattoos.

I hardly recognise the girl staring back at me. My blue eyes have a sapphire-like sparkle to them, my cheeks are rosy, and my smile is no longer the fake one I have perfected over the years. They say love changes you, but I didn't believe them for a second. I am living proof that love changes everything. From your appearance to the way you feel inside, that broken, mess of a heart that Callum ripped out of my chest and trampled on the day he cheated on me has now been mended and my heart is growing stronger by the day with every minute I spend with Sam.

The door of the hotel room slamming shut interrupts my thoughts. I step into the doorway of the bathroom and look up, my eyes instantly locking with Sam's blazing green ones. He moves towards me and is in front of me in two large strides. His chest is heaving, and he is so close I can feel his warm breath on my cheek. His familiar Sam scent envelopes me as he runs his thumb across my bottom lip.

"Please don't run from me, angel, I can't stand it."

"I promise I won't run anymore, but you need to start being honest with me, Sam. You can't keep things from me. I have to know what's going on in that head of yours. Don't shut me out, please."

He takes my face in both of his hands and presses his lips hungrily to mine. His kiss is deep and his tongue probes mine. It is as if he possesses me so completely by putting everything he has into one kiss. He pulls away and looks into my eyes.

"You're mine, Peyton, every fucking inch of you belongs to me. I won't let you leave me again."

I shake my head. "I'd never leave you, baby, you're my world."

I stroke his face and he lifts me into his strong arms.

"I need to be inside you now, angel."

I start to wonder what has gotten into him, but I don't want to push him while he is obviously feeling vulnerable, so I decide to give him what he obviously needs, and I wrap my legs around his waist to pull him closer. He takes that as a green light and he crashes his lips frantically against mine. He moves us towards the king-size bed and deposits me in the middle. He tears off his t-shirt and unbuckles his belt. He pulls off his jeans, boxers briefs, and is naked in record time. I know something is off when he doesn't give me a chance to admire his rippling physique. He climbs on the bed and parts my legs with his knee. He roughly pulls off my clothes; his eyes are blazing with lust. I have never seen him this way before, and a large part of me is so turned on by this dominant side of him. He cups my breast in his hand and kneads it. He moves to my other breast and latches onto my nipple, causing me to moan softly.

"Oh, Sam."

He moves up to nuzzle my neck and bites down as if to mark me as his. I gasp in both pleasure and pain.

"You're mine."

I grip the nape of his neck and force him to look at me. His eyes aren't their usual sparkling green, and a lump starts to form in my throat. I swallow it back and try to hide the quiver in my voice.

"I'm yours, Sam, yours. Just yours, baby."

He seems satisfied with my statement. He grasps his steel erection in his hand and he enters me forcefully, I cry out at the invasion. His pace is rapid and unrelenting. With every stroke, he growls, and I moan.

"Look how greedily your cunt swallows my cock. No other man is allowed even a taste of how fucking sweet you are."

My heart constricts at his crass words and how conflicted his thoughts have become. It is as if his body has been possessed and taken over by a complete stranger. He slams into me so hard, my eyes start to water.

"Sam, baby," I say softly to try to make him slow down, but his pace doesn't let up. He pumps into me one more time and he yells out as he comes inside me.

"*Mine.*"

His breathing is laboured as he collapses on top of me. He pulls out of me after a few seconds and silently gets up off the bed. He walks into the bathroom and closes the door behind him, leaving me laid on the bed in a state of shock at what just happened. *What the fuck has gotten into him?* Sam *never* acts this way. Something must have happened for him to behave this way. I get up, wincing in pain. I pull on the hotel robe and pick up my phone off the dressing table. As I go to dial Jax's number, my phone starts ringing in my hand. Cole's name flashes up on my screen, and I answer straight away.

"Peyton, is Sam with you?"

I lower my voice, "Yeah, but he's acting really strangely, Cole. I don't know what to do."

It is taking everything I have right now to stay calm and not freak out at Sam's odd behaviour.

"*Fuck*," he curses.

"Are you back at the hotel?"

"Yeah, he's locked himself in the bathroom."

"*Shit!* He was about to tear the walls down after you left, then he dodged me and just disappeared from the club. I tracked the GPS on his phone, and I'm on the way to you right now, sugar."

"What's going on? Please tell me, Cole, I'm sick of you keeping secrets from me."

He is silent for a second.

"Look, sugar, you just need to trust me and keep him in the hotel room. I'm coming right now. I'll be as quick as I can, and I'll explain everything, whatever you do, don't let him leave."

My stomach flips at his words.

"OK, I'll make sure of it."

"Good girl, I'll be there soon, hang tight, sugar. Bye."

I hang up the phone and am struck dumb at the turn of events. I take off the robe and pull on a pair of comfortable black yoga trousers with one of Sam's oversized Rancid Vengeance hoodies; it smells of him and I inhale his scent. I pull my hair into a loose messy bun and hear the water from the shower running. It is times like these when I miss Ruby so much. I miss our chats and having her around to talk to in times of crisis, so I decide to text her.

Hey babe

Miss you ⬦

P xx

She responds almost straight away.

Hey girl

Miss you too

How's the tour going?

Scratched any groupie's eyes out yet! ⬦

Any gossip?

R xx

I smile at her response; she has such an uncanny ability to make me smile.

Tour going great

Not scratched any groupie's eyes out...yet! ⬦

Sam's acting weird

Could do with a chat ⬦

P xx

I lie down on the bed and wait for her reply.

Are you OK babe?

Please call me

R xx

I am almost relieved at her response and I start to type a reply, when the door taps softly. I get up off the bed and go to the door. Cole and Jax are both in the doorway; I move out of the way to let them both in. They both step into the room and close the door quietly.

"Are you OK, Peyton?" Cole asks softly, and I nod.

Jax looks at me apprehensively. "Where is he, babe?"

I point to the bathroom and pull the sleeves of Sam's hoodie over my hands, suddenly feeling freezing cold. Cole takes charge of the situation.

"Do you want to tell me what happened, Peyton?"

I bite my lip embarrassed at having to tell them exactly what happened between us and Cole rolls his eyes.

"Believe me, darlin', I've heard and seen far worse from these guys so please don't be embarrassed."

I take a breath and he folds his arms waiting for my answer.

"He came back to the room, he started acting weird, and we had sex. He was so distant, rough and forceful. He's never been that way before. He scared me."

My voice trembles. Cole puts his hand to his head and looks at Jax. A look passes between them, which makes me feel oddly nervous and worried.

"*Motherfucker!* Did he hurt you?"

Cole moves closer to me with a concerned look on his face and checks me over. I shake my head and he lets out a relieved breath.

"He's having one of his episodes. You need to pack your stuff right now, sugar, no arguments please. You're going to have to trust me on this one, Peyton, ask no questions, and I'll tell you no lies. I'm going to stay here with him tonight; you're going to take my room down the corridor. Jax will stay with you, is that OK with you, mate?" Cole says calmly and Jax nods. However, by the look on Cole's face, Jax doesn't have a choice.

"It's room four-twenty-four. I'll deal with Sam, I'm the only one who can handle him when he's like this."

My eyes glaze over, and I nod, struggling to process what is going on. He hands me his key card, and I take it with shaky hands. I pull up my suitcase on the bed and start to pack my stuff together.

"Trust me, darlin', he is going to get a whole lot worse before he gets better, it's best that you don't see him this way."

The door of the bathroom opens, and Sam strides out with a towel slung low on his hips.

"Well, well, well, is this a private conversation or can anyone join in?" His eyes are wide and agitated. "Don't mind me," he says flatly. He drops his towel; Jax and Cole don't seem at all fazed by Sam's blatant nakedness. He pulls on a clean pair of boxers and a pair of loose-fitting combat shorts. "What the fuck is this, some sort of intervention?"

Sam laughs, and I zip my suitcase up. Sam's eyes widen at the sound. He looks between Jax and me.

"Come on, babe, we need to go now," Jax says softly and he picks up my suitcase.

"You can't take my girl," Sam says, his voice trembling. "I won't let you take her from me, you can't fucking take her. Peyton, baby, please, I can do better, please don't leave me."

My heart breaks at hearing him so upset and distressed. A tear rolls down my cheek, and Sam goes to step towards me, but Cole is so fast and exudes pure strength as he holds him back with an iron grip.

"Sam, mate, it's just for tonight."

"No, no, no, you can't fucking take her. I need her, she needs to stay with me. She fucking promised me she wouldn't run anymore."

He breaks free of Cole's grip, collapses in a heap on the floor, and sobs uncontrollably. His hands run frantically through his still damp hair. I push past Jax and kneel down in front of Sam.

"Sam, baby, I'm here, I'm not running," I say softly. I cup his face in my hands and he looks at me. His eyes are so sad and pained.

"I fucked up, please don't leave me."

Sam reaches for my hand, but Cole touches his shoulder and stops him.

"Mate, just let her go with Jax, yeah? It's just for tonight; she's going to be right down the corridor."

Sam stands up and moves towards Cole until they are toe to toe.

Sam raises his voice. "You can't fucking stop me from being with my girl, you've got no right!"

"Sam, please, mate, you need to calm down."

Sam's nostrils flare and he has gone from uncontrollable sobbing to boiling rage in the matter of seconds.

"Jax, get the lady out of here now, please."

My eyes widen. "He needs me. Look at the fucking state of him!"

Cole shakes his head. "You don't need to see him like this, darlin', trust me." He nods at Jax and Sam moves forward.

"Jax, please I'm begging you, don't do this, mate," he pleads and Jax shakes his head. It breaks my heart to hear him in such distress. Jax picks me up and throws me over his shoulder; Cole holds Sam back.

"Jax! Fucking put me down now!"

He strides out of the hotel room and slams the door behind us. I can hear Sam's raised voice as we walk ten yards to Cole's room with me pounding on Jax's back to put me down. He inserts the key card and kicks the door open with his boot. He strides in and sets me on my feet, closing the door behind us.

"You didn't need to throw me over your shoulder and act like a fucking cave man, Jax!"

I narrow my eyes and shoot daggers at him. He smirks and shrugs as I sit down on the identical king-size bed. Jax goes over to the other side of the room, opens the mini bar, and takes out a miniature bottle of whiskey. He pours it in a glass and hands it to me.

"You look like you need it, babe."

I manage a smile; I take a long sip and enjoy the burn as it slides down my throat. His face is marred with concern and he crouches down in front of me.

"Listen to me, that wasn't Sam back there, he's not himself right now. You need to understand that he has some ... Erm ... Issues. He gets like this every now and then."

A tear slides down my cheek, and he rubs it away with the pad of his calloused thumb. I finish my drink and put the glass down on the floor.

"Hey, none of this your fault, babe, you have to trust me on that one."

I look at him and the tears don't stop falling for my gorgeous, handsome, fucked up, rock star, boyfriend. Jax gets up from the floor, sits down next to me, and pulls me into his arms. He strokes my back reassuringly.

"Shhh, everything's going to be all right, I promise."

I pull away from him, but he keeps me tucked safely in his arms.

"What's wrong with him, Jax? Why was he acting like that? Please don't fucking lie to me. I need you to start telling me the truth, I can handle it."

I sniff and Jax closes his eyes for a second. He opens his eyes and his wide hazel eyes lock with mine; he takes my hands in his.

"Sam's ill. He has been for years. Day to day he is usually OK, he manages it, he takes his meds like second nature, and he's totally fine. Since he met you, he decided he didn't need his medication anymore and he has been off it for a few months. He's—*fuck* he is going to kill me for telling you this, but I can see it's getting serious between you two and you have a right to know. I've been on at him for a while to tell you the truth, but he was terrified you would run from him again. Sam has severe manic depression. We thought he was handling it until you had the car accident, then he started behaving oddly, being stupidly possessive and very aggressive. We noticed he wasn't sleeping, working out excessively, self-medicating with the drugs, not eating properly, and burning himself out. Cole knows how to handle him in these types of situations; the guy is a total fucking legend. He's been around at some of Sam's lowest points and he's the only one who he listens to for some reason. If anyone can get through to him, it's Cole but you need to let him work his magic and he will be back to being regular Sam in no time at all, I promise you, babe."

I am struggling to take all this new information in. Sam has severe manic depression? It certainly explains a lot of things, his need to protect me after the accident, the fights and his drug taking. *How the fuck did I miss the signs?*

"He thinks you're more of a tonic for him than his medication. I begged him to carry on taking it, but you know Sam well enough by now to know that he's extremely fucking stubborn and ridiculously pig-headed."

Jax shakes his head, and he looks as if he wants to say more but he doesn't. He runs his fingers through his unruly, dirty-blonde hair and lets out a sigh. I sit wondering how this day could possibly get any worse and wish it would end sooner rather than later.

I yawn, suddenly feeling exhausted from the day's events. I look at the clock and it reads twelve midnight.

"You should get some sleep, love, you look exhausted."

I smile, knowing that Jax is right. I take off Sam's hoodie and get into bed wearing my yoga trousers and a black vest. Soon, I drift off into a deep sleep.

I'm not sure how long I have been asleep, but I wake to a darkened room and Jax is sleeping fully clothed on top of the duvet with his arm thrown over his eyes a few inches away from me. I lie awake for a few minutes thinking about Sam, and I feel the overwhelming urge to go to him; I need to know that he is OK. I pull the covers back quietly and pull on Sam's hoodie. I pull on my UGG boots and tip-toe out of the room, shutting the door silently behind me. I walk the ten yards to what was mine and Sam's room.

I hear a loud crash, the sound of Sam shouting, and the faint sound of Cole's deep soothing voice trying to calm him. My heart clenches at the sound. I insert the key card and push open the door. I am shocked at the state of the room—it is completely trashed. There is a lamp smashed on the floor, glass everywhere, and all of the furniture is upturned. Sam is sitting in the corner of the room with his knees pulled up to his chest. He looks like a frightened animal: trembling, his eyes are glazed, and he looks terrified. I look from him to Cole, who is sitting on the edge of the bed shaking his head as if to say, '*you shouldn't be here*'. Sam's eyes meet mine and a lone tear falls down his cheek. I go to move towards him and Cole stands up. He clears his throat.

"Can I have a word in private please, Peyton?"

I nod, and Sam's face looks stricken.

"It's all right, try and stay calm; we'll just be a sec, mate, I need to talk to, Peyton." Cole tries to placate him; it seems to be working as Sam lets out a shaky breath. He leads me towards the bathroom and pushes the door, so it is ajar but not completely closed. He turns on the tap to drown out our voices.

"What the fuck is going on, Cole?" I snap, and Cole lets out a breath.

He lowers his voice. "I can't get through to him Peyton; it's like he's stopped listening to me. After you left, he went completely crazy, he's so far gone I'm starting to worry he won't come back from this. The only other person who can talk to him and get through to him when he's like this is his dad, but Marlowe is my last and final resort."

I look at him and he scrubs his hands down his face. "What a fucking mess."

I brush his arm in reassurance. "Please let me try."

He nods, and I leave the bathroom. I crouch down in front of Sam and his pained eyes meet mine. I cup his face in my hands.

"Baby, you're breaking my heart," I tell him, my voice thick with unshed tears. "Please let me in. I need you to talk to me, Sam."

He holds my gaze and puts his hand over mine on his face.

"I'm so sorry angel," he says, his voice hoarse.

"You don't need to apologise to me, you're ill and you're not yourself right now. Jax told me everything"

His eyes widen but he is silent.

"Why didn't you tell me all of this before?"

He shakes his head. "I was ashamed, you're the only good thing to come out of all this; you don't deserve to be involved in this fucking mess, angel."

I get to my feet and offer him my hand. He looks up at me and takes it; I lead him over to the bed and lie down. I pat the space next to me and he complies, lying down beside me. I lay my head on his chest and we get comfortable on the bed.

"Start talking, rock star."

I hear him chuckle softly. "Where do I start?"

I laugh. "How about the beginning, baby?"

I take his hand in mine and stroke it gently. His knuckles are bruised and covered in dried blood.

"I need you to tell me one thing before I start. Did I hurt you? I couldn't bear to think that I hurt you and laid my hands on you while I was like that."

His voice is pained and my heart clenches, I shake my head.

"No, you didn't hurt me baby; you were a little rough but nothing I couldn't handle."

He strokes my arm. "I'm so sorry angel," he whispers, and in a gesture of reassurance, I kiss his knuckles.

"My medication makes me feel dead inside, Peyton. Why do you think I only ever had sex without feelings for so long? Because I couldn't fucking feel anything! I flushed my pills a few days after I met you, that first morning you woke up in my bed, in a rare moment of clarity. I promised myself I wouldn't be just an emotionless shell anymore; if we were going to do the whole relationship thing, I didn't want anything in the way. I didn't want you to be just another conquest; I wanted it to be real."

He moves closer to me and wraps his strong familiar arms around me.

"J.D. thought it was a bad idea from the moment I told him. He called my dad and told everyone in the crew to keep an eye on me. I had a grip on it, I was fine! I was finally alive for the first time in a long fucking time. I have emotions and feelings now, feelings that weren't there before. Up until the accident. I started to lose control, and I'm so fucking sorry for that, angel. I know I fucked up and I was suffocating you, but you have to understand. It's like all the stuff I didn't feel before was rushing to the surface and it completely overwhelmed me."

I suddenly feel responsible for all this happening to him and as if he reads my mind, he says, "None of this is your fault, angel, you have to believe me when I say that. I take full responsibility for everything that's happened since I've been off my meds. But I wasn't totally honest with you about why I was in rehab I had a drug problem, but it was also because of my depression. I'm sorry I was economical with the truth, but everything I've done, my actions, are all because I was trying to protect you. Shield you from this fucking shit storm. If you want to go I wouldn't blame you, angel, the door is right there."

I shake my head. *How could he possibly think I would want to leave right now?*

"I'm not going anywhere, Sam; I intend to stick around for the long haul. I love you, so much."

He kisses me gently on my forehead and strokes my hand.

"I took it out on the people closest to me. I've been lashing out at everyone, and I don't know how I'm going to make up for that, but I'll spend my life trying if that's what it takes."

I snuggle closer to him, hoping to offer him some sort of comfort. I hate seeing my strong man hurting like this, knowing there isn't a single thing I can do to make it right.

"I'm so fucking sorry for everything I've put you through, I'm such an idiot."

We lie there for a while just listening to each other breathing, revelling in the silence and Sam's quiet calmness. As I am lying on his chest, I hear his breathing even out, and before I glance up, I know he has fallen asleep. Cole comes out of the bathroom, and a look of relief washes over his features. He sits in an overstuffed armchair in the corner of the room.

"How do you do that, sugar?" he whispers, and I smile.

"I must have the magic touch!"

He laughs. I slide out slowly from Sam's arms and sit on the edge of the bed.

"I love him so much, Cole, and he's everything to me. Seeing him that way earlier broke my heart. It makes me feel like I hardly know him at all."

Cole regards me intently.

"You're the first girl in a long time. I have never seen him look at anyone the way he looks at you. He might be off his medication, but the way he feels about you isn't in question, not for a second. The thing with Sam is that once he has his mind set on something he does it regardless of the consequences. He's a kind of a do now think later kind of guy."

I smile at Cole's accurate description of Sam. I look at him and decide now is the time for answers.

"Who's Lyla?"

Cole lets out a sigh. "She's in his past, you're his future."

I shake my head.

"Don't give me that generic bullshit, Cole, and don't insult my fucking intelligence. Who is she? Why is she here?"

He leans forward in the chair and rests his elbows on his knees.

"It's complicated."

A loud pounding on the door prematurely halts our conversation. Sam flinches at the sound, and his eyes fly open as he sits bolt upright. Cole gets up from his chair and strides towards the door. He opens it and standing in the doorway is Marlowe Newbolt.

Sam's calmness is short-lived, and I see him visibly tense. "What the fuck, Cole?"

Marlowe walks slowly into the room. "Sam, I'm here to help." Marlowe's voice is soft and calming. I shake my head at Cole and get up from the bed, I jab my finger in his chest.

"I had it under control! You saw that I had finally calmed him down! What the fuck!"

"I'm so sorry Peyton, I know you're upset, but I didn't know what else to do. I called him right before you got here, he wouldn't listen to me. I had no choice."

"I was handling him, and I was in the room right down the corridor the whole time. You could have come and got me."

Sam stands up and Marlowe moves closer to him. I anxiously watch the exchange between father and son unfold in front of me.

"Sam, you're ill, son, you just need a little bit of help that's all. You'll be back to your old self in no time at all."

Marlowe smiles warmly and goes over to the mini bar, slinging his jacket over the arm of the chair as he goes. He takes out a bottle of water and starts to pour it into a glass tumbler with his back to us. Sam shakes his head and scrubs his hands down his face.

"Don't you get it? I don't want to be back to my old self! I'm happier this way! I don't feel fucking dead inside, I finally feel alive, Dad. It's thanks to Peyton that I'm still here."

Marlowe brushes Sam's arm. "Here drink this, son, you'll feel better."

He turns around and hands Sam the glass of water. I can't help but think there is something going on that I don't know about. I narrow my eyes at Cole, and he looks to the floor, avoiding eye contact. Marlowe moves closer to his son, and as Sam takes a long sip on the glass of water, the glass crashes to the floor. I scream and freeze in place at what just happened. Marlowe put something in his own son's drink. *What the fuck?*

"Sam!" I scream. Marlowe and Cole catch him before all six foot four of him hits the floor and his eyes lock with mine.

"Angel, I'm sorry."

With those words Sam's eyes close and he is out cold on the hotel room floor. I sob uncontrollably and sink to the floor beside him. I stroke his hair gently and Marlowe crouches down next to me.

"It was for the best. Peyton, you have to understand that. I didn't have a choice."

"Of course you had a fucking choice! He's not some animal you can put down, he's a human being!" I shout. I take Sam's hand in mine and plant a kiss on the back. "It's going to be all right, baby, I'm here."

I am more than a little gobsmacked at the turn of events that have unfolded. Marlowe placing his hand gently on my shoulder interrupts my thoughts.

"Come on, love, we should talk."

I shake my head. "Don't you dare fucking touch me, Marlowe," I choke out. Marlowe removes his hand from my shoulder and takes a step back from me. "I can't leave him. What if he wakes up and I'm not here?" A tear rolls down my cheek.

"He's going to be fine. It was just a mild sedative mixed with his medication. Completely harmless, and he'll come round in an hour or two, right as rain."

I swipe the tears away and look up at Marlowe.

"How could you do that to him? Your own son?"

Marlowe scrubs his hands down his face and he looks exhausted. I let go of Sam's hand and get to my feet. I brush past Marlowe and Cole, walk into the bathroom, and close the door. I lean on the counter and try to compose myself.

Get it together, Harper, Sam needs you. I take a deep breath and splash cold water on my tear-stained face. A few minutes passes and the door taps softly.

"Peyton," Marlowe's soothing voice filters through the door. "Can I come in, love?"

I open the door and look up into his green eyes, which remind me so much of Sam. He pulls me into his chest and wraps me in his arms. Even though I am spitting mad at him for doing that to Sam, I can do nothing but cling to him and sob. I sob for my beautifully broken man who is currently out cold on the hotel room floor. He strokes my hair.

"Shush, it's all right, my love; he's going to be just fine in the morning. I know it's hard seeing the man you love crumbling, but he's strong. I know you're upset but don't blame Cole for this, he was just doing his job. He's kept Sam on the straight and narrow for almost ten years. When Sam first got famous, he was so out of control he wouldn't even listen to his mother or me, he let the fame go to his head in a big way. Twinned with Sam's addictive personality it was a total recipe for disaster, he needed someone to take care of him when we weren't around."

I look up at him, knowing where this is going.

"You orchestrated the whole thing with Cole that night at the club?"

Marlowe is silent for a moment. "Cole is ex-military and an ex-cop, he is extremely intelligent, and he's engaged to Milo's step-daughter, Amy. The bloke who smashed the glass was an old friend of mine, and the girl Brody felt up wasn't his girlfriend, it was his sister. But Cole and Sam becoming close friends wasn't my doing. Sam is an extremely good judge of character and he chooses his friends carefully, which is a trait he inherited from me."

He smiles proudly, and I pull away from our embrace, hearing voices outside the bathroom door. Marlowe opens the door; Jax is in the hotel room with us. Sam is passed out on the bed now; Cole must have moved him. Cole is at least three or four inches taller than Sam is and definitely a lot stronger. I step out of the bathroom followed by Marlowe. Marlowe sits on the edge of the bed and lets out a sigh.

"Was it bad?"

Jax's face is marred with concern for his friend.

"Pretty bad, the state of the hotel room is a clear indication, mate," Cole replies and gestures to the mess on the hotel room floor.

"*Fuck!*" Jax curses and runs his hand over the stubble on his chin. "Bollocks!" he curses again. "Shit! I need a fucking drink."

He goes over to the mini-bar and Marlowe looks at his watch.

"I think we all need some sleep. It's late. Things always look better in the morning."

Jax takes a long pull on a large glass of vodka.

"I should stay with him," I say.

Marlowe stands up and brushes my arm. "It's better that you stay with Jax, sweetheart. We don't know what mood he'll be in when he comes around."

I look at Marlowe, and he smiles reassuringly.

"Go with Jax, flower, he'll look after you. I'll call you in the morning."

Marlowe kisses my forehead. Jax finishes his drink and wraps his arm around me.

"Come on, love."

He smiles and leads me out of the room. Jax opens the door of Cole's hotel room and we both step in, closing it behind us.

"I was woken up by Ruby calling your mobile, repeatedly. That's when I realised you'd gone. Ruby was fucking frantic. You hadn't called her back and she said she was worried about you, I had to talk her out of coming to get you." He smirks. "*Christ*, that woman is a fucking force of nature." We both laugh for a moment before his face turns serious as he looks at me. "Seriously, though, babe, I was genuinely concerned when I woke up and you were gone."

I look to the floor.

"I'm sorry, I had to go to him, Jax, I was terrified."

He sits down on the edge of the bed and pats the space next to him. I sit down beside him.

"He finally opened up to me, Jax."

"Believe me, that's a good thing. Sam keeps things bottled up a lot. It usually takes a lot of fucking vodka for him to say what he is really feeling. He is lucky to have you, babe, you're good for him."

I smile and there's a light tap on the door. Jax gets up to answer it and Marlowe is standing outside.

"Can I come in, Jax?"

Jax nods and Marlowe steps into the room, closing the door behind him.

"How is he, Marlowe?" Jax enquires and Marlowe nods.

"He's asleep; he should be fine by the morning. I actually came to speak to Peyton, if that's OK with you?"

Jax nods. "No worries, I'll go to Lucas' room, he should still be awake. Will you be OK?"

"I'll be fine and thanks for tonight, Jax."

"You don't have to thank me, babe, you're one of us now. I programmed all of our numbers in your phone, if you need anything at all, call me." He winks and leaves the room.

Marlowe sits in the overstuffed armchair in the corner of the room and steeples his fingers underneath his chin.

"It's easy for me to see why Sam's fallen for you. You're beautiful, intelligent; all the boys in the band seem to be taken with you. They've accepted you as one of their own, which is extremely rare. You made an impression on my wife, such an impression that she's already planning her wedding outfit."

He chuckles, and his dimples remind me so much of Sam. It is actually scary how much they look alike.

"I keep thinking you're too good to be true. I have to say when Sam told me he'd met someone, I had Cole run a background check on you, but you came up squeaky clean, whiter than white."

I am actually offended that he did a background check on me when all I have ever done is fall in love with his son.

"I'm sorry for doubting you, Peyton. You must understand that being in the music industry most women are just after a one-night stand and to make money by selling their sordid little stories. I saw that you weren't like that, I saw the way you and Sam were together at the album launch, and he was quite smitten." He smiles.

"When you smile you remind me so much of Sam, the eyes, the dimples."

"You really love him, don't you?"

My eyes glaze over, and I nod. "God, I love him so much it physically hurts. He consumes me, every single part of me. It broke my heart seeing him in such distress tonight."

Marlowe pauses for a second before he speaks. "He's been off his medication since he met you; against my better judgement, might I add. I thought he could handle it. He seemed to be doing so well, but then you had the car accident and I could see him spiralling out of control. I saw the signs, but I did nothing. John managed to convince me he'd snap out of it once he saw you were recovering."

Fucking J.D. God, now I really hate him, I never thought it was possible to hate a person this much.

"The night of the accident, Sam disappeared from the hospital and Cole tracked the GPS on his phone. Him and Jax found him passed out in the bathroom in his apartment. That boy has the biggest self-destruct button I have ever seen. While Ruby was trying to get in touch with your parents and Sam was having his meltdown, I came to the hospital to sit with you. I stayed for two whole days. I wanted you moved to a private hospital, but we didn't know if you were going to make it. I saw then how much you meant to Sam. I've never seen him like this with anyone, he was devastated. He never brings girls back to meet us; we knew you must be special."

I smile at Marlowe's words, also shocked at the revelations he is revealing to me. *He was with me for two days at the hospital?*

"I don't know what to say. Thank you for staying with me at the hospital."

"You don't have to thank me, my love."

With those words, my mobile signals a text message. I swipe my finger across the screen and open the message, it's from Cole.

He's awake, and he's asking for you

I'll leave the door unlocked

Cole

I look at Marlowe. "That was Cole. Sam's awake, and he's asking for me."

Marlowe nods. "Go and be with my son." He smiles brightly, strides across the room and envelopes me in a hug. "Welcome to the family, my love."

He kisses the top of my head tenderly, and I feel so much pride at that moment I squeeze him tighter. I feel elated that I have been accepted into the bosom of Sam's family and it means everything to me.

"Thank you, Marlowe, for everything."

Marlowe pulls away from our embrace.

"I'll even let you call me Dad if you want!" We both laugh. "Now that's enough of that soppy bollocks. Go and be with Sam, he needs you."

He winks, and I leave the room. I practically run down the corridor and push the door open. Sam is sitting crossed-legged in the middle of the king-size bed. As I step into the room, his eyes lock with mine. He releases his lip from his teeth and I see his tense shoulders visibly relax. He climbs off the bed and moves fluidly across the room, his eyes never leaving mine. In a few strides, he is in front of me and towering over me.

"Angel," he rasps and tucks a strand of my hair that has come loose from my ponytail behind my ear. He moves his hand down and strokes my face, I lean into his touch. I stroke his lightly-stubbled cheek and Cole carefully observes the exchange between us.

"I'll leave you two to it; I'm on my mobile if you need anything."

Sam and I are silent for a few minutes, just standing there silently observing each other not knowing how to react. A feeling, which is completely alien to me, especially in Sam's presence. He cautiously steps closer until his chest is pressed against me and I can feel his warm breath tickling my cheek. I am not used to cautious and careful where Sam is concerned. I am not sure whether it's a good sign or a bad sign.

"I'm so fucking sorry, angel, please forgive me," he whispers. Those are the only words he says before he wraps his strong arms around me and I melt into his arms, clinging desperately to him. It is as if we need each other to stay rooted to the floor. He runs his hands up and down my spine; I relish the feeling of closeness and safety being in his arms.

"Lie with me for a while?"

His voice is unsure, and I let him lead me to the bed. He lies down, and I lie next to him in complete silence. He pulls me closer to him and I have never encountered this side of Sam before. The careful, cautious, unsure, and vulnerable side. He is so gentle, and his eyes search my approval at every turn. He wraps his arm around me, and I rest my head on his chest, listening to the sound of his thundering heartbeat under my cheek. In that moment, I know everything is going to be OK. I feel completely and utterly content being with Sam despite his faults. I vow to spend the rest of my life with him because he is everything to me.

9

Peyton

A month passes, and I have travelled the length and breadth of the country with Rancid Vengeance. From Glasgow, to Manchester, Birmingham, Cardiff, Liverpool, Nottingham, Sheffield and back to London tonight for the band's farewell gig. It is my last night on the tour bus, and I am due to return home tomorrow while Sam and the boys go on the European leg of their tour for two months. It has definitely been an experience, and I have gotten an insight into life on the road with a high-profile, world famous, successful rock band. I have met some interesting people from, Lex the tour bus driver, to the roadies, and even some of the bands diehard fans. I have witnessed the ups, downs, and everything in-between.

The night of Sam's meltdown was one of the worse nights of my life, but it feels like it has pushed us closer together as a couple. That was the only good thing to come out of that night. He is back on a low dose of Seroxat to control his moods, and he is back to his usual charming self. *My Sam.*

Today is the twenty fourth of August, and it is my twenty-seventh birthday. I wake up to Sam's gorgeous smiling face.

"Good morning, my beautiful birthday girl."

I smile sleepily and sit up. Sam hands me a mug of steaming coffee.

"Thank you, baby."

He smiles that dazzling smile I love so much and climbs onto the bed.

"I've got a surprise for you, angel"

I look at him and raise my eyebrows. "Does it involve you naked?"

He cocks his pierced eyebrow and laughs. "That can *always* be arranged, angel," he says huskily and kisses me gently on the lips. "Get dressed, baby, and I'll show you. You're going to love it, I promise."

He gets off the bed and winks, leaving that phrase hanging in the air as he exits the room. I shower in record time, dry my hair, and get dressed. I pull on my Converse trainers and head down to the lower deck of the bus.

"Happy birthday, Peyton!" all the boys say in unison and I grin widely.

"Aww, thanks, boys, you didn't have to!"

There is an array of presents on the table along with achocolate birthday cake topped with candles. Sam moves to my side and puts his arm around me.

"You deserve it for putting up with us, baby."

"Blow out your candles, Peyton!" Jax says enthusiastically.

Bless his heart. We've actually become really close during the tour and he is definitely going to be a lifelong friend. I tuck my hair behind my ears and lean down to blow my candles out, to a personal rock rendition of '*happy birthday to you*' from the boys, with Brody on acoustic guitar.

"You have to make a wish, honey." Lucas smiles; I close my eyes and make a wish.

I wish for a long and happy future with Sam.

The boys whoop and clap their hands. Sam pulls out a familiar scrap of black material from his pocket, and I bite my lip at the memory of being tied up, blindfolded, and completely at Sam's mercy. I feel liquid heat between my legs and Sam cocks his head, leaning close to me, he whispers so only I can hear him.

"Remember this baby?"

I look at him and his eyes are hooded with lust. I nod, and he winks, pulling the blindfold over my eyes.

"Oi, oi! You could at least wait until we're off the bus before you start getting kinky, dude!" Brody shouts and the boys laugh. Sam leads me down the bus steps and out into the morning sun. He holds my hand.

"Keep walking forward, angel, I won't let you fall. I've got you."

I do as he says, and we stop suddenly. He pulls off the blindfold.

"Surprise!"

He shakes a set of car keys in front of me and there in the car park at Wembley Arena is a brand new Chevy Camaro ZL1 Convertible in an identical purple colour to my old car and a white racing stripe on the centre of the bonnet. It is beautiful; I jump up and down excitedly.

"Do you like it, angel?"

I throw my arms around Sam. He picks me up and I wrap my legs around his waist, clinging to him like a monkey.

"I love it! Thank you so much, baby."

I press kisses all over his face and we both laugh.

"You're very welcome, angel, I'm glad you like it. I wanted to surprise you. You loved your old car, and nothing can replace that, but I wanted to treat you to something special. You deserve it, for being you, and for putting up with my shit."

He kisses me passionately on the lips and sets me on my feet.

"Do you want to take her for a spin? She is fast, five hundred and eighty brake horse power, a V-8 engine and she goes from zero to sixty miles an hour in three point nine seconds."

I raise my eyebrows; I am impressed. I nod enthusiastically, and Sam laughs.

"Come on then, angel."

He clicks the key fob and opens the driver's door for me. I get into the driver's seat; the seats are bucket seats, which hug you as you drive. They are a gunmetal grey colour and the leather is so soft and comfortable. Sam gets into the passenger seat and we both buckle up for my first test drive in my brand new car.

Happy birthday to me!

The day passes by in a haze of presents, birthday surprises and calls from my family and my friends. They all wish me a happy birthday and say they are eagerly awaiting my return home.

"Hey, sis, happy birthday," Dexter's familiar voice fills my ears.

"Hey, little brother. Thanks. I'm officially old!"

He snorts. "Twenty-seven isn't old! I'll be there soon enough! How are you?"

I smile. "I'm great, thanks, Dex, I'm actually enjoying being on the road with the boys."

"Who would have thought it? Have we lost you to the lifestyles of the rich and famous?"

I roll my eyes to myself. "Hardly! How are things with you and Grace? How was Paris?"

Dexter took his fiancée Grace to Paris for the weekend and he was going to propose. I haven't had a chance to catch up with him about it.

"Paris was amazing, sis. I asked her to marry me at the top of the Eiffel Tower, and she said yes!"

I shriek, and I start to think to myself that Ruby's dramatics have rubbed off on me!

"Oh, my god, Dex! That's fantastic! I'm so happy for you. Congratulations!"

"Thanks, Grace wants you as a bridesmaid, so she is going to be in touch in the next few weeks. She is turning into a bridezilla with wedding planning! I'm up to my fucking neck in seating plans and bloody colour schemes." I chuckle, and he says, "Fuck me, her and Mum are a force to be reckoned with. I've actually never done so much overtime at work!"

"You should come and visit us soon; it's been too long, Dex. Sam's going on the European leg of the tour tomorrow he's going to be gone for two months."

He pauses and asks, "How are things with you and Sam?"

"Things are great. Actually, more than great."

"There are stories all over the internet and the papers about him having some sort of breakdown while he was on tour?"

I tut. *Typical Dexter, I would bet money that my mum has put him up to this.*

"He has severe manic depression, Dex. He was off his medication, but he's totally fine now."

He pauses, and I know he is probably frowning.

"Did he hurt you? If he's laid a finger on you, I swear. I already gave him the 'you hurt my sister and I'll kill you' speech."

I smile to myself. "He hasn't laid a finger on me, Dex. I love him so much. He's everything, and I can't imagine my life without him in it. I can finally see a future with him."

I hear him let out a sigh of relief. "It's so good to hear you happy again, Peyton. There were times when I thought it was impossible, but it sounds like he is good for you." He swiftly changes the subject, which seems to be a Harper family trait. "So what did the flash bastard get you for your birthday?"

"A new car. A Chevy Camaro ZL1."

Dexter splutters, "Fucking hell! It must be love! Could we be looking at a double wedding?"

I snort in the most unladylike fashion. "I don't think he *is* the marrying kind, Dex."

With those words, Sam walks in and cocks his pierced eyebrow curiously at me. I stick my tongue out and he heads into the kitchen.

"Every man is the marrying kind; it just takes a certain type of woman, sis. I never in a million years thought I would ever entertain the idea of marriage until Grace and I took that break from each other a few years ago. While we were apart, I knew in my heart I wanted to spend the rest of my life with her, it was definitely a turning point."

"My little brother, the romantic. Who knew! Besides, you and Grace have been together *forever*."

"You should try it sometime; he might surprise you. Just because you've only been together a few months doesn't mean it's completely out of the question, and just because you got your fingers burnt in the past with Callum doesn't mean all men are the spawn of Satan!"

We both laugh. There's nothing like a conversation with Dexter to put things into perspective.

"You're getting way too deep for me, Dex, I have to go. I'll call you once I'm settled back at home and we can arrange that visit."

"You got it, sis. I'll hold you to that; catch you later."

"Bye, Dex, love ya."

"Back at ya, Peyton, bye."

With those words, we both hang up and Sam leans over the table drinking orange juice from the carton. He cocks his pierced eyebrow and smirks.

"So, I'm not the marrying kind?"

Shit! He heard that? I feel my face burn with something that resembles embarrassment but also terrified of his reaction to the idea of marriage, as we have never had the whole marriage conversation before. I sit opposite him at the table and he takes my hand in his, stroking my knuckles softly.

"I'd love nothing more than to spend the rest of my life with you, Peyton. I want to spend my life proving to you that I'm enough for you. I want to prove that I can be the man you deserve. Do you want me to propose? I'll get down on one knee now if that's what it takes, tell me what to do, baby, and I'll do it." My stomach does a flip and I am surprised at his reaction. "Marry me?"

I laugh. *Really?* Did he really just propose sat at the table of his bands tour bus? *No way, Newbolt!* His face turns serious and he puts his hand on his heart.

"I'm wounded, angel."

He smirks, and I raise my eyebrows.

"If you want me to marry you, baby, you're going to have to do much better than that. I want romance, hearts, flowers, a bedroom window serenades, the whole nine yards!" I quote a conversation we had at the beginning of our relationship. He throws his head back and laughs.

"Consider it done, babe."

He winks and gets up from the table, kissing me on the end of my nose. With that simple gesture, I know Sam Newbolt is going to be forever mine, lock, stock and barrel.

***

The boys perform their gig at Wembley Arena and they are amazingly flawless as usual; giving an immense, show-stopping, all-out rock performance to their beloved fans. Sam and the boys are on top form tonight.

"How the fuck are we doing, London? It's so good to be back on home turf, we have missed you guys. Are we ready to rock?" The crowd cheers. "I can't hear you; I said, are you ready to fucking rock?"

The crowd erupts into rapturous screams, and the whole place vibrates with the noise. Every time I see Sam up on stage doing what he loves, I am in awe of him. His stage presence, the way he interacts with the fans, his enthusiasm, and a true showmanship that would rival the likes of Freddie Mercury and Robbie Williams. He plays each gig as if it is going to be his last; he puts his heart and soul into every performance.

After the gig, we all pile into a waiting black limo and make our way to the after show party at Neon Nights, the club where the album launch was held. I am wearing a daring, black-lace mini dress with leather panels on each side. It is very short, backless, and way out of my comfort zone, but I feel sexy.

I have teamed it with silver hoop earrings and black studded ankle boots. My hair is in soft tousled waves.

After braving the press gauntlet with Sam and the boys, I step into the familiar surroundings of the club. It is just as decadent as I remember.

Sam has his arm wrapped casually around my shoulders and he is more relaxed than I have seen him in weeks. He is smiling his dazzling, dimpled, panty-dropping smile, and I know it is all for me. He leans close to my ear and his breath tickles my neck.

"Even though that dress is obscene, you look absolutely fucking stunning. It's taking everything I have not to take you to some dark corner and fuck you until you can't remember anything else but my name," he rasps, and I shiver as I feel that customary heat between my legs. "Your tits are looking fucking exquisite. I think I'm going to have to do a lot of arse kicking tonight, you're attracting a lot of attention, angel."

I laugh. "It's lucky I'm not wearing any underwear and I'll be going home with you at the end of the night."

He groans at my words and I chuckle softly. He licks a trail up my neck and bites my earlobe. I mewl softly.

"*Jesus Christ*, you're going to be the death of me, angel."

He growls, and I get a secret thrill knowing that I have that effect on him. A man approaches us, and he smiles a dazzling smile as he reaches us. He is tall, lean, but muscular, tanned, and has short brown spiky hair. He has pale-blue eyes and he is wearing a black suit, a crisp, white shirt with the top button undone and a loose turquoise tie. He is clutching a glass of amber liquid and he pulls Sam in for a manly one-armed hug.

"Ryan, my man, how's tricks?"

He pulls away from the embrace.

"Sam, so good to see you, mate, it's been a while. Yeah, it's all good, thanks, how are things with you?"

Sam smiles and nods. "Can't complain, mate."

Ryan looks me up and down. He licks his lips provocatively and raises his eyebrows.

"Aren't you going to introduce me to this extremely beautiful creature on your arm, Sam?"

Sam looks at me. "Angel, this is Ryan, he's Alistair's brother and the owner of this club. Ryan, this is my beautiful girlfriend, Peyton."

Ryan nods and he offers me his hand. I take it and smile shyly.

"Nice to meet you, Ryan."

He kisses my hand and Sam rolls his eyes.

"It's a pleasure to meet you too, petal. I've heard so much about you and I've been looking forward to meeting the beauty who has stolen the famous Bolt's heart."

Sam throws his head back and laughs.

"So you can turn on the charm and try to get in her pants? That's the reason I haven't introduced you before!" Sam jokes and both men laugh. But the way Sam says those words makes me believe that there is a hidden warning in there somewhere.

"Can I get you both a drink?"

Sam nods. "Yeah, that would be great, cheers, mate."

Ryan nods and winks.

"Coming right up. I'll see to it myself. If you need anything at all, give me a shout, mate. If you'll excuse me."

Ryan nods, slaps Sam on the back, and strides off. As he strides off, he exudes confidence and charisma. I can't help thinking that he has 'heartbreaker' written all over him. Sam wraps his arm around me again and nuzzles my neck.

"Now, where were we before we were rudely interrupted?"

I laugh.

"What's got into you tonight, baby?"

Sam chuckles softly. "Need you ask, angel? You've got into me, in more ways than one. I don't know how I'm going to hold out until we get back to the bus; I intend to make our last night together a memorable one."

"Good things come to those who wait, Newbolt."

I wink cheekily, and two tall, muscular, tattooed men approach us.

"Newbolt."

The taller of the two is an inch or so shorter than Sam, muscular, heavily tattooed and has long black hair flowing past his shoulders. Sam tightens his grip on my waist and I look up to see a look I haven't seen before; it looks like pure hatred.

"Draven," Sam says flatly through clenched teeth. "You've not been hit by that bus then yet, I see?" Sam says coldly. I feel like I am at a tennis match looking back and forth between both men.

"No unfortunately, I see you haven't been pushed off that cliff yet." Draven laughs and then turns his attention to me.

"Hey, gorgeous, what are you doing this with this fucking loser?" he asks in a soft American drawl. I narrow my eyes at him, instantly disliking him.

"Step into the dark side, babe, I'll show you a good time."

He winks. Everything about this man screams out slime ball, and I can't quite believe the cheek of him. The man next to him steps forward, putting distance between him and Sam.

"I'm sorry about him, darlin', he seems to have misplaced his manners again. I'm Mitch Masters, and this fuck face is Draven Michaels. I'm the drummer, and he is the lead singer in The Devil's Henchmen, we've been supporting Rancid Vengeance on this tour. He's not normally this rude."

I shake my head. "Don't apologise for him, honey, it's not your fault he's a complete fucking arsehole."

Draven raises his eyebrows and laughs.

"She is feisty, I love it, and do you have a name, sweetness?"

"Yep, but maybe I don't want to give it to you."

"OK, let's start again, I'm Draven."

He offers me his hand, but I don't take it. He tries to disguise my rejection and he casually tucks his hand behind his back. Mitch offers me his hand, I shake it and smile.

"I'm Peyton, nice to meet you, Mitch."

"I believe you've rendered *the* Draven Michaels speechless with your blatant brush off. I salute you, hot stuff!" He salutes, and I laugh, instantly liking him.

"So, how's Lyla these days? I heard on the grapevine she's back in town."

Sam smiles slyly, and it's the first time I have ever heard Sam be anything but nice to someone. I see Draven tense and clench his fists at the mention of Lyla's name. Before I know what's going on, Draven has drawn his fist back and punched Sam square in the jaw. Sam head snaps back and his nostrils flare. He punches Draven in the nose and blood drips down his face. I am still none the wiser to who this woman is, and I might have known the hostility would be down to a woman. We are soon joined by Jax, Lucas and a tall, slender woman with an hourglass figure to die for. She has long red hair, wide green eyes, and full red lips. She is wearing skinny jeans and a red bustier emphasising her ample breasts.

"Boys, y'all need to calm down." Her voice is soft, breathy, and has a Southern American drawl. She brushes Draven's arm. "Draven, a word, please."

Draven's eyes don't move away from Sam. "This isn't fucking over, Newbolt, not by a long shot."

The woman turns to me and smiles.

"I'm Phoenix King, I'm the manager of The Devil's Henchmen. I'm so sorry for his behaviour, if there's any more trouble, don't hesitate to come and find me."

Phoenix goes to lead Draven away.

"Oh, Draven, make sure you give Lyla my love." Sam smirks and he can't resist having the last word. Draven spins around and punches Sam in the face again. "I didn't realise how much you loved my sloppy seconds, Michaels."

Mitch and two other men, which I assume are the other two members in their band, try to hold Draven back, but he is too fast and strong. He rugby tackles Sam to the ground and both men are full-scale brawling on the floor. Fists are flying, and chaos has ascended around us. Jax, Lucas, Mitch, and two other men are trying to stop the fight, but they end up being caught in the fracas. There is blood, limbs, and fists flying from every direction. I realise there is nothing I can do to stop it; I am rendered helpless and useless watching the violent drama unfold in front of me like something from a bad soap opera. *Where the fuck is Cole?* I feel like my feet are rooted to the floor and I can do nothing but stare. Unexpectedly, I am pulled away from the fight by a delicate hand.

"Oh, dear, all this because of little old me." Lyla smirks smugly.

How does she have the ability to just appear out of nowhere?

"Who the fuck are you, Lyla?"

She pulls me towards the bar area where Cole and the club's security are descending from all directions trying to diffuse the whole situation.

"I'm Lyla Hudson; I used to be in one of the biggest female rock bands, Hell on Heels."

I thought her face seemed familiar, I remember seeing her on the cover of one of Ruby's gossip magazines.

"We supported Rancid Vengeance for a while on tour. We did some rock festivals together, and we got to know each other pretty well. Sam and me we had a fling of sorts; it was just sex to him but never to me. That handsome bastard made me fall in love with him, I was besotted. When I found out it was going to be nothing more than sex I, went off the rails for a while. I had a highly publicised fall from grace, the band split up, and I lost everything. I hit the booze and the drugs hard, I did a stint in rehab, and it was all his fucking fault."

Her voice sounds so bitter it actually makes me feel sorry for her. I cock my head and regard her intently, not knowing what to make of the information she is telling me.

"Don't you fucking dare feel sorry for me, my only crime was falling in love with a man who I could never have. He was so emotionally detached. We'd fuck like bunnies, and he'd just lie there afterwards with this look on his face." She frowns at the memory and I bristle at the thought of Sam with another woman. "It was like the shutters came down and he just totally switched off. I knew we were toxic together, but I couldn't help myself, I was addicted to him. It was fun, exciting, and dangerous. I saw you together; when I saw him look at you that way it hurt because all those years I wanted him to look at me the way he looked at you."

She laughs resentfully.

"Why are you so interested in mine and Sam's relationship? It's none of your business." The tone of my voice is brusque, and she nods curtly.

"You make a fair point. I've followed his career closely for years now, and I was curious as to what all the fuss was about with this—" She looks me up and down, I feel my temper spike. I ball my fist at my side. *How fucking dare she look at me that way as if she is superior to me?* "—ordinary, plain, tattoo artist who captured the heart of *the* Sam Newbolt, famous ladies' man. So tell me, Peyton, what did you do to grab his attention? Is your vagina made of platinum and encrusted with diamonds?"

I suddenly feel intense anger towards this woman standing in front of me. I sense a presence at my side, and I instantly know it's Sam. I catch his familiar scent before I see him and a feeling of calm washes over me. I turn to him and his face is a bloody mess. My heart clenches at seeing his beautiful face covered in blood. He swipes his hand across his nose.

"It's nothing, angel, just a little blood, that's all. I'm fine."

He smiles. Lyla moves closer to him and his face drops.

"What the fuck are you doing here, Lyla?" he spits out angrily.

"Don't be like that, baby. Aren't you pleased to see me? I've missed you."

How dare she call him baby! I feel the anger bubbling up inside of me, and I'm not sure if I can hold it back. She drapes herself over him and gropes his crotch. That is all I can take. I push her away from him, grab hold of her hair, and punch her in the face. I have never been this angry in my entire life. I am so consumed by rage and before I gather my wits, my forehead connects with her nose, spraying blood all over her face.

"You fucking bitch!" she screams, grabbing my hair and managing to get a punch to my nose before Cole drags her off kicking and screaming. Sam lifts me from the ground and carries me over his shoulder. He strides off across the club and into the corridor, setting me on my feet.

"You're bleeding, angel." I touch my nose, dismissing him. "Is it wrong that I'm hard?"

He laughs and runs his finger down my arm, causing goose bumps over my whole body.

"God, I need to be inside you, but I'm not sure if I should be kissing your feet or spitting mad for that floor show," he says huskily, and I look at him.

"I'm so sorry, I don't know what came over me, and I was so fucking angry."

He smiles crookedly. "Green is a colour that definitely suits you, babe."

I suddenly start to feel angry towards Sam for not telling me about Lyla before.

"Why didn't you tell me about her before?"

"She's not important; she's in the past, babe."

I fold my arms, suddenly filled with an overwhelming sense of jealousy.

"She doesn't seem to think so, she was in love with you, and she still is by the looks of it."

He tips my chin up, and I look into his eyes.

"She's nothing to me, angel, you have to believe me, I'd never do anything to hurt you."

"I can't be around you right now, Sam, I'm so fucking angry," I say through clenched teeth and he frowns.

"Please don't be like that, angel, I'm sorry." I shake my head and jab my finger in his direction. "I need to be on my own for a while, please don't follow me."

I spin around and run towards the club exit. As I run towards the exit, I collide with a hard chest. Strong arms catch me before I fall, and I look up to see Brody standing in front of me.

"Whoa! Where's the fire, sweetheart?"

His eyes are wide and glossy. As I look at him, I realise he is completely off his face on drugs.

"*Jesus Christ*, you're high."

"As a kite, babe!" He winks and clicks his tongue. "You didn't answer my question, where's the fire?" I roll my eyes. "You're bleeding, babe, come on. Let me take you back to the bus and get you cleaned up."

He grabs my arm and pulls me towards the exit. We step out into the cool night air and Skip drives us back to the o2 arena car park where the bus is parked. My emotions and the events of the night start to flood into my consciousness. I start to shake uncontrollably in the back of the car.

"Hey, I've got ya, sweets."

Brody pulls me close to him, drapes his arm around me, and I look at him. He smirks.

"Not that I care, but Sam would kick my arse all over the bus for letting you bleed everywhere."

"God, do you have to be such a prick?"

"It's all part of my charm, babe."

Skip parks the car and makes his way over to the bus. He checks the bus for unwanted guests, and when he deems it safe, Brody and I step out of the car and onto the tour bus. He steers me to the sofa and sits me gently down.

"I'll be right back; Lex has a first-aid kit here somewhere."

He strides off, and I realise that it is the first time I have been alone with Brody. A few minutes later, he comes back with two shot glasses. He puts down a bottle of Jack Daniels on the table and places the first-aid kit next to it. He sits on the table in front of me and is inches away from me. He opens the first-aid kit in his lap, taking out some antiseptic wipes and some cotton wool. He looks at me and I cock my eyebrow at him.

"Are you not familiar with the concept of personal space?"

He laughs, and I can feel his warm breath on my cheek.

"You really don't like me very much, do you?"

He leans closer to me and cleans the blood from my nose.

"I didn't say I didn't like you."

He raises his eyebrows. "So there's hope for me yet." He winks, and I wince as he swipes the antiseptic wipe under my nose.

"Ouch."

"Are you always such a baby?"

I hit him on his arm. "You could at least be a little gentler."

He holds his hands up in defence. "OK, I'll be gentle, I promise, scout's honour." He salutes. He smiles, and he actually looks sincere.

"By the looks of it, you had the pleasure of being introduced to the delightful Miss Hudson?" He laughs, and I narrow my eyes.

"Why didn't he tell me about her before? Surely, you were all aware I knew nothing about who she was."

Brody shrugs. "Look, babe, I'm not interested in yours and Sam's proclivities, sexual or otherwise. If he wanted you to know, it was down to him to tell you. Personally, I don't give a shit, it's always been bros before hoes, that's just the way it is, darlin'. I know I come across as an arrogant prick, because, well, I guess I just am, but he's turned into a cockless wonder since he met you. We used to have fun before you came along, he was my best mate, we shared women, we took drugs, and every night was a party."

He stands up, throws the antiseptic wipe in the bin, and goes to the sink to wash his hands. He comes back over to where I am sitting, pours us both shots of Jack Daniels, and he pushes the shot onto my side of the table. We both down them at the same time, and I grimace at the after burn as it slides down my throat.

"I know you think I've taken your best friend away from you, but it doesn't have to be that way. I don't want us to be enemies, Brody. Look, I know what happened to your mum, and I can't even begin to imagine what you went through—"

"Wait, Sam told you about that?"

I nod, and he pours us both a second shot of Jack. "*Motherfucker!* He had no fucking right; it wasn't his story to tell."

"Brody, it's OK to talk, I'm a good listener, and I'm actually kind of starting to like you. You've shown me a different side of you tonight, you didn't have to take care of me tonight, but you did, and I'm grateful for that."

I smile, and he knocks back his drink.

"Let's play a game, if you're up for it?" he says, completely changing the subject. I raise my eyebrows and knock back my second shot.

"OK, I'm up for it."

He takes a seat next to me and crosses his legs at the ankle. He pours us more shots and smiles.

"Let's play a little truth or dare game."

I nod.

"Here are the rules, if you choose truth you have to take a shot."

I smile, suddenly enjoying Brody's company.

"You start."

I lean back and take off my heels. I get comfortable, tucking my legs underneath myself.

"Truth."

He points to the shot glass, and I take my shot.

"OK, has Sam fucked you in the arse yet?"

I almost choke on my drink.

"Using the whole 'I want to be the first and last man back here'," he says putting on Sam's deep voice. He seems amused and I can feel myself burning with embarrassment. I pause, not knowing how to answer, I just feel pure humiliation. I vow to talk to Sam as soon as he gets back. Brody laughs. "From the silence, I'm assuming that's a yes? I fucking knew it! That boy has no shame; it's his signature move."

I feel the tears stinging my eyes. *How could he discuss something as personal and intimate as that?* He leans forward sensing my unease.

"Seriously, don't sweat it, babe."

I swallow back the lump in my throat and shake my head. Then I remember I am close to my period, which explains the mood swings, sore breasts, and extreme fatigue I have been feeling lately. I suddenly feel silly for over reacting at such a trivial thing, boys will be boys after all. I smile.

"It's fine, really."

"OK, my turn, I take dare."

A few hours passes and a whole lot of truth or dares later, Brody and I are extremely drunk, after polishing off a whole bottle of Jack Daniels and half a bottle of tequila. I have had such a good night getting to know Brody and his quirks. We definitely got off on the wrong foot, and my drunken mind thinks it could be the start of a beautiful friendship. I giggle at the thought and Brody gets to his feet.

"I'm off to bed, babe, I'm fucking fucked!" We both laugh. "Care to join me?"

He wiggles his eyebrows, and I attempt to roll my eyes, which makes Brody laugh hard.

"You wish, rock star!"

He laughs.

"You don't know what you're missing, sweetness!"

He winks cheekily and staggers to the bunks at the back of the bus, leaving me to pass out in a drunken haze on the sofa.

I am not sure how long I have been here, and I don't remember how I got here. My mouth feels dry, and I feel the start of an epic hangover. I am woken to a heavy weight pressing me into the sofa. My eyes fly open expecting it to be Sam on top of me, but I am terrified at who I find. *J.D.* It takes me a few seconds to gather my wits and I go to scream, but he covers my mouth with his hand.

"Shhh, do not fucking scream, if you make a sound, I'll hurt you," he whispers harshly.

Even though his frame is tall and wiry, I struggle to push against and break free of the iron grip he has on my wrists. His eyes are wide and maniacal adding to his frightening demeanour. My heartbeat is thundering in my chest, and I can feel myself trembling underneath him. I am trying to fight back the tears that are threatening to escape. My thoughts turn to what is actually happening. *He is going to rape me.* I try to get my erratic breathing under control, but he laughs.

"I can feel and smell your fear; good, you're finally frightened of me."

He laughs wildly. I find my strength and I try to buck him off me. He pushes himself further onto me.

"If you're going to act like a whore, I'll treat you like one. You deserve to be used and abused. Once I've had you, you'll be tainted. Sam doesn't do damaged goods."

I struggle and thrash against him. He releases my wrists, grabbing and roughly pawing my sore aching breasts. I cry out in pain. I expect Brody to come to my rescue, but nothing happens.

"Get the fuck off me, J.D., you're sick," I choke out, still fighting to get him off me. He rolls his eyes dramatically.

"Blah, blah, blah, every time I hear you speak I feel my brain cells committing suicide one by one."

He thrusts his hips into me, and I let out a strangled sob.

"Don't worry, I'll make this quick, it will be over soon. The sooner you get the fuck out of Sam's life, the better; you'll be just another one in a long list of whores."

I fight him wildly and I manage to scratch my nails down his face.

"I always knew you'd be a fighter."

He slaps me around the face with the back of his hand, and I am stunned at the brute force. He reaches down and undoes his belt.

"Get the fuck off me now!" I spit angrily.

"All in good time, angel. That's what Sam calls you, isn't it?"

My heart clenches at the thought of Sam, and I can't fight back the tears anymore, I sob hard. J.D frees himself from his trousers. He strokes my face and as he goes thrust himself closer to me, I hear the thud of loud footsteps across the tour bus floor. Before I know what is happening, J.D. is removed from on top of me and being flung across the floor like a rag doll. I look up and Lucas is standing over J.D. with his foot pushed into his chest. Lucas' usual gentle features have become harsh and he looks positively murderous.

10

Peyton

"What the fuck, J.D.?" he shouts. J.D. is breathing heavily, and Lucas drags him up from the floor. He pins him to the wall. "Give me one good fucking reason why I shouldn't get Sam and let him fucking deal with you?"

Lucas raises his voice, and J.D shakes his head nervously.

"Let's not be hasty. Luke."

Lucas clenches his fists.

"You were going to fucking rape Sam's girl; you're a piece of shit. Just when I thought you couldn't get any lower, you do something like this. What the fuck, J.D.?" Lucas bellows and I don't think I have ever heard Lucas raise his voice before. He is usually so quiet and laid back. I manage to pull myself up shakily and sit up on the sofa. I am shaking and sobbing softly.

"You need to get the hell out of dodge, J.D.," he says, his voice barely a whisper now, a stark contrast to a few moments ago.

"Please, please, Luke, don't tell Sam, I don't know what came over me," J.D. pleads.

Lucas pushes him harder into the wall, lifting him a few inches from the ground, draws his fist back, and punches him square in the jaw. Lucas lets go of J.D. and runs his hands through his hair. J.D. side-steps Lucas and runs off the bus. Lucas crouches down in front of me, I look at him and lose it completely, sobbing uncontrollably.

"Shhh, honey, it's all right."

He gets to his feet, sits down next to me, and I flinch as he moves closer. His face is marred with concern.

"I'm not going to hurt you, honey, and I won't let him hurt you, I promise."

He pulls me into his strong arms; I cling to him tightly and sob into his warm chest.

"*Fuck,*" he curses softly and pulls me tighter against him, trying to soothe the trembling. He strokes my back softly. "I've got you, he can't hurt you anymore," he says tenderly. "*Shit*, I should have come sooner, what if I'd been a few minutes longer?"

He sounds genuinely distraught at the thought and I start to wonder if something happened in his past for him to react like this. I pull away and look up at him, stroking his cheek softly.

"None of this is your fault, babe," I say in reassurance and he shakes his head.

"We should tell Sam, honey, he needs to know, he can deal with J.D."

My thoughts turn to Sam, and I start to thinking would he still feel the same about me knowing what J.D tried to do? Sam would most likely kill him if he found out and I swiftly change the subject.

"Where is he?"

Lucas pulls away from our embrace and scrubs his hands down his face.

"He's been trying to sort things out at the club with Ryan; it was one hell of a fight. Tate's been on the phone all night trying to keep it out of the papers, but the police were called. Sam and Draven were taken in for questioning, but they got released around an hour ago. Sam's been going out of his mind wondering where you were, he said you just took off."

"Brody bought me back here, we were chatting and drinking."

He nods.

"Since when have you and Brody been buddies? Last I checked he couldn't be friends with a girl without trying to get into her panties!"

"Looks like he's proved you wrong, he was quite the gentleman."

Lucas cocks his eyebrow. "Right, are you sure we're talking about the same guy?" he says with a smirk. "I should call Sam, but first you need to tell me what happened, honey."

I close my eyes, reliving what almost happened, and I let out a shaky breath. I recount the events of the evening, and by the time I'm finished, I feel a little better for sharing it with someone.

"We should call the cops on that fucking son-of-a-bitch," Lucas says flatly. I am about to reply when Sam strides across the bus floor. He crouches down in front of me and cups my face in his hands.

"There you are. Thank fuck, I was going out of my mind."

His hair is dishevelled and looks like he has been constantly running his fingers through it. He has the beginning of a black eye, stitches in his lip and eyebrow, a swollen nose, and a dark bruise marring his cheek. Even with cuts and bruises all over him, he still looks ruggedly handsome, the ultimate bad boy rocker. He frowns at my obvious rumpled look. My hair all over the place, my tear-stained and mascara-streaked face.

"Are you sure everything's OK, angel?"

My stomach flips, and I shudder at the term *angel* after J.D used it. Lucas looks at me and I turn my gaze to Sam. I put on a fake smile and nod.

"Everything's fine, baby."

Sam turns to Lucas and narrows his eyes as if to say, *'you're going to tell me what's going on'*. I shoot Lucas a look, silently pleading with him not to tell Sam.

"I'm so sorry I took so long, angel, I wanted our last night to be special. But if you want, we can go to bed and just snuggle. After tonight, I just need to feel you in my arms."

I nod. "Yeah, I'd like that."

I smile, and Sam kisses me gently on the corner of my mouth.

"I'll be up in a second, babe, I just need to speak to Lucas."

He winks in reassurance, and I go up the stairs to the upper deck. I go into the bathroom, take off my make-up, step out of my dress, and throw it in the laundry basket, not wanting a constant reminder of the events of tonight. I spend five minutes in the shower washing away the remnants of the night's events, enjoying the sting of the hot water as it cleanses my skin. After my shower, I crawl into bed in my underwear, and a few minutes later Sam opens the door. I can't see his expression, and I start to wonder whether Lucas has told Sam about J.D.

"Are you still awake, angel?"

The light from outside the bedroom filters in, casting him in shadow. He strides across the room stripping his clothes off with each step. He stands next to the bed looking glorious, shirtless, with his boxer briefs hanging off his narrow hips. He climbs into bed and pulls me close to him, my back to his warm, muscled chest. His arms feel so good wrapped around me; I am going to miss him so much. He nuzzles my hair.

"I'm going to miss you so much, angel," he whispers in my ear and it's taking everything I have not to cry.

"I'm going to miss you too, baby, so much."

He pulls me tighter to him, and before I know what's going on, Sam flips me onto my back and straddles me.

"Tell me to stop if you don't want this, angel."

I shake my head and whisper softly, "I need you Sam"

The truth is I need him to erase J.D.'s touch and replace it with his own. He kisses a trail from my neck to my collarbone and his hand snakes the length of my body.

"You're so fucking perfect," he whispers huskily, and I am apprehensive at being intimate after being almost raped by J.D, but I try to push the thought from my mind and just feel Sam. *My Sam.*

"You looked amazing tonight, that dress was magnificent on you, and you made me so fucking hard," he rasps. "I want to make love to you, angel; I don't want to just fuck tonight. I want you to feel me, every inch; I want to explore every beautiful inch of your perfect body. I promised you I would make our last night together memorable, and I intend to keep my promise."

With those words, he cups my breast softly in his large hand, and it is a contrast from the rough grope I felt earlier. He leans his head down and takes my nipple between his teeth. He bites down gently, and I gasp.

"Tender, angel?" he says against my breast.

"Just a little."

He soothes the bite with a gentle suckling, and I run my hands through his hair.

"I'll be gentle, I promise."

I feel his erection press into my stomach.

"Do you feel that, angel? You have no idea what you do to me."

Oh, I think I do, Newbolt, because every time he is within an inch of me, my whole body lights up and I ache for him.

"Where do you want me to touch you, baby? Tell me," he whispers. He moves his hand lower to my stomach. "Here?"

I shake my head. He moves lower to cup my sex, and I gasp at the contact.

"Here?" I nod and bite my lip. "Say the words, angel, let me hear you."

He massages my sex through my knickers and I am writhing underneath him.

"Sam, oh, God, touch my pussy. Please, baby. Make love to me, I need you," I say, and I sound breathy and desperate. He chuckles softly.

"Just lie back and relax; I'll take care of you, angel."

He rips my knickers off in one swift movement and reaches round to unhook my bra. He pulls it off, and I am naked beneath him.

"So perfect," he whispers, proud of his handiwork at getting me naked in record time. He removes his boxer briefs and the flex of his muscles drives me to distraction.

How is it possible for a man to look so perfect?

"See something you like, baby?" He takes his throbbing erection in his hand and I cup his testicles in my hand. He growls. "Easy, angel, you'll make me come in a second like a fucking teenager if you're not careful."

I chuckle softly, and he kneels between my legs. He strokes his finger up my cleft and I shudder with excitement.

"*Jesus*, you're always so wet and ready for me."

He smiles his dazzling smile. He grasps his erection again and slides gently into me, inch by glorious inch.

"You feel like heaven, angel."

He moves painfully slow, and I feel every warm throbbing inch of his marvellous cock. I moan softly and wrap my legs around his waist to pull me deeper into me.

"*Oh, Sam.*"

He thrusts his hips forward. The rhythm he sets is slow and sensual, he leans forward and pins my wrists above my head. He kisses my neck and nips my earlobe while tirelessly pumping in and out of my soaking wet pussy.

"Peyton."

He lets out a low growl and with each languorous thrust, I feel my orgasm rising higher.

"You're close," Sam pants.

"So close, baby."

"I can feel you around my cock, angel."

He swivels his hips and with each plunge of his cock, I can feel him deep inside me, hitting my g-spot. An intense orgasm builds with each deep drive.

"Peyton, I'm close, baby, come with me," he rasps, and with those words, I feel my orgasm tear through me so powerfully I see stars. A second later, Sam finds his release and fills me with his hot seed, shouting out my name repeatedly. No man has ever brought me to climax the way Sam does. His deft expert fingers, his talented mouth, and his glorious cock, teasing and coaxing every ounce of pleasure out of my body. He is so in tune with my needs sexually, physically, and emotionally, it overwhelms me. He knows my body better than I do. I have no doubt in my mind that we were made for each other, he is my soul mate and I am eternally in love with him.

11

Peyton

The next morning after an emotional goodbye to Sam, and a bout of throwing up due to a hangover of epic proportions courtesy of Mr. Jack Daniels, I arrive back at the flat after being driven by Cole. He was under Sam's strict instructions for him to deliver me right to my door. Cole lets me out of the car; I look up and there is scaffolding scaling the building. It looks as if I have stepped right onto a construction site. Under the watchful eye of Cole, I walk up the flight of steps and into the foyer. There is plastic sheeting and workmen in hard hats. I am suddenly curious at what has been happening while I have been away. I take the stairs up to the flat, dragging my suitcase behind me, and open the door.

"Rubes?" I call out, and she comes out of the kitchen in her dressing gown. She runs towards me and enthusiastically throws her arms around me.

"Peyton! I'm so glad you're home, babe," she says in her familiar singsong voice that I have missed so much. I smile at her fervour.

"I missed you, babe, I'm so glad to be home."

She pulls away from our hug and looks at me carefully.

"So, you haven't become accustomed to the rock star lifestyle? You're not wearing sunglasses indoors and you haven't turned up with an entourage, that's always a good sign!"

We both laugh.

"What's with the work men downstairs babe?"

She smiles and has a knowing look on her face.

"Yeah, about that, I should have mentioned it. We got a letter a few weeks ago; apparently, an unknown benefactor has bought out the building. We're getting brand new state-of-the-art security, twenty-four-hour concierge service, and a guard is being permanently stationed in the new reception area. It all sounds pretty impressive; it's going to be like living in one of those fancy pants apartment buildings," she says excitedly, and I narrow my eyes. I can't help thinking this has something to do with Sam.

"What's the name of the construction company?"

She picks up a letter from the worktop and skims through it.

"AMS Construction, I know what you're thinking. You think this has something to do with Sam?"

I nod and flop down on the sofa. "It all seems a little too convenient if you ask me."

"So what if it something to do with Sam? It's sweet that he cares so much, he just wants to protect you that's all, babe. Besides he's a world famous rock star, he can afford it!" She chuckles. I regard her intently and she swiftly changes the subject. "How was it being on tour with a bunch of sweaty rockers?"

"Yeah, it was an experience," I say with a giggle that Ruby quickly joins in on.

I am happy to be back home after a month away. I feel refreshed and ready to take on the world. I spend the rest of the weekend doing my washing, catching up with Ruby, my family, and Seb.

By the time Monday morning rolls around, I am in work mode and ready to take on my role as manager of Saint Sinner Ink. I am about to leave for work when my mobile starts ringing.

"Good morning, beautiful," Sam rasps down the phone and I smile widely.

"Good morning, handsome."

Ruby rolls her eyes as she sips her coffee.

"I was just calling to wish you good luck on your first day as shop manager, angel."

I grab my coat.

"Thanks, baby. God, I miss you."

He sighs. "I miss you too, angel, so much. Go down to your parking garage; there's a surprise for you."

I smile and kiss Ruby on the cheek promising to meet her for lunch. I leave the flat and walk to the parking garage with the phone still to my ear.

"What are you planning, Newbolt?"

He chuckles softly, and I am curious as to what my surprise might be.

"Is it against the law to surprise my girl?"

I walk into parking garage and there parked in my usual parking spot is my new Chevy Camaro ZL1. I shriek with excitement and Sam laughs.

"Thank you so much, baby."

"I'm glad you like it, angel, my work here is done. I've put a smile on your face, and I hope to keep it there for the rest of the day."

"I love you so much, Sam."

"I love you too, angel, but I have to go. Duty calls. Think of me."

With those words, he hangs up, and he is right: I am left with a grin plastered across my face for the whole journey to work. Twenty minutes later, I breeze into the shop. Seb looks up from his tattoo magazine and his face lights up.

"Good morning, honey."

I have missed his usual morning greeting, and I am glad to be back. He leaps up from his chair, sprints across the shop, picks me up, and spins me around. We both laugh. He sets me on my feet and pulls me into a bear hug.

"It's so good to have you home, honey; the place is never the same without you."

I pull away from our embrace to say, "I've missed you, Seb."

"I got you a coffee, your usual Starbucks special." He winks. I stand on my tiptoes and kiss him on the cheek.

"Thanks, babe, you're a star."

I take the lid off my coffee and go to take a sip. My stomach roils, and I suddenly feel the overwhelming urge to throw up. I put my cup down and rush to the toilet. As I sink down to my knees and vomit, I feel a presence at my back.

"Seb, you don't need to see this, babe," I manage to say between bouts of being sick.

"Don't be silly, honey, it's nothing I haven't seen before." He kneels down, rubs my back, and holds my hair out of my face. "What's wrong, is it something you ate?"

I pause. "I'm not sure, maybe."

He rubs my back soothingly.

"Take your time, honey, your first appointment isn't until eleven. But if you need to take some time, I can reschedule it if you need me to. I need to leave at lunch time, though I'm taking a flight to California early this evening; I need to oversee the new shop opening."

I smile to myself and I am so happy for Seb in expanding the shop. It is as if everything he touches turns to gold, and I am glad he is taking me along for the ride as shop manager.

I clean myself up and out of curiosity, I check my calendar on my phone. I am shocked at the discovery I make. My period is late, and it's never late. It's always regular as clockwork, I can literally set my watch by it. According to my calendar, I am four weeks late. How the fuck did I not realise? *Shit.* The morning passes quickly in an endless flow of ink, but it is made more difficult with the underlying thought lingering in the back of my mind. *I might be pregnant with Sam's baby.* With that thought at the forefront of my brain, I say goodbye to Seb and wish him luck on his shop opening in California and walk to Swingin' Eli's for lunch with Ruby. By the time Ruby gets there, I am chewing on my bottom lip and deep in thought.

"Earth to Peyton." She snaps her fingers. She plonks herself on the seat in front of me and drops her bag on the floor.

"Come on spill it, sister, you look like you could use a chat." She smiles, her face filled with concern. I look up at her with glazed eyes.

"My period's late."

Her eyes widen. "Fuck me, Peyton."

I take a sip from my glass of water. She reaches over the table and grasps my hand.

"Everything will be OK, babe, we'll do a test, and if it comes back positive, we'll deal with it. I'll be here for you, every step of the way, just like last time."

She smiles softly and reassuringly. I always feel better after I have spoken to Ruby. Her reassurance, her uncanny knack of reading me like a book, and her ability to say the right things make me grateful to have someone like her in my life. We eat lunch, even though my appetite seems to have abandoned me, and after settling our bill, we head to the pharmacy down the street. I buy a pregnancy test and go back to work, promising Ruby to meet her back at the flat later.

The rest of the afternoon is busy. In-between tattooing, cashing up, and sorting out the rest of the week's bookings, I am rushed off my feet. Parker is on hand to help which I am grateful for. He offers to lock up the shop, and I head back to the flat after a long, busy day.

The heavy rush-hour traffic means it takes twice as long to get back to the flat and by the time I finally get back, I am tired, anxious, and extremely pissed off. I throw my bag down on the counter top in the kitchen and hang up my coat. I go straight to the bathroom, wanting desperately to get the test out of the way. Ruby leans in the doorway with her arms folded.

"I can't pee while you're watching."

She giggles. *"For fucks sake!* I'll turn around, although it's nothing I haven't seen before, babe. I know what your lady garden looks like! How long have we known each other?"

She cocks her eyebrow and we both laugh hysterically. *If you don't laugh about it you'll cry, right?* I make a turning motion with my finger; she rolls her eyes and turns around. I pee on the stick and wait while the results develop.

"How late are you?"

I bite my lip. "Four weeks. Being on the road with the boys, it was hard to keep track, but how the fuck did I not realise?"

She brushes my arm reassuringly. A few minutes pass and I look at the result. The test reads *'pregnant'*. I put my hand to my mouth and start sobbing. This is not happening. *Fuck.*

Two little blue lines—pregnant. *Those blue lines are going to change everything.*

"Hey, what's with the tears, babe, it's good news, right?" Ruby says gently, and she pulls me in for a hug.

"How could I have been so fucking stupid?" I sob, and she strokes my hair.

"I should be congratulating you, not comforting you, sweetie."

It's easy for her to say—she hasn't got herself knocked up by a handsome rock star that could quite easily bolt if I tell him. *At least he would be living up to his stage name.* I decide to keep the news to myself for the time being and swear Ruby to secrecy. At least until I come to terms with the situation. I will tell him. *Soon.*

12

Peyton

Two months pass by quickly in a haze of morning sickness, busy days at the shop—which seem to all blend into each other—and daily phone and Zoom calls from Sam. It is the end of October almost and I still haven't dropped the baby bombshell. Every time I speak to him, I can't seem to bring myself to say the words. A trip to the doctor's confirmed that I am now twelve weeks pregnant. I have taken to wearing bigger clothes to try to hide my ever-growing baby bump. I feel exactly like I did when I was with Callum.

Today is Saturday, and I have a well-earned day off from the shop after working gruelling twelve-hour shifts at the shop. I am curled up on the sofa in my pyjamas and Ruby comes storming in with her hands on her hips.

"You're getting off that fucking sofa and you're coming shopping with me. I can't stand seeing you so miserable and wallowing in your own bloody self-pity. When the fuck are you going to tell Sam? When your waters break or when you're actually in hospital giving birth?" she snaps, and I avoid her stern gaze. I know she is right, but I can't. *I just can't.* He'll run, I just know it.

"Stop overthinking." Ruby looks at me and sits on the sofa next to me. "Look, Peyton, you need to hear this, I've kept my mouth shut for long enough."

She narrows her eyes and she has a look on her face that tells me she is serious.

"I was the one who mopped up your tears, I was the one who picked up the pieces and put you back together. I was there through the nightmares, I was the one who held you while you screamed and cried because of him, Peyton. It broke my heart to watch you go through that. *Christ*, you tried to take your own life because of Callum-fucking-Kennedy. Sam isn't Callum, babe; he'll stand by you no matter what because he worships you. That boy would walk through hell for you; any fucking idiot can see that except for you. You're just waiting for him to prove you right and you're going to end up losing your happily ever after because of that selfish prick. You're carrying Sam's baby and you *have* to tell him, he deserves to know, babe. He might not have been my favourite person in the beginning, but he is a genuine, kind, caring bloke and he loves you. He might be a pig-headed, egotistical, hot-tempered dick that makes the wrong decisions sometimes, but only because he loves you. I'm not going to sit back and watch you ruin the one good thing in your life; best friends don't do that." She clasps my hand in hers. "Everything's going to be all right, babe, I promise. Sam's due back next week, isn't he?"

I nod.

"You need to tell him." She gets up from the sofa. "Or I will," she says nonchalantly.

My eyes widen, and I rush after her. "You wouldn't dare," I challenge, and she raises her perfectly-plucked eyebrows.

"Don't dare me, babe, this isn't some game. You're pregnant, and you're refusing to tell the father. Maybe I should call your mum and get her to talk some fucking sense into you."

By the tone of her voice, I know she really means business.

"Ruby, please don't call my mum. I'll tell him as soon as he gets back, I promise."

She smiles brightly.

"Good, mission accomplished. Now, get your fat pregnant arse up off that fucking sofa and get dressed; we're going shopping."

I smile at her feistiness and drag myself into the shower. I dry my hair, apply my usual natural makeup and get dressed into a simple, purple, polka-dot dress and black pumps. I admire myself in the mirror; I am beginning to think they're right what they say that a woman in the early stages of pregnancy is glowing. My hair is glossier than usual and falling down my shoulders in a dark brown cascade, my eyes are wide, and even though they are incredibly sore and tender, my boobs look amazing! I stroke my stomach and start to wonder what's Sam's reaction will be. *Will he be angry? Will he run? Will he be happy?* I try to push my wayward thoughts to the back of my mind as I grab my bag and my coat. I go out into the living room and Ruby is waiting for me.

"See, that wasn't so hard, was it, babe? You look gorgeous as always."

She smiles brightly. She links my arm and we leave the flat. We walk down the steps and as we start to make our way down the street, a motorbike roars close to us.

"Boys and their toys."

Ruby rolls her eyes. We carry on walking; the motorbike circles us and comes to a halt at the kerb inches away from us. The person on the motorbike pulls off their helmet and there in front of us is Sam. He smiles lazily, and he looks absolutely delicious. His raven black hair is longer than I remember, and he looks thinner, more defined, and extremely hot. My mouth forms a perfect *O* shape as I take in the sight of him.

"Angel," he rasps, and it is taking everything I have not to melt in a puddle at his feet. He climbs off his custom black Harley Davidson Sportster Iron 883 motorbike, kicks the kickstand, and strides towards me. He wraps me in his strong arms and I cling to him tightly. Ruby is standing off to the side taking in the sight unfolding in front of her. I take in his scent and nuzzle my face into his neck.

"God, I've missed you, baby," he says into my neck.

"I missed you too so much, Sam."

I feel him smile against my skin. He pulls away from me and looks at me.

"You're even more beautiful than I remember, angel."

He moves closer to me and presses his lips urgently to mine. His lips are so soft, his tongue carefully caresses mine, and I am lost in his kiss right in the middle of the street.

"I thought you weren't due back until next week."

He smiles his dazzling melt-worthy smile.

"I wanted to surprise you; it's just a flying visit, though. We fly out to Las Vegas next weekend for our ten-year anniversary gig."

I still can't believe he is standing in front of me after so long apart. I feel so overwhelmed I feel like I might burst into tears. I swallow back the lump in my throat.

"Come home with me?"

I am about to protest and Ruby jumps in.

"It's fine, babe, honestly. Go and be with Sam. You deserve to spend some time together, plus, it's kind of sickening watching you."

She makes a vomiting motion with her hand. We all laugh and Ruby brushes my arm.

"Go, I'll find something or someone else to entertain me, babe. I'll be fine." She winks.

"Are you sure, babe?"

She pulls me in for a hug. "'Course I'm sure, you silly tart. Call me once you've told him, we'll have some celebrating to do," she whispers so only I can hear her, and she pulls away. "Enjoy your day together, love birds."

She laughs and walks off down the street, leaving Sam and me looking at each other.

"You look ... *Fuck*, you look amazing. Our video calls are no match for the real thing, angel."

I smile shyly.

"Should we go up to your flat and get some clothes for you? Although, while I was away, I hired a personal shopper and got you a whole new wardrobe full of clothes at my place."

I raise my eyebrows.

"I'm not sure whether to be flattered or creeped out that you did that for me."

He laughs. "You should definitely be flattered, angel."

He pushes his bike nearer to my flat, secures it, and we head up to the flat.

"Did you have anything to do with this?" I say as we step into the new state-of-the-art reception area, complete with security guards and twenty-four hour surveillance. He smirks.

"I might have."

He guides me towards the stairs with his hand at the small of my back.

"I just wanted you safe and protected while I was gone. If you're still adamant that you don't want to live with me then it's the least I can do. Besides, Diego owed me a favour."

I smile, and I get a fuzzy feeling inside that he is so protective. I start to think that maybe telling him about the baby won't be so bad. We go up to the flat and he stands in the living room. I pack some things in my overnight bag, zip it up, and join Sam in the living room. I lock the door on the way out and we head out onto the street. Cole is waiting at the kerb in Sam's sleek black Mercedes SL convertible.

"Cole's going to take you to my place. I'm going to take the bike back and I'll meet you there."

Cole smiles brightly and tips his hat. Sam kisses me gently on the lips and I get into the car. We make the journey back to Sam's place in relative silence. I am lost in thought for the whole trip and I hardly notice as we pull up at the kerb.

"Peyton?" Cole's deep rumbling voice interrupts my thoughts. I look up into his deep brown eyes, and I manage a smile. "I thought I'd lost you back there, sugar." He smiles warmly. He opens my door and I step out of the car. "Are you sure everything's OK, Peyton?" Cole asks as we walk into Sam's building. I don't hear him as I take in the opulence; it never ceases to amaze me, the marble floors, and the sleek clean lines and despite the feeling of wealth within the building, the warm inviting atmosphere soothes you as soon as you step inside.

"Peyton." I spin around. "I said, is everything OK?"

I nod and smile, knowing that my smile doesn't quite reach my eyes.

"Yeah, everything's fine, thanks, Cole."

He smiles and nods, but something about the way he looks tells me he doesn't believe me for a second. Cole calls for the lift and we step in. I am silent and a slave to my thoughts as the lift ascends to Sam's apartment. I step into the foyer and Cole steps out behind me, he hands me a purple key on a Rancid Vengeance key ring.

"Sam asked me to give you this." I take the key from him, open the apartment door, and go to hand the key back to Cole. He shakes his head. "He said you can keep it, just in case."

I go into Sam's apartment and Cole follows me. I put my bag down and take off my coat. I notice four mounted photographs wrapped in bubble wrap leaning against the kitchen island. Sam's luggage and a guitar case are leaning against the wall. I am curious as to what other adjustments Sam has made to his apartment while he has been gone. Cole stands stock-still with his hands behind his back.

"Do you need anything while I'm here Peyton?"

I look up at him regarding me intently and shake my head.

"No, thanks. I'm good."

I smile. He nods, and I wonder if he is under orders from Sam to stand guard until he comes back. I move into the kitchen and I suddenly feel dizzy. I stumble and lean into the kitchen island for support. Cole is at my side in seconds.

"Are you sure you're all right, sugar? You look pale; come, sit." He guides me to the sofa and sits me down. He crouches in front of me. "Do you need me to get you anything?"

I look at him and smile at his concern. "A glass of water would be great, please."

He nods, and as he gets to his feet, the door closes and Sam strides across the apartment. He takes Cole's place crouching in front of me. His face is marred with concern, and a frown line jumps into place on his forehead.

"Angel, is everything OK?" I am suddenly sick of being asked if I'm OK. I go to rise from the sofa and fall back down as another dizzy spell takes hold of me. "*Jesus*, angel."

I look at him.

"I'm just tired, babe, that's all, it's been nonstop at the shop lately."

"I'm taking you to our room, you look like you could use a lie down."

"I'm fine, babe, I promise, I just need you to hold me for a while. I've missed you."

He smiles and nods. He picks me up and carries me into the bedroom. He sets me down on my feet and moves me, so he can look at me.

"God, you're beautiful." He strokes my face and tucks my hair behind my ear. "I have a surprise for you, angel."

I raise my eyebrows and he smirks mischievously. We both stand facing each other and he strips off his t-shirt. I lick my lips as he reveals his perfectly ripped torso.

"Don't get any ideas, angel," he rasps. He throws his t-shirt on the bed and looks at me. "Do you see that?"

He points to a spot above his right pectoral and there in bold, flowing script is a tattoo of my name *'Peyton'* with two elaborate black and grey angel wings either side.

"That's how much I love you, angel. There is nothing I wouldn't do for you, you're my good luck charm, my angel; you are my life, my whole world. You own me."

My eyes glaze over at his words, and I can't believe he has my name permanently etched on his skin. I trace over the lines of his tattoo, and I lose it completely. I collapse in floods of tears in his arms, mentally cursing my hormones to hell.

"Hey, what's with the tears, babe?" he soothes. "Shhh." He kisses my forehead and I snuggle closer to his warm chest. "I'll never let anyone hurt you, angel."

I don't doubt for a second that he means every word. We spend the rest of the day catching up and spending some quality time together. I have missed being in his presence—it calms and soothes me. By the time the evening rolls around, we order takeaway and snuggle on the sofa. After we finish eating, I literally fall asleep in Sam's lap; I didn't realise how tired I was. I am only aware of him lifting me from the sofa and carrying me effortlessly to his bedroom. I am awake as he lays me down on the bed.

"I've got you, angel."

I shake my head. "It's fine, baby."

I smile, and he kisses me gently on the lips. I get up and go to the walk-in wardrobe. I take out one of Sam's oversized Rancid Vengeance t-shirts that I have become accustomed to. I go into the bathroom and close the door, not wanting him to see me naked. I take off my dress and quickly pull on Sam's t-shirt—he doesn't knock, and he opens the door.

"Hey, what's with the closed door, babe? You're not normally so shy about getting undressed in front of me. Is something wrong? Have I done something?"

"Everything's perfect, babe, I've just put on a little weight since you've been away. Too many late nights at work, too many takeaways, and too much Ben and Jerry's. I should get back to the gym."

I smile but something in the way he looks at me says he knows something is wrong and he doesn't believe me for a second. I brush my teeth and tie my hair in a loose ponytail. I go back into the bedroom and Sam pats the bed.

"I'll stay with you until you fall asleep, angel, I've got some unpacking to do, and I've got some stuff that needs taking care of, but I'll be in soon."

He lies next to me, and I fall asleep in his arms.

***

I'm not sure how long I have been asleep, but I wake up screaming to Sam softly calling my name.

"Peyton, wake up, baby, you're having a nightmare."

He strokes my hair. My breathing is laboured, and I have a thin sheen of sweat forming on my forehead.

"*Jesus*, angel, I'm here. Are you OK? You scared the shit out of me," he says quietly.

He goes to pull me into him, and I flinch as if he has burned me. *I can't do this.* I jump out of bed and run into the bathroom. I slam the door and lock it behind me. I slide down the wall and onto the floor in a hysterical sobbing heap, with the remnants of my nightmare still clinging to me. Sam rattles the doorknob.

"Angel, *fuck!* Open the door, please talk to me."

I sob hard. I am shaken by the nightmare and realise it has been such a long time since that particular nightmare has haunted me. Except it wasn't Callum, it was Sam, and the image of that cold green gaze makes me sob harder. I pull my knees up to my chest.

"The door's coming down if you don't open it, angel." His voice is soft. "I'm not going anywhere until you talk to me, babe"

I hear him sit down outside the door.

"Please just go away," I choke out.

"Not happening, baby, I'll sit out here all night if I have to."

A few minutes of silence passes.

"Do you want to tell me what your nightmare was about, angel?"

As he says those words, something inside me just snaps, I really can't do this. He is going to run; I just know he is. I can't put myself through that; my heart has been trampled on enough. I shakily get myself to my feet and lean on the sink. I look at my reflection in the mirror—my face is pale, my eyes are red, and my hair is sleep mussed. I pull my hair loose, run a brush through it and splash cold water on my face. I unlock the door; Sam is sat outside leaning against the wall, shirtless, and wearing only a pair of tight grey boxer briefs. He stands up as I open the door and reaches his hand out to me. I know if I touch him, I will give in and talk myself out of the decision I have made. I need to get out of here and I need to get out now. I push past him and run into the living room. Sam is following me.

"*Fuck*, where are you going, angel?" His voice is panicked but I don't answer him. I frantically start throwing my stuff back into my overnight bag. "Peyton, will you just fucking stop for one god damn second!"

He makes me stop in front of him and he tilts my chin up to face him. I look into his eyes.

"Don't leave me, angel."

I shake my head. "I can't do this anymore Sam, being with you is unpredictable. Every time I'm near you, I lose myself."

I swipe the stray tear that has escaped from my eye. *Be strong, Harper.*

"Why are you doing this? What have I done? Tell me what I've done, and I'll fix it, I'll make it right."

I force myself to look at him, and as I see the look in his green eyes, my heart breaks.

"I thought we were OK, please stop and fucking talk to me. Please don't run from me, tell me you'll stay." His voice is broken. I move closer to him and he reaches for my hand. I let him take it and he strokes my knuckles softly. "What's wrong? Please talk to me."

I release my hand from his grip and put my hands to my face. I sob.

"*Jesus*, please don't cry, what can I do? Tell me what I can do, angel."

I try to gather myself. "This is all such a fucking mess, Sam, and it's all my fault."

He shakes his head. "Everything's going to be OK as long we have each other; I'm not going anywhere I promise you, angel." He moves towards me and he pulls me into his hard chest. I cling to him and sob as he holds me close. "Tell me what's going on in that beautiful mind of yours, angel," he whispers.

Then Ruby's words start to echo in my mind, *"Sam isn't Callum, babe; he'll stand by you no matter what because he worships you. That boy would walk through hell for you; any fool can see that except for you."*

I take a deep calming breath and look up at him, my blue eyes locking on his green ones. *Here goes nothing.*

"I-I'm pregnant," I choke out, waiting for his reaction. Waiting for the inevitable to happen where he walks out and leaves me. He doesn't say anything at first, and I start to tremble with fear in his arms.

"Hey, shush, I've got you angel," he soothes. "You're pregnant, wow!"

The biggest dimpled grin spreads across his handsome face. He cups my face in his hands and presses his lips to mine.

"Angel, you've just made me the happiest fucking man to walk this earth! I'm going to be a dad!"

A feeling of relief washes over me like a tsunami. I sag in Sam's hold; he releases me and holds me at arm's length.

"You thought I was going to leave didn't you, angel?" he says so softly I barely hear him. "Look at me, baby." I look up at him and nod, my eyes brimming with tears. "How could you think that, angel? After everything we've been through?"

"I don't know I just panicked. I was terrified."

"I'm not going anywhere; you're stuck with me." He smiles his dazzling smile and his green eyes sparkle. He lifts up my t-shirt and strokes my bump gently. "How far gone are you?"

I watch his hand trace my small bump; I put my hand over his and smile. "Twelve weeks."

He takes a breath, curses to himself, and walks over to the balcony. He pulls open the doors and drops down on the lounger. He is visibly annoyed, and I don't blame him for one second, I follow him.

"Why the fuck didn't you tell me, angel? That night you told me about Callum I promised you if that ever happened to us I would stand by you."

He scrubs his hands down his face. I hang my head, and I actually feel ashamed that I have kept this baby a secret for almost three whole months. Three months where he could have supported me, through the morning sickness, and through the hospital appointments. That thought makes me burst into tears again and Sam wraps me in his strong arms.

"Shhh, it's going to be all right, angel. I promise, we'll be a family. The three of us, you, me, and our little rock star!"

He laughs.

"What if it's a girl?"

Sam cups my cheek and kisses me on the end of my nose.

"Then she is not leaving our house until she is at least thirty and I'm not letting any boys near her!" We both laugh, and I let out a yawn, suddenly feeling exhausted. "Tired, angel?"

I nod. He picks me up and carries me into the bedroom.

"I can walk you know; I do have legs!"

He laughs.

"I know, but you're carrying precious cargo!"

I chuckle softly. He sets me down gently on the bed and lies down next to me. He pulls my back to his chest and wraps his arms around me. He gently rests his hand on my stomach and snuggles into my back. At that moment, I know everything is going to be all right. We will be a proper family and finally get our happily ever after.

13

Peyton

The next morning, I turn over to find Sam's side of the bed empty and my phone ringing. I look at the clock—eight AM. *Who could be calling me at this hour?* I reach for my phone and see Lori's name flash up on my screen. *Why would Sam's mum be calling me?* I swipe my finger across the screen and answer with curiosity.

"Hello?" I try not to sound like she has just woke me up.

"Peyton, good morning, sweetie. I hope I didn't wake you," she says in her familiar cheery American drawl and I clear my throat.

"No, of course not, Lori, is everything OK?"

I lie and she pauses. "Yes, everything's fine, honey, I'm just calling to remind you and Sam that I've organised a birthday dinner for him."

I knew Sam's birthday was coming up, but he hasn't mentioned anything. I am silent for a moment and Lori chuckles.

"Let me guess, he hasn't mentioned it? He is a little sensitive that it's his thirtieth birthday."

I smile. *Typical Sam.*

"He hasn't mentioned it, but we would love to come."

"Fabulous, darling. It's on Saturday before the boys fly out to Vegas on Sunday. I was just calling to invite your parents, brother, sister, and that lovely boss of yours, Sebastian, too."

I find myself smiling that our families are finally going to get to meet each other.

"That sounds really great, Lori."

"The boys are all coming, Cole, Amy, Milo and Seth from Marley's band. It going to be quite a gathering, I'm getting the caterers in."

I start thinking to myself that it isn't any normal gathering and what do I get for the man who has everything for his birthday?

"Wow, that sounds amazing, Lori."

"Tell Sam I'll call him later, sweetie, and I'll see you on Saturday."

"See you on Saturday, bye."

I hang up and Sam walks into the bedroom with a pair of dark jeans hanging off his narrows hips, a black t-shirt that clings to his muscles, his hair is wet from a recent shower and he is bare foot. He is clutching a mug of coffee and he leans in the doorway.

"Good morning, beautiful, how are you and our little rock star this morning?"

I chuckle softly. "Good morning handsome, we're all good, thanks."

I rub my stomach and suddenly feel a wave of nausea hit me. I leap up off the bed and run into the bathroom. I sink to my knees and throw up in the toilet. Sam is instantly at my side rubbing my back soothingly and holding my hair out of my face.

"*Jesus*, are you all right, angel?"

I manage to nod.

"I'll be fine babe, honestly, just morning sickness, that's all."

Unexpectedly, I hear a woman's voice. "Sam, are you here, sugar?"

I recognise it as Amy, Cole's fiancée. *Shit.* The last thing I want is for someone to see me throwing up and putting two and two together, especially since we haven't told our families about the baby yet.

"She's bringing my washing back that's all, angel; she has a key in case of emergencies," he says, as if to clarify my unspoken question. I hear tiny footsteps running through the apartment.

"Uncle Sammy!"

Addison's voice shouts and Sam chuckles.

"I'll be right back, angel, I promise."

He steps out of the bathroom and blocks the doorway with his large frame.

"Hello, beautiful!"

Sam scoops Addison up in his arms and she giggles. It makes me wonder what Sam will be like with our baby, and it warms my heart that we're going to be parents to a little me or little Sam.

"Found him, Mummy!" she shouts and looks over Sam's shoulder at me on my knees practically hugging the toilet. *Nice.*

"Is Aunty Peyton sick Uncle Sammy?"

Sam swings her around.

"Aunty Peyton isn't feeling well right now, Princess, so we have to be really quiet." Sam lowers his voice and put his finger to her lips. "Shhh, can you be a quiet little mouse while Aunty Peyton is sick?" She nods. "Good girl."

He kisses her on the end of her nose and he strides out of the bedroom with her in his arms. Twenty minutes later, I feel the sickness starting to wear off, splash my face with cold water, brush my teeth, and run a brush through my sleep-mussed hair. I pull on a cream jumper with a black *&?* Logo across the front and a pair of loose fitting black jeans. I walk through the apartment and into the kitchen where Amy is perched on a stool drinking coffee with Sam. She always looks immaculately dressed, with her flawless coffee coloured skin and wide eyes. Her curly black hair sets off her tall, slim frame dressed in a black pencil skirt, a pink silk camisole, and black heels. She looks like a catwalk model. Sam has Addison sitting quietly on his lap with her colouring book and crayons.

"Hey, hon, are you feeling better? Sam said you weren't feeling too good?" Her voice is filled with concern. I smile and nod.

"Yeah, I'm good thanks, Amy. I feel much better now."

She eyes me suspiciously and Addison tugs on Sam's t-shirt.

"Uncle Sammy, can you take me to look at your shiny bikes?"

Sam laughs.

"You had better ask your mummy, baby girl."

Sam turns his green eyes onto Amy and she rolls her eyes.

"Go on then and don't spoil her, you!"

Amy laughs and Sam salutes. He lifts her up, piggybacking a giggling Addison down to the garage, leaving Amy and me in Sam's kitchen.

"Congratulations by the way, hon."

My eyes widen. *How did she know?* She chuckles.

"Sam called Cole. Don't look so worried, your secret's safe with me."

She winks, and I smile. I feel happy to share our news with someone other than Sam and Ruby.

"How far gone are you?"

I stroke my stomach. "Twelve weeks."

She nods and regards me intently.

"Wow! I'm so happy for you both, babe," she says brightly and brushes my arm.

"Thank you, it means a lot."

She takes a sip of her coffee. "Please don't hurt him, Peyton, that boy worships you. I've never seen him like this with a woman ever, he is crazy about you."

"I would never hurt him, I love him too much. He has made me feel alive again, and I can't imagine my life without him in it."

She smiles.

"I remember the night Addison was born. Cole almost missed the birth because he was working a gig with the boys. They were halfway through the gig when Cole got the call from my dad. Sam caught Cole's eye and he knew straight away that something was wrong; he jumped off stage and cut the show short. He drove Cole to the hospital and he made it just in time."

I smile, and it warms my heart to think that Sam did that for his friend.

"He was one of the first people to hold her, ever since that moment he was smitten with her. He's her godfather; they love the bones of each other. She's at that stage where she wants to follow him everywhere; she's the most popular kid in her class at nursery because her god father is in a famous rock band!"

We both laugh. I can see Amy and me being good friends. She is warm, friendly and easy to chat to; I feel as if I have known her all my life.

"She bosses him around, and he's total and utter mush around her. She has definitely got him wrapped around her little finger. Both of you are going to be great parents. Sam and Cole have been friends for a long time. Cole has seen the highs, the lows and everything in-between, but he won't give up on him no matter how much he screws up. But these past few months since he met you it's like looking at a completely different person, he's changed so much, because of you, babe."

I am so grateful for the insight Amy is giving me on Sam.

"The boys, their crew, they're all like family and for them to accept you into their fold is a victory in itself, honey. Even though they don't show it, the guys all love you and they speak very highly of you." I smile shyly. "They're just typical boys, babe, you clearly know how to handle them, they need a female influence around them, and you're the perfect woman for the job, trust me."

She brushes my arm reassuringly, and I am grateful for her kind words. I feel as though I have been accepted into an extended family and it feels good to belong.

"Lori called this morning, she's organised a birthday dinner for Sam next weekend."

Amy chuckles.

"Ah, the infamous Newbolt birthday dinners, you haven't lived until you have been to one. Lori goes all out; she's a force to be reckoned with, trust me. She has each and every one of her boys wrapped around her little finger, Sam included, even though he swears she hasn't."

I smile, and I am looking forward to getting to know Sam's family better.

"It's Sam's thirtieth birthday, what do I get the man who has everything?"

She takes my hand.

"Just you being there is a present in itself, babe, that and the fact that you're now carrying Sam's baby. He might be a rock star and he might like extravagant things, but the simple little things have more meaning behind them, trust me on that one."

I smile, and Addison runs into the room with Sam trailing behind her.

"I winned, Uncle Sammy!" she declares and giggles. Sam pretends to catch his breath.

"You beat me; you're just too fast for me, sweetie."

He winks at me, and I feel my stomach flip. After all this time, he still has that effect on me. He has the power to turn my insides to jelly with just a look. At that moment, I know that this is the beginning of a beautiful future with Mr Samson Newbolt.

***

A week passes, and we are busier than ever at the shop, it's all hands to the pump. Reluctantly, I have asked Harley Hernandez from Black Tiger Ink to step in while Seb is tying up a few loose ends with the new shop in California before his return to the U.K to join us to celebrate Sam's thirtieth birthday. Over the week, I have officially moved out of the flat I shared with Ruby and

I have permanently moved into Sam's apartment. I expected it to take a while for us to adjust to living together as a couple, but it has all just fallen into place.

Today is the twelfth of November, Sam's thirtieth birthday, and I wake to an empty bed. As his birthday has drawn ever closer, Sam has woken before me every morning and put his body through a daily gruelling three-hour work out. It is as if he keeps himself fit enough he'll avoid turning the big three-oh. His muscles are looking more sculpted and defined, his shoulders are broader, his arms and neck are thick and corded with muscle. He walks into the bedroom taking a long pull on his water bottle and a black towel around his neck. He is wearing a grey vest covered in sweat with long black shorts. He looks good enough to eat; I lick my lips sleepily at the sight of him. Instantly becoming more alert and aware as I take in his large frame. Being pregnant, I am so horny, and I crave Sam's body like a drug.

"If you keep looking at me like that, angel, I'm not going to be held responsible for my actions," he rasps, and I feel heat pool between my legs. *God, I want him so badly*. He chuckles softly. "You are insatiable, baby."

I bite my lip. "Only for you."

He sits on the edge of the bed and plants a soft kiss on my lips. I move forward to deepen the kiss and he moves back.

"Easy, angel."

I pout. He throws his head back and laughs.

"That pout is adorable. How are my two favourite people this morning?"

Swiftly changing the subject, he strokes my stomach softly. Over the course of the week, Sam has been attentive and treating me like glass as if I am going to break at any second. I explained to him that I'm pregnant, not ill. After a lot of gentle persuasion, lots of epic shagging, and mind-numbing blow jobs, I seem to have placated his neurotic side. He kisses the end of my nose and gets to his feet.

"I'm going for a shower, angel."

He goes into the bathroom. Time for me to put my birthday surprise into action. I decided to go with Amy's idea, the simple things mean more. So with that in mind, I strip naked and tie a length of pale yellow ribbon around my stomach in a neat bow. I run my fingers through my sleep-mussed hair and lie back on the bed. Ten minutes later, Sam steps out of the bathroom with a towel hanging loosely off his narrow hips. His mouth drops open as he catches sight of me.

"Happy birthday, handsome," I whisper, and his eyes glaze over. "I wanted to get you a present no one else has ever given you, baby."

He sits on the edge of the bed.

"It's perfect, thank you so much."

He plants a kiss on my bump and pulls me close to him. His body is still damp from the shower and he smells of his familiar Sam smell, it is intoxicating.

"I have a few other surprises up my sleeve for you, Mr. Newbolt."

He smiles that dazzling smile, and I feel myself melt in a pool all over the bed.

"You didn't have to, angel; I'm not big on birthdays."

I cup his cheek. "I know, but I couldn't resist, I want to spoil you the way you spoil me."

He puts his hand on top of mine.

"Just being with you is enough, angel, it isn't a competition."

He gets up from the bed, dries himself off, and pulls on a clean pair of boxers. I lay back and watch the show unfolding in front of me with hungry eyes. He laughs; he pulls on a pair of loose-fitting jeans and runs his fingers through his wet hair.

"Your present is on the shelf inside the wardrobe."

He pulls it open and takes out the large box.

"You better not have put this up here yourself, babe."

I bite my lip and he growls, taking the box down. He lays it on the bed and unwraps the gift. His eyes light up as he sees what's inside the box. A Les Paul Gibson nineteen seventies tribute electric guitar, which Marlowe helped me pick out. Apparently, it was the first guitar that Sam was given by Milo—one of Sam's heroes.

"Angel," his voice is barely a whisper and his eyes are glazed. "Words fail me."

I cock my eyebrow at him. "Wow, *the* Sam Newbolt rendered speechless; that's a first."

He pulls me close to him, holds me tightly, and buries his face in my hair.

"Thank you, thank you, so much, angel."

"I take it you like it then?"

He nods against my neck and pulls away. We sit cross-legged opposite each other on the bed and he inspects the front more closely. I called in a favour and got Seb to design a faceplate for Sam's guitar. Seb has custom designed a large skull with angel wings and vibrant red roses spanning the outside. This is similar to the tattoo I designed for him when we first met. Inside the skull is an old style microphone and the wire of the microphone is a figure eight infinity symbol, meaning *forever*. Also, Seb has incorporated the Rancid Vengeance logo, a tattoo machine, and a motorbike with a skeleton rocker playing a burning guitar. Along the fret board is Sam's band name *'Bolt'* in old English lettering. He runs his fingers over the artwork and a tear slips down his cheek.

"It's fucking perfect. This means more than you'll ever know, angel."

I wipe the tear away with my thumb and kiss him softly on the lips. His morning stubble tickling my face as he wraps his arms tighter around me.

"I don't deserve you, Peyton Harper."

I push him down on the bed until he is laid flat on his back and I straddle his hips.

"You need to unwrap your gift now, Mr. Newbolt," I say in my best seductive voice and he cocks his pierced eyebrow. I wriggle against him, and he growls; I can feel his erection through the soft denim of his jeans. He moves his hands up to the ribbon and slowly unties it. Once the ribbon is untied, he lets it drop to the floor and runs his hands up the length of my body. He doesn't take his eyes off me for one second.

"God, you're so fucking beautiful it makes my chest ache," he rasps, and I run my fingers gently down his chest. I feel the erratic beat of his heart and his hands skating all over my body, leaving goose bumps in their wake. I pull up his t-shirt until his chest is bared. I lick my lips at the sight of his hard, muscled, tattooed chest and the V, which disappears under the waistband of his jeans. He is so perfect it makes heat pool between my thighs and I can only think of how much I need him inside me.

"Sam, I need you." My voice is a soft plea and he smiles wickedly.

"I'll take care of you, angel," he says huskily. I grind on his straining erection and cup my aching breast in my hand.

"Oh, God, please," I moan, and he lifts me, so I am pinned beneath him. He trails kisses down from my breasts, down my stomach, and softly blows air onto my pussy. I shiver at the coolness of his breath. I am aching for him, and I don't think I have ever been this desperate for him to fuck me.

"I need you inside me Sam, please."

He pulls off his jeans and throws them onto the floor. He is gloriously naked in front of me and his hard cock is standing to attention.

"Are you sure I won't hurt the baby, angel?"

I bite my lip and shake my head.

"Just shut up and fuck me like you mean it, rock star."

He stalks towards me like a predator about to devour its prey and positions himself between my legs. He runs his finger up my slit and collects the moisture that has gathered there.

"You're such a bad girl, always so wet and ready for my cock."

Just the sound of his voice could get me off right now, I am aching for him. But I can tell he is in the mood to tease me. I reach for his hardness, but he grips both of my wrists in one of his hands and holds them prisoner above my head trapping me. He leans down, kisses me passionately on the lips, and trails soft nips along my collarbone.

"Do you want me to fuck you, angel?" he whispers in my ear.

"Oh, God, yes!"

I feel his smile against my skin.

"Beg me to fuck you, beg me to ram my cock deep inside you."

He grinds against me and I am so frustrated by his teasing.

"Please fuck me, Sam, God I need you to fuck me! Ram your big hard cock in my pussy!" I scream out and Sam cocks his eyebrow, releasing my wrists from his.

"*Jesus,* that was so hot, angel," he rasps. He positions the head of his penis against my opening and pushes into me. I let out the breath I didn't know I was holding as he moves in and out with an expert swivel of his narrow hips, which causes a delicious friction deep inside me.

"Mmm, Sam."

I writhe beneath him and he leans down taking my already erect nipple in his mouth. He nips it softly with his teeth causing me to gasp, somewhere in between pleasure and pain.

"*Christ,* angel, you feel so good around my cock." He growls as he increases his thrusts and I can feel him deliciously hitting my g-spot with each plunge.

"Oh, fuck, Sam!"

I squeeze my pelvic floor muscles around his cock and he cries out.

"*Fuck!* If you carry on doing that, angel, I'm not going to last much longer."

I smile devilishly and contract my muscles around his cock again, he slows his pace.

"Don't play games with me, angel, because I'll win *every single time,*" he emphasises the last three words.

"Sam, please, I need you. God, I need you," I whimper. He cups my breast in his large hand and massages it gently. His calloused hand feels so good against the soft delicate flesh. He increases his thrusts again, and I can feel that he is close to finding his release.

"*Jesus Christ,* angel, I'm close, so fucking close, come with me."

He moves his hand from my breast and his finger finds my sensitive nub. He strokes my clit, and that's all it takes for us to both find our release at the same time. He growls, and I feel his hot seed coating my insides. I cry out as my own orgasm takes hold.

"Fuck. Oh, *fuck,* Sam. Oh, God. *Yes,*" I scream.

It takes a few minutes for our laboured breaths to return to normal, then he pulls out and lies down next to me. He tucks me under his arm and pulls me close to him. When Sam and I have sex, it feels like the first time every time, and I never get bored of feeling his body pressed against mine. He is an expert in the bedroom department and we satisfy each other's needs like no one else can. We are sexually in sync and I couldn't ask for more in a partner.

"I'm going to miss you so much when you leave for Vegas, babe," I break the silence and Sam stops stroking my hair.

"Come with us then, angel, I looked online and consulted a doctor. You're totally fine to fly and you're out of the danger zone now so there's no reason why you can't. Plus, I've kind of already squared it with Seb."

He bites his lip boyishly, and I smile at his thoughtfulness.

"Yes! I'd love to come to Vegas!"

He kisses me on the lips and we spend the rest of the morning making slow, passionate love in Sam's overly-large bed.

14

Peyton

A few hours pass, and Sam and I are wrapped naked around each other when I hear voices in the apartment.

"Newbolt, you better not be doing the horizontal hula!" I instantly recognise Brody's voice and the raucous laughter of the other boys. "Although, he's entitled to some birthday pussy!"

Sam laughs.

"Come out, come out wherever you are, Newbolt, we need to give your birthday beatings!" Jax shouts. Sam rolls his eyes, kisses me on the end of my nose, and gets up.

"I'll be right back, angel."

Sam walks out into the apartment stark bollock naked.

"Fuck me, dude, put your cock away!" Brody yells.

"Excuse me, but you fuckers are intruding in *our* apartment" I hear Sam say but I can tell he is holding back his laughter.

"Touché!"

I quickly pull on some clothes, tie my hair up in a loose knot, and walk barefoot into the kitchen where Jax and Brody are sitting on the worktop. Lucas is sitting at the table leaning on his elbows, and Sam is nowhere to be seen.

"You need to sort your man out, darlin', I'm going to need fucking therapy after that!"

I laugh. Brody jumps off the worktop and lifts me into his arms; he pulls me in for a bear hug. I am still struggling to get used to the friendly, affectionate side of Brody Hart. Over Brody's shoulder, I see a look pass between Jax and Lucas. The look on Jax's face is bemused and Lucas shakes his head with an adorable smirk on his face.

"Am I going to have to kick your arse for having your hands all over my woman, Brody?" Sam jokes and Brody pulls away from our embrace.

"Happy birthday, you old fucker!" Jax breaks the silence. He leaps off the worktop and gives Sam a manly hug.

I love the brotherly banter between the boys. I can see what Amy was talking about when she said the boys have taken me under their wing and have accepted me as one of their own. Our baby is going to have an extended family, consisting of three doting uncles in Brody, Jax, and Lucas.

Throughout the day, our apartment is like Piccadilly Circus with visitors coming to wish Sam a happy birthday. Soon the evening rolls around and we are getting ready to go to Sam's parents for his birthday dinner. A part of me is really looking forward to seeing how our families interact with each other, and another part of me is really nervous. I am dressed in a red prom style dress with black skulls covered in diamantes. It matches my quirky style and still makes me look lady like. The neckline accentuates my breasts, but the cut of the dress doesn't draw attention to my growing bump, which is good because tonight is the night we have decided to announce the pregnancy. My hair is in loose tousled waves and I have a red rose in my hair. I am putting the finishing touches to my make-up in the mirror when Sam comes up behind me. He looks so handsome in his black suit, white shirt, with a loose black tie and black biker boots. His hair is his usual messy spiky style, and his green eyes are glittering with excitement. He nuzzles my neck and snakes his arms around my waist.

"Are you ready yet, angel?"

I chuckle.

"I'd be ready a lot faster if you weren't being so distracting in that suit."

He cocks his pierced eyebrow and smiles, temporarily disarming me.

"Ah, so you like the suit then, angel?" he rasps. I blot my lipstick and spin around in his arms.

"If you carry on looking at me like that, baby, we won't be leaving here tonight and I'm sure your mum won't be too pleased about that."

He kisses me on my forehead. "You look absolutely breath-taking, angel." He kneels down and rests his cheek against my stomach. "Your mummy looks beautiful, boo."

I love seeing this tender side of Sam, it melts my heart.

"Boo?"

He plants a gentle kiss on my bump and gets to his feet. He takes my hand and leads me out into the living room.

"Yeah, what else are we going to call him or her?"

"Boo sounds perfect."

"Boo it is then."

We leave the apartment and go down to the parking garage. Cole and Amy are waiting for us. Cole is dressed in a black pinstripe suit, black shirt open at the collar, and black shoes. He looks handsome; Amy's slender figure compliments his muscular frame. She is wearing a silver strapless dress which make her legs look like they go on forever, silver and white Jimmy Choo shoes with a black bow on the front, and her hair in a neat, sleek up-do.

"Peyton, you look gorgeous, hon." She kisses me on both cheeks.

"So do you, Amy, you look stunning, I look like a small beached whale next to you."

She takes my arm and rolls her eyes. "Please, I've seen more fat on a butcher's pencil. Tell her she looks beautiful, Cole, sweetie."

Cole smiles brightly. "You look wonderful, Peyton."

He kisses my hand, and I blush. We all climb into Sam's Porsche Cayenne 4x4, Sam and Cole in the front, Amy and me in the back. The journey to Sam's parents' house in Kent goes by quickly as we all chat easily in the car. As we pull into Lori and Marlowe's driveway, I notice the gravel path lined with small tea lights. We climb out of the car and Sam takes my hand.

"I'm sorry, my mum has a thing for all things theatrical," he whispers. The door opens and Lori steps out; she looks like a movie star. Her short hair is styled perfectly, and she is wearing a gold dress with matching accessories. The look suits her and makes her look younger than her years.

"Happy birthday, my darling boy," she croons as she kisses him on the cheek and he wraps her in his arms.

"Thanks, Mum."

She pulls away from their embrace and opens her arms.

"Peyton, sweetie, you look fabulous," she says in her familiar American drawl, which I have become accustomed to.

"So do you, Lori, you look amazing."

She laughs. "This old thing, oh please!" She rolls her eyes and chuckles softly. "Cole, Amy! Come, come inside," she says enthusiastically. She greets Cole and Amy, we all step inside.

"Happy birthday, son." Marlowe hugs Sam and the similarity between the two of them never fails to amaze me. "Peyton, you get more stunning every time I see you."

He kisses my hand, and over Marlowe's shoulder, I see Ruby. I am surprised to see her. *What could Ruby be doing here?* Last I heard, her and Jax weren't on the best of terms.

I catch her gaze and she shrieks, "Peyton!"

She rushes towards me and envelopes me in her arms as if we haven't seen each other in years.

"Rubes! What are you doing here, babe?"

I am actually happy and relieved that she is here; I could do with some back-up.

"Jax and I are seeing each other again, exclusively! Who knew?" she says dramatically, and I chuckle softly.

"You're looking amazing, babe."

She looks me up and down, taking me in. "Thanks, so do you, sweetie."

She can throw any old thing on and look stunning. She is wearing a little black dress with a skinny silver belt round her waist. She is wearing black Christian Laboutin shoes and her long black hair is flowing like a cascade down her back.

"The flat seems so empty without you in it, babe," she pouts, and I roll my eyes.

"We knew this was going to happen eventually, sweetie."

She takes a sip of her champagne.

"Yeah, but I didn't expect it to happen so soon."

I take her hand. "I love you, Rubes, you're welcome at ours anytime, babe, you know that."

She nods and Jax comes up behind her. He wraps his arm around her waist and nuzzles her neck.

"So you told her then, sweets?"

Ruby nods. Her and Jax stare dreamily at each other. I have never seen her this happy with a man in all the years I have known her, love looks good on her. I'm so happy for her and Jax; they will be good for each other. I turn and see my mum, dad, Dexter, Grace, Eden, and Jonah walk into the large open living space.

"Darling," my mum shrieks and throws her arms around me. I am so happy to see my family; it feels like it has been ages since I last saw them all.

"God I've missed you, Mum."

She squeezes me tight. "We've missed you too, sweetie, so much." She kisses me on the cheek. "Now, where's that handsome rock star of yours?"

I look around the room, and it is as if Sam and I are drawn together like two magnets. His gaze locks on mine, he casually walks over to me with a beer in his hand and a glass of orange juice in his other hand. I take it from him and he kisses my forehead.

"Sophia," he rasps, and my mum practically melts at his feet. I am glad it isn't just me that has that reaction to him. My dad hugs me and tells me how happy he is to see me when Dexter taps my shoulder.

"Sis." He envelopes me in his arms and lifts me off the floor. "It's so good to see you."

I laugh. "You too, Dex."

He sets me down on the ground and narrows his eyes at me. "You look different, sis."

Grace hits Dexter playfully.

"Leave your sister alone, Dex, she looks gorgeous as always. I love your dress!" she says in a singsong voice and hugs me.

"It's been forever, we need to set up a meeting to get you fitted for your bridesmaid dress, and we could make a day of it."

I am actually looking forward to Dexter and Grace's wedding, honoured that I have been asked to be a bridesmaid. Dexter rolls his eyes, and it's my turn to hit him on the arm.

"What?" He feigns innocence and we both laugh.

As the evening progresses the conversation is flowing easily, my parents and Sam's parents are getting on famously, much to my relief. Milo, Seth, Brody, Lucas, Willow, Brandon, Elijah, J.D., Savannah, and Callum all join the party. Even though I am less than happy to see Savannah, Callum, and J.D., I feel good for the first time in a long time and I am happy. I am chatting to Amy and Ruby when Sam comes to my side, wrapping his muscled arm around my waist.

"Are you ready to make our announcement official, angel?" he whispers so only I can hear him, and I worry my lip between my teeth nervously. "Don't be nervous, angel, it will be OK, I promise."

He winks reassuringly and kisses me gently on the lips. He taps his glass and clears his throat.

"Excuse me, could we get everyone's attention, please?"

Sam is interrupted by the arrival of Seb.

"I'm so sorry, I'm late," he says, and I see Willow's mouth drop open from the corner of my eye. I chuckle. Sam shakes Seb's hand and runs his hand through his hair.

"Erm, yeah, where was I? First, I want to thank everyone for coming to celebrate the birthday that shall remain numberless." He smirks, and the room erupts with laughter. "Also, Peyton and I wanted to wait until tonight to make our little announcement official. *Christ,* I'm no good at this speech stuff ... We're having a baby."

There are a few audible gasps and then a rapturous round of applause. Our friends and families, happy to be expecting a new addition to the family, enthusiastically congratulate us all. I feel blessed and relieved to have our news out in the open. My sister stands behind me wearing a white dress with a skinny red belt around her waist, sipping champagne.

"Wow, who would have thought, my little sister knocked up by a rock star?" she sneers rather loudly, and I roll my eyes. *Typical Eden.*

"Can't you just suck it up and be happy for us, Eden?" I snap, and she cocks her perfectly-plucked eyebrow.

"Don't you understand? You have my life! You have the life I want so badly! You're with a gorgeous rock star who quite clearly worships the ground you walk on and I'm left with ..."

She gestures over her shoulder where her fiancé Jonah is standing with a bored look on his face. His sandy blonde hair is slicked back, and he is wearing a tan roll neck jumper and dark-blue jeans, his attempt at looking casual. I have only ever seen Jonah wear perfectly-tailored Saville Row suits.

"He doesn't even want to be here, thinks this rock star nonsense is beneath him," she mimics his upper crust English accent, and I can't help but feel sorry for her. "At least you got out of Brighton and made a life for yourself."

I brush her arm.

"Yeah and jumped from one failed relationship to another. I'm standing in my current boyfriend's parents' house with my ex and the woman he cheated on me with."

We both laugh.

"OK, you win on that one, but you're in your dream job and you're doing fantastic."

Wow! Who kidnapped my sister and replaced her with a clone!

"Who are you and what have you done with my sister?"

She laughs. "I know I've been a bitch to you and Dex for years and I can't apologise enough, Peyton. I'm sorry; I love you so much, for putting up with my shit for so long."

We hug tightly, and with that hug, the past few years of us being at each other's throats fade into insignificance.

We all assemble around the table for a three-course meal of mushrooms on ciabatta toast, pie and mash, and banoffee pie, all of Sam's favourite foods. I am sat between Sam and Seb. Sam chooses to eat one-handed, refusing to let go of my hand. I observe everyone, and the table is alive with the cacophony of animated conversation. Marlowe, Milo, and Seth have my dad and Dexter in stitches with their stories. My mum, Grace, Amy, and Lori are locked in a fashion debate. Lucas and Brody are discussing music with Brandon, Elijah, J.D., and Cole. Jax and Ruby are fawning romantically over each other, it is sweet to watch. Eden and Jonah are having an awkward whispered argument; Savannah is shamelessly feeling Callum up across the table in a lame attempt to evoke a reaction from me. Needless to say, it isn't working, and Callum's face is beet red. Willow is staring dreamy-eyed at Seb from across the table and I catch him staring back at her.

I nudge Seb and whisper. "Someone's got the hots for you, babe."

Seb chuckles throatily and shrugs as he takes a sip of his beer.

"She is cute."

I laugh. "You should go for it, honey, you deserve to be happy. She's a smart girl, you could do worse." I wink as I get up from the table.

"Excuse me, I need to use the bathroom, the trouble with being pregnant I need to pee all the time!"

Everyone laughs, and I leave the table. I use the bathroom and as I come out, Callum is leaning against the wall waiting for me; I get a feeling a déjà vu.

"Peyton."

I go to walk around him, and he grabs my arm.

"I've got nothing to say to you, Callum; we've said all we need to, time and time again."

"So you're pregnant? I'd like to congratulate you, but I don't like it, baby cakes, not one fucking bit."

I snatch my arm away from him.

"The last time I checked it has fuck all to do with you and stop calling me baby cakes!" I snap.

"It should be me; you should be carrying *my* baby!" he blurts out and I am taken aback.

Where the fuck did that come from? I quickly recover from the shock of his statement.

"Don't you dare! You had your fucking chance, Callum, but you cheated on me with that ... that fucking whore!" I lower my voice and he smirks.

"Wow, you always were one not to beat around the bush, baby cakes."

"And that was a dick move, by the way, letting her practically wank you off under the table just to get a reaction out of me. Nice, Callum, really fucking grown up."

He hangs his head. "I had nothing to do with that, Peyton, I swear."

I shake my head. *Un-be-fucking-lievable.*

"I fucked up, I know, babe, and I've said I'm sorry countless times, I don't know how many more times I can say it. But you and Newbolt, I fucking *despise* him, Peyton. He's going to hurt you I know him; he walks around with his stupid rock star swagger thinking he is God's gift to women."

I smirk at Callum and he frowns.

"You always were the jealous type, Callum."

"Because you deserve so much better than that prick, baby cakes."

I roll my eyes. "Like you, you mean?"

He tucks a strand of hair behind my ear, and I hear footsteps approaching.

"Get your hands off her, you filthy fucking worm!" Ruby's voice cuts through the silence and she steps behind him.

"I suggest you get the fuck away from her, now." She raises her voice and Brody storms up the stairs towards Callum, grabbing his arm.

"So you're the famous fucking ex?" Brody retorts and regards Callum with a look of pure disgust on his face. "I've got this, babe, take Peyton downstairs and make sure we're not disturbed. Callum and I need to have a little chat, man to man."

Brody winks at me, and I smile warmly at his concern. I am glad we have become close friends; I love all the boys like brothers. Ruby takes my arm and leads me downstairs. The party has spread out onto the outdoor deck area, it is relaxed, and people are still chatting easily as if they have known each other for years. Ruby finds us some spare seats and we sit down.

"What the fuck was that all about, babe?"

I shake my head. "Callum being Callum, he just can't leave it alone."

She takes my hand. "He's just jealous because you've quite clearly moved on and he is stuck dealing with his mistake, fuck him."

We both laugh, and she gets up. "I'll get us some drinks. Don't go anywhere, I'll be right back."

As Ruby vacates her seat, J.D joins me. *Great.*

"Peyton," he snarls.

"What the fuck do you want, J.D?" I snap. I am so not in the mood for his bullshit tonight. He cocks his eyebrow.

"I wanted to congratulate you," he leans in and whispers in my ear. To the observer he is just leaning in to kiss me on the cheek, but he whispers, "Don't think I can't see what you're doing, I know you're trapping him."

What the fuck? I am getting sick and tired of his stupid mind games.

"How the fuck did you work that one out? I didn't force him to make me pregnant, it just happened. I'm getting sick of your twisted fucking mind games, J.D. When are you going to get it into your thick head that Sam and me are for keeps?"

He is about to reply when I see Sam approach and it is as if someone has turned on a switch with J.D. One minute he is dripping poison in my ear the next he is being sickly sweet. He is a good actor and his performance is Oscar worthy.

"Congratulations, darling, I am so happy for you and Sam."

He smiles a little too brightly. He gets up and Sam takes his place at my side.

"I've been aching to get you all to myself all night, angel," he rasps and puts his arm around me. I rest my head on his shoulder.

"You look amazing in that dress, babe; I can't wait to strip you out of it later." I laugh, and Sam nuzzles my neck. "God, I fucking love you, angel," he slurs, and his smile disarms me.

"Are you drunk, Mr. Newbolt?" I raise my eyebrows and he bites his lip in a boyish way.

"Maybe just a little tiny bit."

He closes one eye and chuckles to himself. Marlowe approaches and smiles warmly at both of us.

"Would you mind if I borrowed my son for a moment, Peyton?"

I shake my head. "No, of course not, go ahead, he's all yours."

Sam gets to his feet and leans in to kiss me.

"I'll be right back, angel." He winks and leaves with Marlowe.

I get to my feet and go back inside the large living space. Out of the corner of my eye, I see Seb and Willow looking cosy in the corner of the room; he is standing close to her, his large frame towering over her tiny one. I hear the deep rumble of his laugh and her soft chuckle. I almost feel like I am intruding on an intimate moment, but I can't tear my eyes away. He reaches a tattooed arm out to her, tucking a strand of her hair away from her face then he leans down and kisses her on the lips. I am so happy that Seb followed my advice. Hhe deserves to be happy, and he is such a kind, sweet, gentle, loyal, and genuine man.

When I finally tear my eyes away from Seb and Willow, I see Brody and Callum walking down the stairs. Brody whispers to Callum, and Callum looks as if he has seen a ghost. He shakes Brody's hand robotically and rushes off sheepishly. I narrow my eyes at Brody and approach him. He has his hands tucked casually in his pockets and a cocky grin plastered all over his face.

"What did you say to him, Brody?"

Brody feigns innocence and shrugs. "Nothing whatsoever, babe, we just had a nice friendly man to man chat."

Something in the way he looks at me tells me that is far from the truth. He pulls me in for a hug.

"Don't worry, let's just say he won't be bothering you again, babe." He winks and pulls away from our embrace. "I wanted to congratulate you and Sam on the baby; you're so good for each other. I wanted to take this opportunity to apologise for the way I reacted in the beginning, the night of the album launch. I was in a bad place, I-I lose my shit when I'm on drugs. I say stuff I don't mean, I do stuff I regret. That night on the tour bus was probably one of the best nights I have had in a long time, I felt like I was myself again. You make me that way, Peyton, I can be myself around you, and I'll always be grateful to you for that. I know I'm no good, I lead people astray, but you make me want to be better. Let's be clear I-I don't fancy you or anything and I definitely don't want to get into your pants. You're the first girl I've ever wanted to *just* be friends with and not fuck!"

My eyes glaze over at Brody's words, and it warms my heart to think that I make him want to be a better person.

"The other boys don't know what happened on the bus that night between us. I haven't told them and I'm grateful that you didn't, either. That night felt pure and I saw clearly for the first time ever. I don't want to be that man anymore, Peyton. I don't want to constantly be off my face, shagging random birds and waking up wondering how the fuck they got in my bed. You see me; I mean you really see *me*, the man I am in here." He puts his hand to his chest and I can see it in his face that he is struggling so I brush his arm to reassure him. "I was such a prick to you in the beginning and I'll never be able to apologise enough for that but you're a close friend, Peyton, you're family to me now, to us all, you're one of us. You brought Sam back to life, you made him whole again."

I am actually crying now, and I curse my pregnancy hormones to hell for making me react so strongly. I will always be grateful for that night on the bus with Brody because it showed me a different side of him and made me see him in a completely new light. Brody pulls me in for a massive bear hug.

"I can't wait to be an uncle," he says against my shoulder and I chuckle softly. I pull away from him and give him a watery smile.

"This baby is going to be so spoilt!"

He strokes my stomach gently. "Definitely. Hey, kid, I'm your uncle Brody, I can't wait to meet you."

He laughs in a childlike way, and I can't help but wonder what sort of childhood Brody had. I know his mum died of a heroin overdose because Sam told me, but I never really found out the whole story. I figure now is a good a time as any to probe further because he seems in a talkative mood.

"Brody?"

His hand is still on my stomach.

"Hmm?"

"What happened after your mum died?"

He moves his hand and looks at me. His face filled with something that resembles sorrow and regret.

"That's a story for another time, babe."

He winks and my mum approaches, ending our conversation.

"Sweetie?"

Brody smiles. "I'll catch you later, Peyton."

He winks at me and casually saunters off. My mum looks puzzled.

"What was that all about?"

I shake my head.

"Nothing, mum, that's Brody, he's the guitarist in Sam's band."

She nods and eyes the length of my body.

"Why didn't you tell us sooner that you were pregnant with Sam's baby?"

I hang my head actually feeling ashamed that I kept the baby secret for so long.

"I-I was in a bad place, Mum. I was certain he was going to leave me once he found out, so I kept putting it off."

Her face is filled with concern and she hugs me.

"Oh, my darling girl, not every man is like Callum. Surely you can see that now?"

I nod, willing myself not to cry again.

"I was terrified he'd run, but he's over the moon. I feel so ashamed that I kept it from him. I'm sorry we didn't tell you sooner, we wanted to wait for the right moment, tell everyone together."

She smiles brightly.

"I understand, sweetie. I'm so happy I'm going to be a grandmother, but I want to be Nana not Granny. Granny makes me sound old!" We both laugh, and she kisses me on the cheek. "Your father and I are going to go back to the hotel soon."

"Thank you so much for coming, Mum, I miss you." I see her lip tremble. "Don't start crying, Mum, please, you'll set me off."

"I'm so proud of you, my darling; you're making your father and me grandparents. It looks like I'm going to have to buy another hat for your wedding."

I roll my eyes. "I'll call you tomorrow, Mum, I promise."

She hugs me and kisses me on the cheek. "Love you, Peyton."

I smile. "I love you too, Mum."

She pulls away and leaves me standing in Lori and Marlowe's living room. For the first time in a long time, I am actually genuinely happy and looking forward to the future.

15

Peyton

The next morning, I wake to the sound of Sam vomiting in the bathroom. Cole had driven us home around two AM this morning and Sam was completely wasted. I am so glad he had a good time, and I have to say, he makes an adorable drunk! Cole and the boys had put him to bed and I was grateful for the help.

Today is the day we leave for the boys' ten-year anniversary gig in Las Vegas, the city of Sin. I have only ever seen Vegas on T.V and I am curious to know what it is actually like. I have sorted cover for the shop and I know I have left it in the capable hands of Seb, Parker, and Harley while I am gone. I did mine and some of Sam's packing when we got home this morning. I feel rested and ready for our ten-hour flight on the boy's private jet. I pull on Sam's t-shirt and walk to the bathroom. Sam is hugging the toilet, a term that Ruby and I used to call *'worshipping at the porcelain throne and praying to the porcelain God'.*

"Baby, are you OK?"

He groans and covers his eyes with his hands.

"Fuck me, angel, I'm hungover to shit. I'm never drinking ever again."

I laugh, and I can't recall the number of times I have said the exact same phrase when I am suffering from a killer hangover.

Two hours later, Sam and I are at the airport, and after being almost mobbed by a crowd of Rancid Vengeance fans, we are ready to board our flight to Vegas. Sam is wearing a black hoodie, dark-blue jeans, biker boots, a black beanie hat and aviator sunglasses—the epitome of a rock star. As we walk to the boys' private jet, the sight in front of me takes me aback. The aeroplane is sleek and black from the outside with the band logo emblazoned on the side and the name 'Air Vengeance' in large silver lettering; it looks extremely impressive.

As we step on board, I am in awe of what I see. The interior of the jet resembles a large living room. It is decorated in masculine black, white, and gunmetal grey tones with matching furniture and accessories. It has two, large, dark-grey sofas opposite each other on either side of the plane, with a large oblong shaped table in front of it, which seems to be bolted to the floor. There is a large flat screen T.V mounted on the wall, four black leather recliners in a line towards the front of the plane. As I move further inside, I am greeted with a small bathroom complete with modern chrome and black power shower cubicle, a toilet, and a small square glass sink. There is a bedroom with a large double bed and a black bedside table with three drawers underneath. Sam comes behind me and wraps his arms around my waist.

"So what do you think then, angel? Do you approve of our extravagant purchases?" He smirks. *Smart arse.*

"I most definitely approve, baby, this is amazing."

His stubble tickles as he nuzzles my neck. "Glad you like it, babe, we're taking off in the next ten minutes, it takes ten hours to get to Vegas. They're eight hours behind, so it should still be early when we get there."

I yawn and Sam chuckles softly.

"Tired, angel?" I nod. "Hold on until take off and you can sleep for a while? How does that sound?"

"Perfect."

He kisses me tenderly on the lips, and we settle in for take-off. Soon after we are in the air, the seatbelt signs are turned off and Sam reaches over me to unclip my seatbelt.

"Come on, angel; let me take you to bed."

He pulls me to my feet and I stumble into his hard chest. He catches me before I fall and our eyes lock.

"I need you to fuck me, Sam," I whisper seductively in his ear and he cocks his pierced eyebrow.

"Do you fancy joining the mile-high club then, angel?" he rasps, and I nod.

I feel my pussy clench with white-hot lust at his words. He pulls me towards the bedroom and the other boys wolf whistle and cheer as we walk past them. Sam flips them the bird and closes the door behind us. His green eyes are hooded and blazing with pure carnal lust. He backs me towards the wall and traps me with his hands on either side of my head.

"Sam," I whisper, and he lifts my leg, wrapping it around his waist.

"Do you want me to fuck you hard and fast or slow and gentle?"

I feel so desperate for him to take me, I am panting with desire and he hasn't even touched me.

"Hard and fast, Sam, please."

I bite my lip and he reaches down, making me release my lip from my teeth.

"Patience, angel," he says huskily, and I feel liquid heat begin to pool between my legs. He lifts me up effortlessly in his arms. "Wrap those gorgeous legs around my waist, baby."

I do as he says, and he crashes his lips on mine. A moan escapes as he moves fluidly across the room and drops me gently on the bed. He climbs on top of me and unbuckles his belt. I arch my back up off the bed, desperate for my release. He begins to remove my clothes carefully until I am lying naked underneath him. He takes off his belt, wraps it around my wrists, and fastens me to the metal bed frame. He unzips his jeans, admiring his handiwork.

"Tell me if it's too much, angel, and I'll stop."

I nod and am so turned on. He strips until he is gloriously naked, and I lick my lips at the sight of his taut, sculpted muscles. He reminds me of a Greek god with his perfect statuesque body. He begins to kiss a trail down my body from my breasts to my swollen stomach and skips over the part I want him to touch the most.

"Sam."

He blows cool air on my pussy and I writhe beneath him.

"Keep still, angel, I'll take care of you." He moves lower and his velvet tongue sweeps up my slit. "Mmm, you taste so fucking sweet." He breathes against me and his stubble tickles my inner thigh. "Tell me what you need, angel."

"You, I need you, Sam, I want you to fuck me hard and fast."

He chuckles softly. "I love it when you talk dirty to me, angel."

He strokes his already erect cock and positions the head against my soaking wet opening and pushes roughly into me. I gasp at the feeling of him filling me to the hilt. He pistons in and out, driving deeper with each thrust.

"Oh, God, Sam. Harder. Fuck me harder," I cry out.

"*Jesus,* angel, you're going to be the death of me."

He lifts my legs over his shoulders, and I feel him so deep inside me, hitting my g-spot with each hard drive.

"Oh, Sam."

He increases his hard thrusts.

"Tell me you like feeling my cock deep inside you."

I bite my lip.

"Oh, God, I love feeling your hard cock inside me, fuck me harder." I see a thin sheen of sweat across Sam's forehead. "What's wrong, rock star, can't keep up the pace?" I tease.

He cocks his pierced eyebrow, slowing his pace. "Never underestimate me, angel, I can go all night."

He winks, leaning down to unbuckle his belt holding my wrists prisoner. He frees my hands and scoops me up from the bed, as he moves across the room pressing my back against the wall. He rams his cock deep inside me, pushing me further up the wall, creating a delicious friction. He nuzzles my neck and nips a trail with his teeth down to my collarbone.

"Sam, please, I need you, I need you to make me come!"

He increases his thrusts again and I am so close to finding my release.

"*Fuck me,* angel, I'm so fucking close."

He pistons in and out one final time and we both find our release at the same time. He growls, and I cry out, "Fuck, Sam."

He stills for a moment, coming down from his orgasm.

"Still think I can't keep up the pace, angel?" he rasps, and I chuckle mischievously.

"I never doubted you, babe."

He nips my sensitive nipple with his teeth.

"You little minx!"

He laughs and moves across the room with me in his arms. He pulls out of me and lays me down on the bed. He climbs in beside me and shifts me, so I am tucked under his arm. I lay my head on his chest and he lazily strokes my hair. Soon, I am a slave to sleep.

I am woken to Sam's soft raspy voice whispering in my ear, "Angel."

I look sleepily at him and smile.

"There's my girl, we're about to land in Vegas."

I stretch out and I feel deliciously sore after our marathon sex session.

"I didn't realise how long I'd been asleep."

He tucks a strand of hair behind my ear.

"It's OK, angel, you look so peaceful when you're asleep I didn't want to disturb you."

I get up, pull on my clothes, and run a brush through my hair. Sam wraps his arms around my waist, stroking my stomach gently. He moves my hair over my shoulder, giving him access to my bare neck, and he kisses me softly.

"God, you're beautiful, to think you've got a part of me growing inside you, it's amazing."

I turn around in his arms and wrap my arms around him, needing to feel as close as possible to the man I love.

"We're going to be one big dysfunctional family," I joke and Sam laughs.

"Three rock star uncles and a rock star granddad, what more could a kid ask for?"

Our moment is interrupted by a voice coming through the speaker system.

"Ladies and Gentlemen, as we have commenced our final descent into North Las Vegas airport, would you kindly return to your seats, fasten your seat belts, and return your seat to the fully upright position. Please ensure that your tables are stowed, all personal items and articles of hand luggage are stored securely in the overhead lockers or under the seat in front of you, and that no items are obstructing the exits. After landing, please remain seated with seat-belts fastened until the aircraft has come to a halt and the Captain has switched off the seat-belt signs."

We go out into the main living area of the aeroplane and take our seats as instructed as we begin our descent into Las Vegas.

After we land, we all exit the aeroplane, and as I step off I am hit with a wall of heat from the blazing sun. There is a black limo waiting for us on the tarmac of the local private airport. Sam, me, Jax, Brody, Lucas, and J.D. all step into the spacious black limo which is driven by a private chauffeur. Cole gets into the front passenger seat with the driver and by the way they are talking, they know each other. Sam wraps his arm around me, takes off his beanie hat, runs his hand through his hair raven-black hair, and pulls his sunglasses up on top of his head.

"I can't wait for you to see my place, Peyton," Lucas says excitedly, and I smile at his animated enthusiasm.

I look to Sam and he leans to whisper in my ear, "When we come to Vegas, Lucas always insists that we stay at his house instead of a hotel. It's more private, and he grew up here."

I nod at Sam's clarification and we begin our journey to Lucas' house.

Some time passes, and the car has pulled to a stop. We all exit the limo and we have entered the circular driveway through a set of black wrought-iron gates. There is a large water fountain in the middle and I am in awe of the building in front of me. From the outside, the house is brown brick and looks to be on two levels. Lucas opens the white, double front doors and punches in a code to disarm the beeping alarm system. We step into an open foyer with a dark wooden floor throughout. There are a series of abstract art paintings framed and hung on the walls. The boys are chatting and laughing with each other, they seem to be in good spirits.

"Do you guys want some coffee? I can fix up some breakfast if you're hungry," Lucas says.

All the boys nod and follow Lucas through the house. I am informed that the house is a four-bedroom property, with three bathrooms, a double, and a single garage. There is a large elaborate staircase leading to the second storey of the house. The house is decorated in light taupe, cream, and warm brown tones. It is warm and inviting.

"Make yourselves at home. I can get someone to bring your luggage up to your rooms, the kitchen should be stocked up on food and beer so we're all good to go."

Lucas chuckles, and the boys all cheer. The boys disappear off upstairs, Sam included, and I am left to explore the house. The view from the floor to ceiling kitchen windows is breath-taking. The house looks out onto its very own swimming pool and miniature golf course. I move closer to the window and admire the view in front of me.

"I inherited this house from my parents. I grew up here, but you already knew that, right?" Lucas' voice startles me, and I jump at the sound of his American drawl. "I'm sorry, honey; I didn't mean to scare you."

He strides towards me and stops when he reaches me. He tucks his hands in the pockets of a loose pair of combat shorts.

"My parents were killed, my dad escaped from prison, he raped and murdered my mum. He murdered and brutally beat my step-dad to death with a baseball bat. That's the reason I moved to the UK. I was seven years old."

My heart clenches at the thought of Lucas as a little boy, scared and in a country he wasn't familiar with.

"Don't feel sorry for me, Peyton, my childhood was awesome after I moved to London. I moved in with my Aunt Ava and my Uncle Kyle, they adopted me as their own. I was loved. I grew up seeing my cousins as the brothers and sisters I never had. Uncle Kyle is a movie director and the actors that came to our house for BBQ and grill nights were just regular Johnny, Leo, Brad and Sam. At school I was the weird kid with the weird accent until Sam, Jax, and Brody took me under their wing."

He smiles a dazzling smile at the thought.

"Coming here, having them here, erases the bad memories and replaces them with happy ones. I've renovated the whole house and added to the original property since I've been in the band."

I turn around to face him and look at him. He hangs his head and his face looks so conflicted.

"That night on the tour bus, the night J.D. had his filthy God damn fucking hands on you—" He closes his eyes and clenches his fists. "—it brought back memories from all those years ago. I saw my mum silently pleading with me to help her while he was on top of her. I was hiding in the laundry bin, I was frozen, fucking terrified. If he knew I was there, he'd kill me too."

He wipes away a tear that has escaped from the corner of his eye, and I take his hand in mine.

"There was nothing you could have done. You were just a kid, you can't blame yourself, babe," I try to reassure him.

"I know there was nothing I could have done; believe me, I've been through enough therapy over the years. But I felt so helpless, so fucking useless. She was my mom, Peyton, the woman who gave birth to me, and I couldn't save her," he says through clenched teeth and I feel privileged that he has chosen to open up to me. I move closer to him and throw my arms around his neck, hugging him tightly to me. He reciprocates the embrace and buries his face in my hair.

"Thank you," he whispers.

"Don't thank me, babe, I'll always be here to listen any time day or night."

Someone clears their throat behind us.

"Sorry, I didn't-didn't mean to interrupt you," an unfamiliar female's voice interrupts our moment.

"It's all good, Kendall, everything's awesome."

I hear heels clicking across the floor.

"I didn't know you were seeing anyone, Luke," she drawls in an American accent.

Lucas pulls away from our embrace and turns around to her. She is extremely beautiful with short blonde hair, violet eyes, and she is tall, tanned and slender. She is wearing a white all-in-one playsuit that emphasises her long tanned legs.

"I'm not. This is Peyton, she is Sam's girl."

She nods and smiles a fake smile.

"Oh, I see. So you guys like pass her around? A live-in groupie? Nice!"

She looks me up and down.

"Who the fuck do you think you are?" I spit out and Lucas looks at me.

"I got this, Peyton." He winks then goes over to her and grabs her wrist. "You're going to fucking apologise for that now, Kendall. I don't take kindly to people insulting my family."

My heart swells at the prospect of being welcomed into the Rancid Vengeance family so openly. She looks up at him, and I observe the exchange between the two of them. There is definitely a history there.

"Apologise now," he says sternly.

"I'm sorry." She rolls her eyes and snatches her hand away from him. "Fucking let go of me you prick! We need to talk, Luke."

He scrubs his hand down his face.

"*Shit!* I have to take care of this, Peyton. I'll see you later?" I nod, and he kisses me on the cheek. "Thanks, for listening, honey, I really appreciate it," he whispers and leaves me standing in the kitchen wondering what the fuck just happened. I am curious at the history and clear animosity between Lucas and Kendall.

"So, you had the unfortunate privilege of meeting Queen Bitch, I see?" Brody chuckles and I spin around. Brody is leaning against the doorway with his arms folded.

"Something like that, who the fuck is she?"

He strides towards me and hops up to sit on the worktop. He opens the cupboard and takes out an unopened jar of Nutella. He unscrews the lid and starts digging his finger into it.

"That's Kendall Savage, she is Lucas' ex. They had a bad break up. She was pregnant with his baby, and her parents forced her to get rid of it. They're billionaires, Lord and Lady Savage of some la-de-da American estate. Sounds quite far-fetched I know, but those Americans are definitely like a completely new breed; it's fucking shocking. Our British scandals are nothing compared to theirs," Brody explains while digging his finger into the Nutella jar and licking it clean.

Our conversation is brought to an abrupt halt by J.D. entering the room followed by Jax and Sam. Sam strides across the room and pulls me close to his side. He nuzzles my neck.

"I missed you, angel." He has freshly showered; his hair is still damp, and he smells so good. "Lucas made sure we got the best room in the house."

I smile, I am so happy and content with life. It feels so good, I have a job I love, a man I adore with everything I am, my large extended family are amazing, and I am expecting a baby. Life is perfect for once and it's everything I wished for and more.

J.D's voice interrupts my thoughts, "Right, boys, where the fuck is Lucas?"

Brody pauses and smirks. "Kendall showed up, she said she needed to talk to him." Brody air quotes with his hands and J.D rolls his eyes.

"That fucking crazy woman, every time we come here." He storms out of the kitchen. "Lucas! Get your fucking arse in the kitchen now!" he bellows.

Sam looks from Brody to Jax and shakes his head.

"What's going on, babe?"

Sam kisses my forehead.

"Nothing you need to worry about, angel, let's just enjoy being here together."

He smiles, but it doesn't reach his eyes and I start to wonder what is really going on. A few minutes of silence passes, and Lucas walks in the kitchen with scratches down his face. I go to pull away from Sam and he digs his fingers in my hip.

"Leave it, angel," Sam whispers. I look at Lucas and he winks in a silent reassurance.

"Right, now you're all together; I'd like to take this opportunity to welcome you all to Las Vegas, the city of Sin. Whatever happens in Vegas stays in Vegas, apart from STDs, that shit will follow you anywhere." J.D laughs at his own joke. "The gig tonight is at The Mandalay Bay Events Centre. It's your ten-year anniversary gig, so I want you all to give the fucking performances of your lives. You're performing to twelve thousand fans, you're doing some press junkets, and a photo shoot before the gig so you all need to be on top form, that includes you, Brody."

Brody salutes at J.D and we both smirk at each other.

"Security is going to be tight at the venue and each of you has been assigned a personal body guard. The gig starts at eight p.m. and the limo is picking us up at six forty-five sharp. Until then, the rest of the day is yours. That's all for today, boys."

Brody jumps off the worktop. "Class dismissed!"

We all laugh. J.D strides out of the room, followed by Lucas and Brody.

"I'm going to call Ruby," Jax says and he disappears, leaving Sam and me alone in the kitchen.

"So, what do my two favourite people want to do while we're in Vegas?" Sam smiles.

"I'll be happy to do whatever as long as I'm with you, babe." I smile and snuggle closer to him.

"Well, I plan on getting you naked before the gig, so we can do whatever you want to, angel." He strokes my stomach softly. "Go and grab a shower, get changed, and I'll meet you back down here in say an hour?"

I nod, and he smiles his dazzling smile. He kisses me gently on the lips, my raging hormones take over and I deepen the kiss, wanting nothing more than for him to be buried deep inside me.

"Angel," he rasps, and I stroke his growing erection through his ripped, faded denim shorts.

"Take me to bed Sam," I whisper seductively.

"Angel, stop, as much as I'd love nothing more than to fuck you right here, there's something I need to show you."

I try not to pout at his rejection.

"I promise I'll make it up to you later, angel, multiple orgasms and I'll make you scream so loud the whole neighbourhood will know my name," he says huskily, and he kisses me gently on the lips. "Now go, before I change my mind."

He winks and swats my bum as I walk up the stairs.

"Second door on the left, angel," Sam's voice echoes through the house and I begin to explore the second storey.

The upstairs is decorated similar to the downstairs of the house in warm creams, light browns and taupe's; it is very open and spacious with windows spanning the landing, which makes the room appear light and airy. There is a series of doors along the landing that read bedroom one to four, bathroom, office and gym, in silver plaques hanging on the doors. I open the door that Sam indicated that is our bedroom and I am in awe of what is inside. The room is extremely opulent and reminds me of a luxurious five-star hotel room. It is decorated in a cream and chocolate brown colour, with dark oak flooring throughout. There is a large queen-size four-poster bed dominating the room with brown fur throws, silk scatter cushions and chocolate brown bed sheets. Scattered around the room is a range of matching furniture and accessories in cream and chocolate brown. There is a dark marble fireplace with a cream fur rug in front of it. It reminds me of something from a film. There are floor to ceiling patio doors leading out onto a small balcony. I am suitably impressed with our room and make my way into the spacious en-suite bathroom.

After a long, hot shower, I dry and style my hair, apply natural make up and slick on some clear lip-gloss. I pull on my clothes opting for a blue, striped, halter-neck sundress, which hugs my figure and compliments my growing bump. I team my outfit it with a silver skull pendant, silver hoop earrings, and black diamante flip-flops. I place my sunglasses on top of my head and I grab my bag, ready to spend the day with the man I love. I make my way down the large staircase and Sam is at the bottom waiting for me. He turns around and catches sight of me.

"Angel, you take my breath every time I see you."

My stomach flips at his words. I grin widely at him and he smiles his dazzling smile. I will never get tired of seeing him smile; it disarms me every single time. I make my way down the stairs and he moves up, meeting me halfway.

"Hey," he whispers and offers me his hand.

"Hey yourself."

I take his warm, calloused hand in mine and he escorts me the rest of the way down the stairs.

"I've got a new additional bodyguard and chauffeur for this trip, I'm not exactly happy about it, but he's a friend of Cole's. His name is Jace."

I nod and wonder where Cole is. We open the doors and step out into the Vegas sunshine. I didn't really get to take in the grounds around the house when we arrived, but I look around and I am awestruck with my surroundings. The perimeter of the house is lined with a high grey stonewall and exotic palm trees. The driveway is circular in shape and in the centre is a large fountain.

Sam leans in and whispers in my ear, "Imagine me fucking you naked in that fountain, angel."

I feel slick heat between my thighs. I bite my lip and Sam growls. We make our way across the gravel driveway and a black Hummer H1 is parked beyond the fountain. A muscular man is leaning against it with his arms folded. He is wearing a black suit and a black chauffeur's hat. As Sam and I approach, he smiles and nods.

"Sam, Cole's told me a lot about you."

He has an Irish accent is average height, muscular, and his salt and pepper curly hair is pulled back into a ponytail. He has a five o' clock shadow on his chin, indicating that he hasn't shaved for a few days. He has pale blue eyes and an infectious grin.

"This must be the famous Peyton, the girl who stole this lucky fella's heart."

Sam grins and squeezes me around the waist as if he is staking his claim on me. I smile shyly, and I feel my face flush. With the introductions done,

Sam whispers to Jace and he nods. As he nods, another car pulls into the driveway. The car is a fire engine red Ferrari GTO. My eyes widen at the sight and I think I am instantly in love! The car pulls to a stop and Cole steps out of the car.

"Peyton." He nods in my direction.

"Cole's going to take care of you, angel, I'll meet you there."

Sam winks and gets in the car with Jace. The iron gates open and Jace speeds off through them. A puzzled look crosses my face and Cole smirks.

"What's going on, Cole? Where are you taking me?"

Cole is silent for a moment.

"If I told you that, sugar, I'd have to kill you!"

He winks and breaks out into a full-on rumbling belly laugh. He opens the passenger side door signalling for me to get into the car. I reluctantly get in, but don't ask any more questions. We climb into the car and with the roar of the car's engine, we begin our mysterious journey.

16

Peyton

We have been driving for at least an hour and I see the familiar bright lights of the Las Vegas strip come into view. I crane my neck to take in the sights and Cole chuckles softly.

"Curious, sugar?"

I grin and nod.

"You should be."

We remain in a comfortable silence for the rest of the journey and soon the car pulls to a stop. Cole gets out of the car and comes around to the passenger side to open my door. He offers me his hand and helps me out of the car. He closes the door and I pull my sunglasses down to shield my eyes from the blazing sunlight. I look up and notice that we are outside the Mandalay Bay Aquarium. There is a sign outside and yellow tape cordoning off the entrance. The sign reads *'Closed until further notice'*. A young woman with short red hair approaches us and whispers to Cole. Cole nods his response and brushes my arm reassuringly.

"This is where I leave you, sugar."

The young woman takes down the tape and signals for me to enter the aquarium.

"Good luck, Miss Harper," she says brightly, and I am suddenly feeling apprehensive of what is to come. I take off my sunglasses and place my hand protectively on my stomach.

"What is your daddy planning, boo?" I say softly as I walk through into the dimly-lit main atrium of the aquarium. There is a large curved tank in front of me and a bench. I sit in front of the tank on the bench and there is a single red rose with a note next to it. I pick it up and read it.

Peyton

When you walked into my life, you made me complete. You are my angel, my saving grace and my light in a world filled with darkness.

S x

I smile to myself, I love romantic Sam. Unexpectedly, the room is filled with music. I recognise the tune as Avenged Sevenfold's <u>Dear God</u>. I let the dulcet honey tones of Matt Shadows wash over me. My eyes fill with tears at the lyrics and Sam's husky voice comes over the speaker system.

"Watch the tank, angel."

I look up and I see a large figure swimming in the tank, the figure resembles Sam. I watch his large frame bobbing in the water, complete with scuba diving gear and snorkel. The music continues, and Sam holds up a white sign with black writing on it, which reads:

You made me the happiest man alive...

When you told me you were expecting our first child...

He drops the sign and reveals another one.

Now will you do the honour...?

Of becoming my wife...?

He drops the sign to reveal another one and as I take in the words, a tear rolls down my cheek.

Peyton Harper

Will you marry me...?

I grin so wide my jaw begins to ache, and the tears are falling freely now. I am so overcome and overwhelmed with Sam's gesture I realise he is waiting for an answer. I look at him and nod enthusiastically.

"Yes! Yes! I'll marry you!"

He makes a heart shape with his fingers and disappears. After what seems like an eternity, Sam appears fully dressed and his hair is damp. He drops down to his knee and pulls a ring from the pocket of his jeans.

"Marry me, Peyton?"

I nod.

"Yes! I'll marry you, Sam."

I sob, and he places the ring on my finger. He places a single kiss on the ring and gets to his feet. He picks me up and spins me around. He nuzzles his face into my neck and breathes me in.

"God, you've just made me the happiest man on this fucking planet, angel."

We look at each other and Sam's eyes are glazed too. I take in the ring that he has placed on my finger and gasp at the sight. It is truly beautiful. It is a platinum band with a large princess-cut diamond surrounded by small purple diamonds. It looks exquisite—expensive yet simple and understated. Sam lifts my hand and places a gentle kiss on my palm.

"Do you like the ring?"

I nod.

"It's beautiful, Sam, it's perfect," I tell him, my voice thick with happy tears. He crouches down on his knees and places his hand on my stomach.

"Did you hear that, boo? Your mummy said yes! She's going to be Mrs. Peyton Newbolt."

A tear escapes from the corner of his eye and rolls down his chiselled cheek.

"We're going to be a proper family, boo: you, me and mummy, we're all going to live happily ever after and you and mummy are going to want for nothing. I'll protect you both and do whatever it takes to make you happy, I promise."

His voice is shaky as he gets to his feet. He wraps his strong arms around me and pulls me to his hard chest. I wrap my arms around him and in that moment, everything is perfect. Life is truly perfect.

After Sam's romantic proposal at the aquarium, we go for a celebratory dinner at the famous Eiffel Tower restaurant. The view is spectacular and looks out over the whole strip, it is truly breath-taking. The food is wonderful and throughout dinner neither of us can stop grinning, we can't take our eyes off each other. From the looks we get from the other diners, it is obvious that they recognise Sam but none of them approach us which both of us are grateful for. After dinner, we make our way down to the waiting car, which is a sleek black Mercedes. Cole is waiting beside the car with a huge grin plastered across his face.

"I take it congratulations is in order, mate?"

Sam nods. He and Sam shake hands and he kisses me softly on the cheek.

"Congratulations, sugar."

He opens the car door. Sam and I climb in and we pull away from the kerb. I snuggle closer to him and he wraps his muscular corded arm around me. His other hand stroking my stomach gently.

"Hey, boo, this is your daddy."

He begins to sing softly; his vocals never fail to amaze me. The soft rasp of his voice as he sings brings my skin out in goose bumps.

I recognise the song as "Heaven Sent" by Hinder. I let the lyrics and Sam's voice wash over me. I am comforted feeling his hands on me and as he continues to sing softly I feel the baby moving. Sam stops singing and his eyes widen, telling me he felt it too.

"Did you feel that?"

I chuckle softly and nod. His eyes glaze over.

"Do you think boo heard me singing?"

I nod.

"Quite possibly, baby. Do you like your daddy's voice, boo?" I say softly, and I feel it again.

"Wow!"

For the remainder of the journey he keeps his hand protectively on my stomach and soon the car pulls to a stop in Lucas' driveway. We both get out of the car and walk into the house hand in hand.

"Hello? Is anyone here?" Sam's voice echoes through the hallway.

"In the kitchen, hot stuff."

My grip on Sam's hand grows tighter as we walk into the kitchen. The kitchen is a hive of activity, all the boys are sat around the breakfast bar, J.D is talking loudly on the phone and the rest of the band's entourage have appeared including Alistair, Blu, Skip, Caleb, Donovan, and Lex. They all nod a greeting to Sam and me.

"Now that everyone's here, me and Peyton have something to say."

Every eye in the room is on Sam and me, and I unexpectedly start to feel nervous. My heartbeat quickens, and my thoughts take a sudden nosedive. *Will they think the only reason Sam proposed is because I'm carrying his baby?* Sam squeezes my hand in reassurance.

"Me and Peyton ... I asked her to marry me, and she said yes!"

Everyone in the room erupts with applause, all except J.D who scowls and leaves the room abruptly. The rest all congregate to offer their congratulations to Sam and me.

A few hours pass, and Sam and me are in our bedroom, relaxing before the gig. I am lying on the bed reading my Kindle and Sam steps out of the bathroom. He is freshly showered, with a towel hanging low on his narrow hips and beads of water running down his washboard stomach. I look up at him and lick my lips at the sight of him.

"See something you like, angel?" he says huskily, and his voice causes the heat between my legs to pool with desire. He drops his towel, giving me a full-unrestricted view of his huge cock.

"I can smell your arousal, angel."

I bite my lip and he strides gloriously naked towards me. I put my Kindle down and as I do; the sight of his cock greets me. It is standing to attention, hard and proud. He steps forward, and I feel so aroused I rub my thighs together.

"Ah, ah, angel, your orgasm is mine tonight. I'm in control, I say when and I say how." I actually whimper softly at his dominant words and he chuckles. "I'm going to take it slow, I want to savour every inch of you. I want to worship you like the goddess you are, no part of you is going to be untouched, angel," he says seductively, and he grasps his erection in his hand. He starts to slowly stroke up and down. "Strip for me angel, let me see that beautiful body."

He helps me to my feet and I lift the hem of my dress, pulling it off slowly until I am standing in my underwear in front of him. He moves closer until I feel his warm breath on my cheek. He reaches behind me and unclasps my bra. He pulls it off and it drops to the floor.

"*Christ,* you have beautiful tits, angel." He cups my breast in his hand and kneads it gently. "So perfect." He takes my nipple and rolls it between his fingers, causing me to moan at the sensation.

"Sam," I moan breathlessly.

"Shhh, patience, angel, we have hours before the gig."

He smiles and leans down to take my other neglected nipple in his mouth. He suckles and laps it with his soft velvet tongue. I run my hands through his damp hair and tug gently. He growls against my breast.

"That's it, angel, grab my hair."

I tug his soft locks again and he nips my nipple with his teeth causing a delicious pain.

"Mmm."

He yanks my knickers and the rip echoes through the room.

"Do you have a problem with my choice of underwear, Mr. Newbolt?"

He takes my nipple out of his mouth with a popping sound and looks up at me from under his eyelashes.

"They were in my way and they were restricting my access, if it's a problem, I'll buy you a new pair. Hell, I'll buy you a whole wardrobe full, how does that sound?"

I smirk. "It will have to suffice, Mr. Newbolt." I mimic a posh accent and he growls.

"*Fuck,* I love it when you're all serious. And soon, you'll be Mrs. Newbolt. This might be the last time we make love as Sam Newbolt and Peyton Harper."

He grins widely, and I practically melt at his feet as his famous dimples make a welcome appearance.

"We had better make it earth-shattering then."

He cocks his pierced eyebrow.

"You fucking bet I'll make earth-shattering, angel, I'm going to blow your fucking beautiful mind," he says huskily. "Everyone within a five-mile radius is going to know my fucking name because you'll be screaming it."

His hand moves down and finds my aching cleft. He swipes his finger up my slit and groans.

"Look how wet you are for me, angel, look how much I turn you on. Your pussy is aching for me to fill her, isn't she?"

I nod.

"Answer me, angel."

My eyes lock with his and his green eyes are blazing.

"*Yes!* Oh God, I want your cock inside me, Sam, so fucking badly. I want to come all over your cock and I want you to fill me with your hot salty come."

He lifts me off the ground and lays me down on the soft fur rug in front of the marble fireplace; he settles his large frame down between my legs.

"Are you ready for me to rock your world, angel?"

"Shut up and make love to me, rock star."

He pinches my sensitive nipple.

"Who's in control, angel?"

I love all the different sides of Sam that come out when we're making love. Dominant Sam, playful Sam, gentle Sam and wild Sam. Tonight I am graced with dominant Sam, and I've never been so turned on in my entire life.

"I said, who's in control?" His voice is low, and commanding and I bite my lip.

"You are, Mr. Newbolt," I pant desperately, and he smiles wickedly.

"Good girl, and who do you belong to, angel?" I writhe on the floor fraught for him to touch me. "Ah, ah, all in good time, baby, now answer me, who do you belong to?"

I look at him, his eyes hooded with lust.

"I belong to you, Mr. Newbolt."

He nods.

"Fucking too right you do, angel, I don't fucking share what's mine, do you understand?"

I nod.

"I need the words, angel."

"Yes, I understand."

He settles between my legs and licks up my slit.

"Now, I think you deserve a reward."

He licks my dripping cleft again and pushes his expert tongue up inside me. I grab my breasts in my hands and arch my back off the floor, it feels so good.

"*Sam!* Oh, Jesus!"

He pulls out his tongue and continues his expert relentless licking. He is so good at knowing what I want.

"*Fuck,* you have such a beautiful pussy, so responsive and always soaking wet for me."

He introduces a long calloused finger and pushes it inside me.

"Please, Sam, I need to come, please make me come," I plead.

"Not yet, baby."

He introduces a second finger and pushes them deeper, finding my hidden g-spot. I buck against him, desperate for any ounce of friction to tip me over the edge.

"Naughty, bad girls get punished, you know that don't you, angel?"

He stops what he is doing and pulls his fingers out of me. He holds his fingers out to me.

"Taste yourself on my fingers, angel."

I take his fingers in my mouth and taste the tangy, sweet flavour of myself. I expertly lick and suck on his fingers imagining they are his cock. He pulls his fingers away from me.

"Bad girl."

I bat my eyelashes innocently at him. He throws his head back and laughs heartily.

"Now we both know you're far from innocent, angel."

He gets to his feet and strides across the room.

"Lie down and close your eyes for me, I'll be right back."

I wonder what he has planned and excitedly lie down, closing my eyes in nervous anticipation. I hear his footsteps on the soft carpet and after a few minutes, he returns to me. He lifts my head gently up and proceeds to tie a silk scarf over my eyes plunging my world into darkness.

"Fuck me, you look so hot. Lift your arms above your head, angel." I do as he says, and he loops his belt around my wrists, securely fastening them in place. "Perfect."

He runs his hand gently from my chest all the way down to my feet, and I love the feel of his warm calloused hands on me.

"You need to trust me, angel."

I bite my lip.

"I trust you, Sam."

I hear him pick up something and then I hear a buzzing sound.

"Can you guess what this is, angel?"

I nod. "A vibrator?"

He chuckles softly.

"Gold star, angel."

The buzzing continues as he presses the head of the vibrator against my throbbing swollen clitoris. I buck my hips and gasp at the contact.

"Sam, oh, God! Fuck!"

He increases the vibration.

"Does that feel good, angel?"

I moan loudly, as he expertly pushes the vibrator inside me.

"God, it feels so good, Sam, so fucking good," I pant.

"I'm going to fuck you deep and hard first then I'm going to make slow sweet love to you."

I writhe as his finger circles my engorged clit, whilst expertly and rhythmically using the vibrator. I moan loudly as I feel my orgasm rising.

"That's it, angel, come for me."

He increases the vibration a third time and increases his slow circles on my clit. I am desperate and panting for my release.

"Come for me, Peyton," he commands and that's all it takes to tip me over the edge of orgasmic oblivion. My orgasm detonates and all I see behind my makeshift blindfold is stars. I find my release screaming Sam's name.

"Oh, fuck. Sam. Oh, god. Oh, god. Sam. *Sam.*"

He pulls out the vibrator and little aftershocks cause me to moan softly, as my orgasm dissipates. He leans close to me and plants a passionate kiss on my lips.

"Mmm, I don't think the neighbours quite know my name just yet, angel. Ready for round two?"

I chuckle softly at his eagerness.

"I think it's your turn, Mr. Newbolt. Let me take care of you; I want to suck that beautiful cock of yours dry," I say, attempting to sound seductive. He takes off the blindfold and unfastens the belt, freeing my hands and restoring my sight.

"Hey, beautiful."

"Hey, handsome."

I kneel in front of him and grasp his painfully hard cock in my hand. I stroke him gently at first and then take him in my mouth. I will never get used to the size of him; he is huge, in girth and in length.

"Get those gorgeous lips around my cock and suck me, angel, show me how much you want me."

I wrap my lips around the tip and sink down until he hits the back of my throat.

"*Oh, fuck*, your mouth feels amazing, take me deeper, angel, take all of me."

I open my throat and take all of him in my mouth, creating a rhythm. Up down, up down, I cup his testicles in my hand and gently massage them. Sam growls.

"God, you feel so fucking good."

I use my tongue slowly swirling around his bell-shaped head, my rhythm increasing as I push him closer to his release.

"*Jesus!* Fuck, Peyton! I'm so close, I'm close, baby."

I feel his cock throb in my throat and I increase my relentless rhythm, massaging his heavy sacs at the same time and his hot salty semen coats inside my mouth.

He cries out as I swallow every drop of his orgasm. He collapses to his knees and gathers me in his lap. He kisses me on the lips, tasting himself on me. He deepens the kiss and lays me back down on the rug.

"Round three, angel."

We both chuckle softly.

"I'm going to fuck you fast, hard, deep, and raw. Angel."

I feel the familiar desire pool between my legs.

"Bend over for me, angel; show me that gorgeous arse."

I bend over with my arse in the air and lean down on my elbows.

"Look how fucking perfect you are."

He grabs the scarf and ties it over my eyes, so I am temporarily without sight again.

"I'm going to make you scream, you'll be so delirious with pleasure you'll be begging me to stop," he rasps, and I wriggle my arse against his muscular thigh. He slaps my bum hard and after the initial sting I feel an intense pleasure wash over me.

"Mmmm, Sam."

He palms my bum cheek.

"Do you like that angel? Do you like being spanked?"

He slaps my bum sharply again and I cry out. This is different to what I have experienced sexually with Sam and I am so turned on by the dominant side of him.

"Oh, God, Sam!"

He soothes the slap with a gentle rub from his hand. A moment later, I hear a squelching sound and I feel his finger against my puckered back entrance.

"You need to trust me, angel, I'll make you feel so good, I promise."

I feel a cool liquid being squirted on my back entrance, Sam's fingers gently rub and probe.

"Relax, angel, I've got you," he soothes as his finger pushes past the tight knot of muscle. I gasp at the initial invasion and once I get past the sting I relax against him.

"Good girl, I'm going to fuck you with the vibrator and I'm going to fuck your pussy at the same time."

I push against his finger, desperate for him to move. He introduces a second finger, stretching me to accommodate the vibrator. He moves his fingers deftly in and out and an intense pleasure pools deep inside my anus. I hear him lubricate the vibrator and he removes his fingers. He soon replaces his fingers and pushes the vibrator deep in my anus.

"Push back against me angel, that's it. Just relax," he soothes. He suddenly rears forward and impales my dripping pussy with his hard cock. He slams forward and moves the vibrator in the same rhythm as his cock. I feel deliciously filled in both holes and I scream.

He rams his cock deep in my pussy and my arse at the same time.

"That's it, angel, feel me, feel how deep I am, feel me fucking you in both of your delicious holes."

He rears forward again, and I can feel him hitting my cervix with each deep thrust. He continues to move the vibrator at the same pace.

"*Fuck,* you feel so good, angel, so fucking good," he pants. His thrusts increase, and I scream.

"Sam. Sam. *Sam.*"

He slams forward again.

"That's it, angel, let those neighbours know my name, let them fucking know who you belong to," he grunts.

His pace becomes forceful and relentless as if he is marking me as his. He growls with each deep thrust and with each intense drive he guides me further up the rug and I wriggle against him, desperate to find my release.

"Give it to me, angel, let it go." He encourages, and grabs my hips slamming me back onto his steel erection. I feel deliciously full of his cock and the vibrator. "Oh, God. Peyton. I'm so close."

He thrusts forward and that's all it takes to tip us both over the edge. I let out a scream and I explode around his throbbing shaft. My orgasm is so overwhelming, and I feel like I'm not going to stop coming.

"Sam. Sam. Oh, fuck, Sam. Oh, Jesus, Sam. *Fuck, Sam*," I scream, and Sam growls his release as he lets loose his seed deep within my cervix.

"Peyton! Oh, Christ, fuck, Peyton! Oh, Jesus, I can't stop."

Both of our orgasms last longer than usual, and I feel like the whole room is spinning. My whole body feels like it is made of jelly and Sam lets out a laboured breath as his orgasm dispels.

"*Fuck,* that was intense, angel."

He wraps his arms around my waist and lays me gently down on the rug. He lies down next to me and tucks me under his arm, pulling me closer to him until my head is on his chest. I feel his thundering heartbeat under my cheek and he kisses me on the top of my head.

"I don't think the neighbours are going to forget my name in a hurry!" He jokes and we both laugh. There is a loud bang on the door, interrupting our moment.

"Are we going to get an encore?" Brody shouts.

"Fuck off!" Sam throws his boot against the door and I hear Brody laugh.

"Can I join in?"

Sam gets up and pads across the room naked. I take the opportunity to ogle his perfect pert arse, and I suddenly have an idea. I get to my feet and walk over to the bed.

"Baby," I purr, and he spins around before he gets to the door.

"You're lucky the missus is begging for round four or I will come out there and fucking kick your arse."

Brody chuckles and I hear his footsteps across the landing.

"God, you're so beautiful."

Sam stalks towards me and I stop him by placing my hand on the middle of his chest, feeling his muscles flex underneath my fingers.

"Let me take control, baby," I whisper and Sam growls, holding his hands out to the side.

"I'm all yours, angel."

"Lie down in the middle of the bed"

He does as I ask and lies down in the middle of the bed. He looks perfect lying there anticipating my next move. I climb onto the bed and settle between his muscular legs. I kiss a trail from his neck and gently suck his nipples. I blow cool air and he shivers.

"*Jesus,* that feels good."

I run my fingernails down his chest and down the ridges of his six-pack. I feel his erection grow with every touch. I lick my way down his torso and kiss the inside of his thigh down his leg and back up the other side. He writhes beneath me and I am enjoying being in control. I settle back between his legs and take his cock in my hand. I stroke him gently and I see him struggling with his self-control with every caress.

"*Fuck,* you feel so good angel, so good."

I straddle his narrow hips and guide his hardness into my dripping wet opening and sink down onto him. He gasps as I take his length inside me.

"*Oh, Jesus,* your pussy feels like velvet."

I lift myself up and sink back down, creating a slow, steady rhythm.

"That's it, angel, ride my cock," he says breathlessly, and I maintain a slow pace, balancing our carnal animalistic fucking with sensual leisurely lovemaking.

"Sam," I moan softly.

"Angel, I love you."

His hands find my hips and he rocks me up and down on him.

"I love you, Sam, so much."

I lean down until our faces are inches apart; his heart is pounding a frantic tattoo as I press my breasts against his chest. I press my lips to his and kiss him sensually. Our tongues colliding and probing each other. I am filled with a pure desperate need for this man. He wraps his strong arms around me and I ride him. I quicken my pace and I am panting softly in his ear.

"Sam."

He pulls me closer to him as if he wants to climb inside me.

"I know, angel, I feel it too, I've got you."

He runs his hands up and down my spine, as I continue to ride him.

"Come for me, baby," I whisper, and he pushes his cock deeper inside me.

With one last thrust, I feel my orgasm burst through me. A few seconds later, Sam finds his release and fills me with his hot seed, shouting my name and telling me how much he loves me. At that moment I feel so much love for this man it brings tears to my eyes. I bury my head in his neck.

"Hey," he whispers. "Hey, look at me, angel."

I shake my head, suddenly overwhelmed by the depth of feeling, which consumes every part of my very being. He lifts me off him and sits up. He pulls me into his lap and strokes my back.

"What's with the tears? You'll give me a complex!"

Sam chuckles and the feelings that I have held in come bursting out like a dam overflowing. The tears flow freely, and he rocks me gently.

"Talk to me, angel." He tips my chin up and I look up at him. "You shred me when you cry, I can't stand it, angel."

His voice sounds pained.

"I'm so happy, Sam; I love you so, so much. You consume my every thought, I need you more than my next breath. I'm addicted to you, and I can't imagine my life without you in it. You're everything to me, you complete me. I love you," I say in a rush and he swallows.

"I love you more than life itself, angel; I need you more than I need my next breath too. I love you so much sometimes it scares the shit out of me. You're so beautiful, don't ever leave me," he chokes out and we sit like that for a while, listening to each other breathe. Content just to sit in silent contemplation, as lovers and as soul mates.

A few hours pass, and it is almost time to go to the gig. Sam is dressed in his full stage costume, complete with stage make-up. I admire my engagement ring and I can't help the ear-splitting grin that spreads across my face. Sam watches me from across the room and chuckles softly.

"God, that smile melts me every time, angel, you're so beautiful."

He pulls me out to the balcony. The sun is just setting, and it is breath-taking. The orange and pink hues on the horizon make it look like a postcard. My back to his hard chest, Sam wraps his arms around my waist and settles his hands on my stomach.

"This is the best day of my life so far, angel, you agreeing to be my wife, you carrying our child. I am so happy right now, I could shout from the fucking rooftops. Today is the first day of the rest of our lives."

We both laugh, and someone clears their throat behind us.

"Just give us a sec." Sam spins me around and presses his lips to mine. "Remember this moment always, angel."

He pulls away and we walk back inside.

"The car's downstairs, Sam," J.D says and Sam nods curtly. I suddenly realise I have forgotten my bag and my phone.

"I'll catch you up, baby; I need to grab my bag."

He smiles his dazzling smile. "Hurry, angel, I need my good luck charm."

He winks and leaves the room. I grab my phone and my bag, as I go to leave the room, J.D. grabs my arm so roughly I know there is going to be a bruise. He leans in so close I can smell the stench of alcohol on his breath.

"This ain't Mills and Boon with guitars, sweetheart. Girls like you don't get happy endings, pregnant or not." He sneers, and the cold tone of his voice makes me shudder. "Remember that, sweetheart."

He winks and lets go of me. There is something off about him. and I can't quite put my finger on it, just his sheer presence unnerves me. I push that thought to the back of my head and go downstairs to join the rest of the boys. For the first time in my life, I am so happy, and this moment is the first day of the rest of my happy ever after with Sam.

17

Sam

I am on stage staring off at the sea of fans that have turned out for our gig. Our American fans are the craziest of all our fans. Their dedication humbles me every time we come out here to perform. I look over to the front row where my girl should be, and I lose myself in my thoughts:

I am on stage performing in front of over twelve thousand fans tonight in Las Vegas at the Mandalay Bay Events Centre, I see only her. She is in the spot where she always is at our gigs. Front row centre, where I can see her easily and clearly. She has become my good luck charm and my sole reason to get up on stage. Our eyes lock, and she smiles holding up a piece of paper. Our marriage license. I can't hold back the shit-eating grin that's plastered across my face. In less than twenty-four hours, she will be my wife. She will be Mrs. Peyton Newbolt. My wife, my whole world, my life, the mother of my unborn child, my Peyton. To me she is beauty personified and I can't quite believe I'm going to spend the rest of my life with this amazing woman.

I want to make my way through the crowd and perform to her, only her. I want to look in her beautiful blue eyes and make her feel just an ounce of what I feel for her in the lyrics of our songs. I need to hold her in my arms, I need to feel her skin on mine, I need to feel the softness of her lips and I need to feel the warmth of her body pressed against me. I need to remind myself that this is real, that this isn't a dream, it's actually happening. I am no longer the shell of a man I once was, for the first time in my life I am finally whole. I'm complete and it feels so fucking good.

I am at the front of the stage singing My Dark Passenger, one of our heavier rock hits. As the lyrics wash over me, I totally lose myself in the music. This is my time to shine...

I am jolted back to the present by Lucas' pounding drum beat and I look over to the front row where my Peyton should be. But she isn't there; she didn't make it to the gig and I'm on edge. This should be the happiest day of my life, and I should be giving this performance everything I have, but my heart isn't in it. My heart constricts as I gaze over at the empty spot where she should be.

Come on, Newbolt, get it together, the fans have paid good money to see you perform. I take a breath and lose myself in the music, trying to ignore the huge Peyton-shaped hole in my chest.

"Good evening, Las Vegas! We're Rancid Vengeance, how are you crazy ass motherfuckers doing tonight? Are we going to fucking rock? Hell yeah, let's do this shit!" I say in my signature growl and plaster a smile across my face.

You can do this, Newbolt.

We have performed the first half of our gig and after the shaky start, I found my stride. I channelled my inner showman and gave the performance of my life, even though my heart and my head were somewhere else. I fly off stage, removing my earpiece and throwing it in the direction of the nearest stagehand.

"Sam, I don't know what happened, we don't know where she is. She forgot her phone and her bag."

Cole keeps up with my stride.

"Where's my girl, Cole? Where the fuck is she? She sent me a fucking text saying she would definitely meet us here," I growl at Cole. "You were supposed to be watching her, for fuck's sake!" I shout. "How hard is it to keep your fucking eyes on her, Cole? Find her!"

A passing stagehand hands me a towel and a bottle of water.

Right now, I could do with something a lot stronger than water.

"Mate, you need to calm down. I've got my best men on it. They're looking for her as we speak, and I've sent Jace back to Lucas' house to look for her, just in case something happened."

He talks into the headset. *How the fuck can I keep calm?*

"Try and calm down, Sam, please, we'll find her, you have my word," he repeats and strides off. I walk down the corridor and J.D runs to catch up with me.

"Sam, Sam, slow down, mate, bloody hell."

I fling the dressing room door open and flop down on the sofa.

"Sam, there's been a delivery for you."

I look up at him.

"I haven't ordered anything, J.D, what the fuck?"

He hands me a folded piece of paper with a DVD disc tucked inside it.

"It was hand-delivered."

He shrugs. I take it from him and unfold the note. My blood runs cold from what I see in front of me. On the note in large black lettering is *'Play this during An Angel's Kiss, or Peyton dies'.* I put my hand to my mouth to stop myself from throwing up at the words.

"What the fuck? Who gave this to you, J.D?"

He looks at me.

"It was hand-delivered to me outside the venue, by a man on a motorbike wearing a motorcycle helmet, I couldn't see his face. I'm sorry, Sam, that's all I can tell you."

My eyes widen, and I feel the sudden need to vomit. I can't bear the thought of someone hurting Peyton. I fly off the sofa and storm out of the dressing room.

"Cole! Where the fuck is Cole?" I bellow as Jax and the boys stop me in the corridor.

"*Whoa!* Where's the emergency, dude?"

I push the DVD and the note into Brody's chest.

"This is the fucking emergency. Someone has my girl!" I shout. This is not happening; this can't be happening. *FUCK!*

"What the fuck?" all the boys say in unison and I run my hands frantically through my hair.

"*Fuck!*" I roar and Jax puts his hand on my arm in a gesture of reassurance.

"She's going to be fine, mate, I promise. We'll get her back, you need to try and keep calm."

If I hear that fucking phrase once more, I swear to God I am going to kick someone's arse. Someone has my girl; she must be terrified. Why didn't I keep a closer eye on her? I should have gone back for her. Christ, this is all my fault. I worry my lip between my teeth and the look that crosses Jax, Lucas and Brody's face mirrors how I feel.

"Are you going to play the DVD during 'An Angel's Kiss' like the note says?" Lucas enquires, and my heart constricts at the title of the song I wrote for her.

The person doing this obviously wants me to suffer and knows the only way to get to me is through Peyton. *This is fucked up.*

"What the fuck else can I do? It's not like I have a choice, what if the person who has her is here watching us? What if I don't play it and they kill her? I have to do this." My voice shakes as I say those words and I try to push that thought to the back of my mind.

"Come on, dude, she's going to be fine. She's going to be back celebrating with us by the end of the gig; it's probably one of the crew playing some sick joke," Brody says, and I smile weakly at his optimism. I wish I shared his glass-half-full theory. A voice comes through the P.A system.

"Five minutes to show time, five minutes to show time."

We all crowd around each other in a circle.

"Come on, boys; let's do this, let's fucking rock," Brody shouts enthusiastically and we have a group hug, part of our show ritual. It has bought us luck over the past ten years; I just hope it works now.

It is almost the end of the second half and the finale of the gig. We have all given the performance of our lives. We have played our hearts out, bantered, and interacted with the crowd. I am sweating profusely from jumping around the stage giving the fans a show. Up on stage in front of the fans I am a true showman, I have perfected my craft over ten years in the music industry. Even through the toughest times in my life, I have managed to get up on stage and act like nothing at all is wrong, this is one of those moments.

I move to the microphone, place it on the microphone stand and wrap my trembling hands around it. I turn to Jax, Lucas and Brody to signal the intro of "An Angels Kiss".

"This next song is called 'An Angel's Kiss', it's on our new album and I wrote it for the angel in my life, my fiancée Peyton Harper; wherever you are baby this one's for you."

The crowd roar, with a rapturous applause. Jax starts his guitar solo and I turn my gaze to Cole, who speaks into his headset signalling for them to play the DVD. Jax's fingers move up and down his fret board, I close my eyes and take a breath ready for the song to start when I am interrupted by a sinister sounding voice, which almost sounds robotic.

"Sam, Sam, Sam, Sam."

The voice sends shivers down my spine and I start to sing, the music flowing through my veins, consuming every part of my body.

"You broke down my guard, shattered my defences. You're my mistress of destiny; I am a master of my own universe. You're my diamond in the rough, a heartbeat in my perpetual darkness. I was the boy who tried to heal a broken heart with a shattered mind and a shattered mind with a broken promise. Like a hurricane, you cure my soul of pain; I've never felt like this, there's no end to this bliss. Our worlds collide with an angel's kiss."

That's when I hear it, the blood-curdling scream of terror coming from the woman I love with everything I am filling the venue. I stop singing, despite the twelve thousand fans in front of us. My throat closes up and my heart clenches at the sound.

"Sam, Sam, please baby, help me, help me," she sobs.

I slowly turn to look up at the large screen that adorns the stage, my knees buckle, and I drop to my knees at the sight that graces me. *My girl*, my beautiful Peyton tied to a chair, bloody and tear-stained, pleading for her life.

"Baby, please, you have to help me, Sam, please, oh God, baby, please," she pleads.

I clench my fists at my sides and a tortured sob is ripped from my throat. The boys step away from their instruments and all three of them are at my side in seconds.

"*Fuck,*" Brody mutters quietly and they all place their hands reassuringly on my shoulders.

"Sam, please, baby, I love you," she whispers and the big blue eyes that I love so much look so wide with fear it tears me open inside. From the corner of my eye I see Cole talking rapidly and frantically into his headset.

"Sam, he's going to kill us, baby. I'm sorry, I'm sorry, I'm sorry, I'm so sorry."

She sobs hysterically and a shadowy figure steps slowly behind her. I notice that the figure is hooded and is unrecognisable. The figure lifts up an arm and the large glistening blade of the combat knife he is brandishing is pressed against her delicate throat.

"No! No! No!" I shout. The camera focuses on her eyes now, wide and full of tears.

"Sam, I love you," she sobs, and a blood curdling scream is torn from her as the figure grabs her hair roughly, so she is staring straight at the camera lens. It feels like she is staring straight into my soul, as I hear myself whimper.

"Dear God, please no."

In one swift movement, the figure reverses the blade and plunges it into her chest. Then the screen goes black and the entire audience goes from silent to a loud audible gasp. That's when I break. I wail and sob hysterically, the love of my life killed on a large screen for everyone to see. A loud voice fills the P.A system.

"If you could all remain calm and make your way to the exits in an orderly fashion, thank you."

I am not aware of what is going on around me, just the image on the screen playing on a loop inside my head. The tears are flowing freely now, and I feel like my heart has been ripped clean from my chest. My whole world has crashed down around me, and I can't breathe, my brain is foggy, tears blur my vision and my lungs are refusing to cooperate.

"Sam?" Cole's deep rumbling voice interrupts my inner turmoil. "Sam, come on, mate, let us get you backstage."

The boys help me to my feet and I am grateful for their support. Somehow, I manage to make my way backstage and I am in total shock.

"Sam? Sam? Sam?"

Brody's voice breaks through my foggy thoughts.

"Sit down, man; I'll get you a drink."

In those few seconds, I go from total shock and disbelief, to boiling rage. A white-hot rage surfaces and consumes every part of me.

"You should have been watching her! All this is your fucking fault! My Peyton is dead because of you!" I bellow, and my fist connects with Cole's jaw. He holds his hands up to stop me, but a look of guilt crosses his face. "This is all your fault! How fucking hard was it for you to keep your god damn eyes on her! I fucking trusted you to protect her!" I shout, not registering my actions and I am trembling with rage.

Cole is a couple of inches taller than I am, he did two tours of Iraq while he was in the military and he is an ex-cop. He also works out like a beast, so he knows a thing or two about fighting and how to handle himself. I cock my fist back to hit him again, but this time he restrains me by twisting my arms around my back and pinning me face forward to the wall.

"Calm the fuck down, Sam," Cole says in his deep baritone voice. I lean my head on the wall and take a few calming breaths, even though deep down I feel anything but calm.

"I'm sorry," I whisper, and Cole releases me from his grip.

"For fuck's sake, Sam, none of this is Cole's fault! Now isn't the time to start placing blame," Jax says sharply. I sit down on the sofa, running my hands frantically through my hair and wondering what the fuck I am going to do now.

18

Sam

The next few weeks pass by in a blur. Peyton's body hasn't been found and there are no suspects, so the FBI investigation has ground to a halt. After the gig at the Mandalay Bay Events Centre, the FBI questioned me and the other band members for hours. Those hours seemed like fucking days. The days after her death I fell into a deep, dark, depression, and my mood swings were giving me whiplash. I experienced pain, sadness, anger, guilt, and denial. I suffered constant nightmares and flashbacks of the moment she died. J.D has been hovering around a lot more than usual and his presence has been a huge comfort to me.

In her memory, I got a memorial tattoo for Peyton, which was done by Seb. The words *'My Angel'* in gothic script spanning from one collarbone to the other in a curved shape. It seemed fitting for her and my feelings for her. I feel empty and have a huge Peyton-shaped hole in my chest. It wasn't just the love of my life that was taken away that night it was the life of our unborn child, and I'll never be able to forget that.

The press constantly hounded us in the days that followed our return from Las Vegas, and I took refuge in vodka and my apartment. I refused to leave and locked myself away, throwing myself a huge pity party. Everywhere in the apartment was a constant reminder of her, everywhere I looked I saw her. She was like a ghost haunting every room I stepped into. I cried a lot and would pass out in a vodka-induced sleep. Everyone around me was worried for my health and my sanity, including the boys, J.D, our entourage, Peyton's family, Seb, Cole, Amy, and Ruby.

Peyton's family and I decide that she deserves some kind of farewell. Seb has insisted that we have the memorial for Peyton at Saint Sinner Ink, the place where she was truly happy. The place where we met, the place where she loved life and created art. Seb has closed down the shop for the day and has placed rows of chairs for the expected guests. He has framed some of her best work and displayed it artistically around the shop with a large black and white photograph of her looking as beautiful as I remember her.

"Sam, sugar? Amy's soft voice interrupts my thoughts and I look up. "Do you need help with your tie, honey?"

She smiles warmly, and I nod. Peyton loved to see me in suit, so today I am wearing black skinny jeans, a white shirt, a skinny purple tie, biker boots, and a black blazer with the sleeves rolled up. Amy steps closer to me wearing a deep-purple dress and she lifts the collar of my shirt up, putting the tie around my neck. She knots the tie perfectly and brushes her hands over my shoulders.

"There you go, sugar" She winks.

"Thanks, babe," I say softly, and I hear tiny footsteps run through the apartment.

"Uncle Sammy!" Addison squeals and runs towards me. This beautiful little girl never fails to cheer me up and put a smile on my face. She holds her arms out to me and I lift her up in my arms. She plants a wet sloppy kiss on my cheek.

"What was that for, princess?"

She looks at me as if I am stupid.

"Because you're sad, Uncle Sammy, I don't want you to be sad anymore, it makes me sad."

My heart melts at her words and even though she is only four years old, she is wise beyond her years.

"I'll be fine. I promise, princess. Uncle Sammy is big and strong like Superman."

She grins and then her bottom lip sticks out.

"Uncle Sammy, where's Aunty Peyton?"

This was the question I have been dreading, and Amy brushes my arm.

"Come on, Addison, Uncle Sammy needs to finish getting dressed."

She holds onto my neck tighter.

"No, Mummy, I want Aunty Peyton, she had pretty hair and pretty drawings on her body like Uncle Sammy's."

My heart clenches.

"Aunty Peyton ... She is ... she is with the angels now, princess, the angels are looking after her."

My voice shakes, my eyes glaze over, and I try to swallow the lump that is forming in my throat.

"Come on, Addison, let's leave Uncle Sammy to it, baby."

Addison kisses my cheek and Amy takes her from me.

"I'm sorry," Amy mouths and I shake my head.

"It's fine, babe, honestly," I mouth back and smile as she strides across the apartment with Addison in her arms.

The boys are all here along with J.D and Cole; I know my parents have told them to keep a close eye on me. I walk into the kitchen and Brody pushes a glass of amber liquid towards me.

"Drink this, dude; you look like you need it."

I smile, and even though it is still barely ten in the morning, I down it in one, relishing the warm burn as it slides smoothly down my throat. As I lower the glass from my mouth, my mum walks in.

"*Jesus Christ*, Sam, it's not even lunchtime yet," my mum snaps and I slam my glass down on the worktop signalling for Brody to refill my glass. He refills my glass and a look passes between my mum and the rest of the boys.

"It's five o' clock somewhere in the world, Mum."

She narrows her eyes on me. "Is it really a good idea to be drinking at ten AM in the morning?"

I roll my eyes as I knock back my second glass.

"Spare me the lecture, Mum, please."

I turn and stride out of the kitchen, practically colliding with Ruby.

"Whoa, careful, babe."

That's when the tears I have been holding back finally come and I break down in Ruby's arms.

"I can't fucking do this, Ruby, I can't," I sob, and she cups my face in her hands.

"Look at me, babe, yes you can, and you know why? Because every single one of the people at this memorial all feel your pain. We've all lost her too, I know it's hard because it's hard for me too, she was my best friend, and she was like a sister to me, I loved her. We dragged each other through the good times and the bad times, I know that she would have fought for you right up until the end." She moves her hands from my face and takes my hands in hers. "Now, chin up, tits out, that's what me and Peyton used to say. Head up, shoulders back and go make her proud."

She winks and kisses me on the cheek. I know deep down she is right, but all I want to do is drown in my sadness and obliterate every negative thought. I need to be so numb I can't feel anything at all.

An hour passes, and I know I have spoken to everyone present at the memorial. I have nodded, put on a smile, and said thank you in all the right places, channelling my inner showman to show everyone I'm OK. When the truth is, deep down I feel like I am dying inside. I'm sitting in the front row with Sophia, Max, Dexter, Grace, Eden, Jonah, Ruby, and Seb. I know that even though they haven't said it I know her family blame me for her death. They blame me for not keeping her safe, for not protecting her and allowing her to be taken. I can see it every time they look at me; the words that usually hurt the most are the unspoken ones.

Seb gets up and steps to the front. He is wearing a light-purple t-shirt, black jeans, a blazer, and black Converse trainers. The theme for today is not black, it's purple, Peyton's favourite colour.

"The day Peyton Leigh Harper walked into my shop, I knew she was special. She showed up to Saint Sinner every single day without fail, begging me to look at her portfolio. She was like a little firecracker, a force of nature with the cutest smile and the personality to match. For weeks, she would show up every day, until I relented and looked at her work; that was the day that changed my life. I taught her everything I knew, and she turned into one of the best female tattooists in the business. She became like a little sister to me, she was my best friend, and I looked forward to coming into work just to watch her breeze into the shop without a care in the world. She was kind, funny, and she lit up a room when she entered it."

Seb pours himself a shot of Jack Daniels and downs it, holding the glass up in the air.

"The shop won't be the same without you, honey, I love ya."

He places the glass down and takes a seat back in his chair. He wipes a stray tear from his eye and Ruby brushes his arm in reassurance. She gets up and steps to the front, her heels clicking across the floor as she walks. She flips her dark hair over her shoulder and starts to speak.

"Peyton was my best friend, the sister I never had, over twenty years of friendship and every day was an adventure. We first met when we were five years old and became inseparable, we brought each other through the good times and the bad times. There's not a day that goes by that I don't miss you."

A tear slips down her cheek and she pours herself a shot. She knocks it back and places the glass down.

"Give em' hell up there. Love you, babe."

She wipes her eyes and goes back to her seat. Sophia puts her arm around Ruby and she quietly comforts her as she sobs softly. Max loosens his tie and stands up from his seat. He steps to the front and clears his throat.

"When Peyton was born, she was such a daddy's girl. Every time I looked into her big blue eyes, she melted my heart. She turned into a beautiful young woman who was full of life and continued to make my wife and I proud until the end. Our lives will never be the same again, sweetheart."

Max pours himself a shot and knocks it back, placing the glass down on the table.

"We love you, my darling."

His voice shakes, and he takes his seat next to me. He nudges me, and I look at him.

"You're up, Sam."

He winks, and I nod—this is the part I have been dreading. *What do I say to do her justice?* I get to my feet and shakily take my place at the front. I can feel everyone's eyes on me and my heart is thundering in my chest. *Come on, Newbolt, man the fuck up.* I take a breath and place my hand on the table for support.

"I'm no good at this, so I'll keep it brief. It was in this very shop where I first laid eyes on Peyton. Her feistiness, her big blue eyes, and her sparkling personality was what attracted me to her. When we first met, she hated the fact that I was a rock star, she had read about my man whoring ways, but as soon as I saw her, I knew that part of my life was over. Her razor-sharp wit and her amazing ability to bring me to my knees with just one look, I think I fell in love with her the moment I saw her. She didn't take my crap and it was refreshing, she was the first woman to ever say no to me."

Everyone in the room laughs.

"She quickly became my addiction, my reason to get up on stage and perform. She was my good luck charm, my angel, and the love of my life. There's not a day that goes by where she doesn't consume my every thought."

A tear slips down my cheek and I look up to the ceiling.

"*Christ*, I'm struggling, angel, I need you."

The tears are flowing freely, and Ruby gets up from her seat. She comes to the front and takes my hand. I am comforted by her presence and I take a deep breath. Suddenly, I am so overwhelmed and crippled by grief and I just can't do this anymore. I want it to stop. I want the pain to stop; I just want it all to stop.

"Sorry ... erm ... *shit*...I really can't do this."

I snatch my hand away from Ruby and I bolt. I head for the door and I run, not looking back.

19

Sam

I am not sure how, but I end up back at my apartment and I am not aware of how much time has passed, I'm a fucking mess. I loosen my tie and make my way into the kitchen. I grab a large bottle of vodka and the grief that threatens to consume me takes hold and firmly grips my very being, until I can't take it anymore. I rush to the bathroom and root around in the cabinet until I find a pill bottle filled with Seroxat. I take the bottle and make my way over to the floor to ceiling windows, looking out across the city, Peyton's favourite view in the world. The apartment is bathed in soft moonlight as the lights across the city twinkle and flicker. I slide down the window and sit down, emptying the pills onto the floor in front of me. I am sobbing hard now, and I unscrew the lid of my vodka bottle, taking a long pull. I drink until the bottle is half-empty. The liquid burns as it slides down my throat and my head feels fuzzy. The thoughts that spin around in my head take over. I can't go on anymore, I can't go on living my life without her in it, and I can't see my future anymore. My life is pointless and totally fucking meaningless. I hear the door pounding frantically and muffled voices shouting outside.

"Sam, open the fucking door!" Jax's voice pleads but I ignore it.

"I know you're in there, you fucking dick! Open the door or I'm going to break it the fuck down!" he roars, but I continue to ignore him. I scramble to my feet; my head feels like it is about to explode, and I just want it all to fucking stop. I can't see a way out of this hell I find myself in. I stumble to the kitchen and grab a bread knife from the chopping block. I stagger back into the living room unable to focus on my surroundings and I collapse onto the floor, hitting my head as I fall.

"*Shit! Fuck!*" I curse. The knife I am holding clatters to the floor and echoes around the room. I reach for the knife and I crawl towards where I left the vodka and pills. My vision is blurry, but I still manage to cut my left wrist deep. The pain bites into my consciousness, but I am relieved to feel something for the first time in weeks.

I hear a loud crash, as the door splinters, and the next thing I know, Jax is beside me screaming, shouting and cursing in my ear for me to wake up, shaking me violently. Ruby is next to him sobbing softly.

"Sam, you fucking prick, what have you done, wake the fuck up, oh, man please don't die on me, please, please."

He taps my face and he sobs.

"Oh fuck, baby, please ring an ambulance. Come on, Sam, stay with me, mate."

The sound of his voice is desperate and pleading, but his voice is muffled. My vision is blurred, and that's when my whole world is plunged into darkness.